"A savory morsel of . . . . culinary goodness. Food lovers will delight in the meal planning and the mystery as both are rich with surprising ingredients. Wiken has a winning recipe with spunky heroine J.J. Tanner and the Culinary Capers Dinner Club. I can't wait to be invited to their next event."

> —Jenn McKinlay, *New York Times* bestselling author of the Cupcake Bakery Mysteries

"Wiken serves up generous portions of suspense and food lore . . . I'm already looking forward to a second helping with book two."

> —Victoria Abbott, national bestselling author of the Book Collector Mysteries

"This story has it all: murder, mystery and food. Wiken weaves a tale that will have readers guessing up until the very end. With the introduction of characters who are fun, quirky and quite charming, fans will want to come back to Half Moon Bay for more. The pace of the book is quick and the writing is solid, so it keeps the interest of readers. Great new cozy series!"

> —*RT Book Reviews*

"A delicious new culinary mystery that is absolutely to die for . . . a great start to a new series and I can't wait to see what happens next for these characters."

> —Moonlight Rendezvous (5 stars)

ROUX THE DAY

LINDA WIKEN

BERKLEY PRIME CRIME
New York

BERKLEY PRIME CRIME
Published by Berkley
An imprint of Penguin Random House LLC
375 Hudson Street, New York, New York 10014

Copyright © 2017 by Linda Wiken
Excerpt from *Marinating in Murder* copyright © 2017 by Linda Wiken
All recipes originally appeared in *The Mystery Writers of
America Cookbook* © 2015 by Quirk Books

ISBN: 9780425278222

First Edition: March 2017

Printed in the United States of America
1 3 5 7 9 10 8 6 4 2

Cover art by Anne Wertheim
Cover design by Katie Anderson
Book design by Laura K. Corless

This is a work of fiction. Names, characters, places, and incidents either are the product
of the author's imagination or are used fictitiously, and any resemblance to actual persons,
living or dead, business establishments, events, or locales is entirely coincidental.

PUBLISHER'S NOTE: The recipes contained in this book have been created for the
ingredients and techniques indicated. The Publisher is not responsible for your specific
health or allergy needs that may require supervision. Nor is the Publisher responsible for
any adverse reactions you may have to the recipes contained in the book, whether you
follow them as written or modify them to suit your personal dietary needs or tastes.

ACKNOWLEDGMENTS

As usual, I'd like to thank everyone who has taken this journey with me: the amazing team at Berkley Prime Crime, including my editor, Kate Seaver; editorial assistant Katherine Pelz; copyeditor Randie Lipkin; and cover artist Anne Wertheim. Their guidance and contributions are very deeply appreciated.

Thanks also to my wonderful agent, Kim Lionetti at BookEnds Literary Agency. I owe it all to her! Of course, I also owe great friend and terrific author Mary Jane Maffini, aka Victoria Abbott, for her ongoing support. To my sister, Lee, as always, thanks for being there for me!

The wonderful gals of the Ladies' Killing Circle, my dangerous critiquing group that's been together for over twenty-five years now—I continue to appreciate your friendship. Thanks also to the two creative and energetic blog groups to which I belong—Killer Characters and Mystery Lovers' Kitchen. These blogs add a dash of fun to the business of writing.

Thanks, in particular, to the amazing librarians and booksellers who believe in the written word and strive to match each book with the readers who will enjoy it. And, of course, thanks to you the reader and all your cronies, for whom we write. I love hearing from you, especially when it's to say how much you enjoyed the book!

CHAPTER 1

"What's the worst that can happen? Another dead body?"

J.J. Tanner stared at her best friend and boss, Skye, her mouth hanging open.

Words eluded her.

Skye noticed the look. "Sorry, I guess that was insensitive, given what happened after your last event. Anyway, it couldn't possibly happen again, so what's got you worried?"

"Only the fact that this is my first event for a nonprofit," J.J. answered, finding her voice. "And, I truly believe in their cause, so I'd hate to see it bomb because I forgot to do something or, even worse, made some wrong choices."

Skye flung her hands up in the air. "I hadn't realized you were uptight about this one. Look, J.J., I've read your proposal and love the idea. You practically forced me to go through your bible for the casino night, and I can attest that you've covered all the bases. This is a casino fund-raiser for the People and Causes Foundation, so any monies coming in—no matter how minuscule, if that's the unfortunate case—will make it a success in their book. And in my experience, it's hard not to make money with a casino night. Now, I'm going to take you out for a glass of wine, some free advice, and a lift home. Grab your stuff."

J.J. let out a long sigh, shut down her computer, and stuffed her makeup bag into her purse. "You've already given me a lot of free advice," she said, closing and locking the door of Make It Happen, Skye's event planning business, behind them.

"Did I say the advice is from me? No, I don't think I said who it's from. Do not assume. You know the old saying."

J.J. made a face just as Tansy Paine exited her office across the hall from them.

"Very dignified, J.J.," Tansy commented, and strode ahead of them, reaching the bottom of the stairs before they started down.

"Four-inch," J.J. said.

"Uh-uh. At least six, I'd guess. One of these days the stiletto diva is going to do a nosedive down these stairs."

"You are in a morbid mood this afternoon, Skye Drake. I think I'd better buy *you* a drink."

"I was hoping it would work," Skye said as she hooked her arm through J.J.'s. They'd made it to the front door of the two-story historic home where they had their office, along with Tansy Paine's law office, when the door to the left opened.

"Drinks?" Evan Thornton sang out. "Am I invited? I am, aren't I?"

"Of course." J.J. glanced at Skye, who nodded. "Are you ready or do you want to meet us at . . . where exactly are we going?"

Skye's eyebrows curved upward and her lips flattened out. "All will soon be revealed."

Evan caught up to them on the sidewalk as they turned left onto Gabor Avenue. He quickly linked arms with J.J.'s free arm, and the three of them walked a block toward

Lake Champlain and then hurriedly crossed the street at the corner of Claymore.

J.J.'s eyes lit up as they approached the outdoor patio of McCreedy's, Half Moon Bay's newest Irish pub. Beth Brickner and Alison Manovich were already seated at one of the tables and waved them over. J.J. glanced at Skye, who shrugged. "I thought you needed your friends around you at a time like this, so I gave Beth a call and she set it up. There's nothing like talking about food to bring back the sanity."

J.J. smiled and squeezed Skye's hand.

"Connor's going to be late," Beth explained. "Something came up at the radio station."

At the mention of his name, J.J. felt her stomach do that flip-flop again. It wasn't that she didn't want to see him, but since she'd signed him on to be one of the emcees at the casino night, Connor Mac's name was now synonymous with her fears for the evening. Skye noticed the look on her face and quickly ordered a glass of Shiraz for them both.

"It might be hard to stay away from talk of the casino night once Connor gets here," J.J. said, "but I'm really hoping we won't be discussing it all night. I really need to think about something else for a while."

Skye jumped in. "And, I hope you don't mind my joining in. I promised her a drink. Or she promised me one. Anyway, we both need it right about now."

"Happy to have you along, Skye," Beth grinned as she plopped a brown paper bag on the table. "Well, I thought I'd take advantage of this opportunity to do the reveal for our next dinner club night." She patted the bag. "It's this baby right here, and you'll have to wait until Connor arrives." She smiled and tilted her glass of wine toward each of them in turn.

"Yikes, I've totally lost track of time," J.J. admitted. "It's coming up way too fast."

"That's because you're thinking too much work and not enough cooking. Hope you at least remember it's at my house." Beth tapped the top of the bag again. "I think this will be a surprise and we'll have lots of fun with it."

"Are you insinuating we haven't been having fun?" Evan asked, a look of affront on his face. J.J. noticed his blue eyes twinkling, and she tried to stifle a grin, waiting to see how this would play out.

Beth looked abashed. "No, of course not. I'd never suggest that." She leaned forward and squinted at Evan across the table. "Nice one, Evan. You really had me going there for a few seconds." She started laughing and they all joined in.

J.J. looked around the table at the three, of four, members of the Culinary Capers club. They all took turns hosting the monthly dinner, and that host got to choose a cookbook and the entrée. The others would bring along an accompanying dish, also from that cookbook. Evan had been the one who'd invited her to join, and now, after many months of shared meals and laughter, she considered them all to be close friends. Food could do that.

"Well, while we're waiting for Connor, can't you at least update us on the casino night?" Alison asked. "After all, you know we'll be there in spirit for you."

J.J. thought about it for a moment. *I'm just being silly.* She nodded. "As you know, it's the big fund-raiser for People and Causes. It's happening next week, and it's on board the *Lady of the Lake*. That's the largest cruise boat in the Crowder Sightseeing Line, so you can imagine how cool that will be. We cast off at six thirty P.M., weave our way along the islands in Champlain Lake, and return to the dock in Burlington at one A.M. Besides the roulette wheel, there'll be blackjack, craps, and three-card poker. We'll serve a buffet dinner at ten P.M., and there'll be a great DJ at the back of the boat for those wanting to dance."

"Aft," Connor said, sinking into the chair beside J.J.

She looked at him.

"Aft. That's the back of the boat. Hi, everyone. Sorry I'm late. Glad you didn't wait for me." He nodded at the drinks.

"And," J.J. said, taking over again, "our celebrity masters of ceremonies are our very own Connor Mac of radio WHMB morning show fame, and TV personality Miranda Myers, host of *Tonight's Entertainment* on WBVT." She looked at Connor and noticed the flicker pass over his face, almost so fast that she wondered if she'd really seen it. And what had it meant?

Connor signaled the waiter and ordered a beer. "No one's ordered any food yet? Are we doing dinner or what?"

"It's my night to cook," Evan explained, "so I'm not eating. Well, maybe an appetizer."

"Okay, then let's get a variety of small dishes on the table." Connor signaled the waiter again and ordered one of each of the four appetizers on the menu. "I hope that's all right with everyone," he asked.

They all nodded, and Alison did the equivalent of a shrug with her eyes.

"Well, I'd like to take over the floor while we're all waiting," Beth said in a loud voice. The patio had filled up quickly, and what with the music and talking, it was getting harder to hear. She stared at Connor. "I'm doing the cookbook reveal tonight." She pulled the narrow but large dark book out of the bag. "There's nothing like a good murder to whet the appetite."

Someone gasped. J.J. realized she'd been the culprit, and she suspected that Beth was pleased with the reaction. The others chuckled and gave Beth their full attention.

"So, my choice for the next Culinary Capers dinner is *The Mystery Writers of America Cookbook*." She handed it to Connor, and he started flipping through the pages. "The recipes are contributed by some of the most dangerous crime writers in the country. And I'm hoping they're all safe to use."

She grinned, and J.J. thought it made her look so much

younger than her sixty-four years. "I'm really sorry, though, J.J. There are only a few full-page color pictures. I know how much you like those, but I'm hoping you'll bear with me for this one time."

J.J. tried to make it look like she was giving her answer a lot of thought. "Okay. But just this once." She smiled to show she was kidding. Sort of. "Have you chosen an entrée yet?"

"I have. I'm going to do the Chicken Gabriella, which is contributed by Sara Paretsky, one of my favorite mystery authors. And I thought it might be fun for us to each talk a bit at the dinner about the authors whose recipes we've chosen. Maybe, if everyone has time, we could each read a book written by our author and just say a few words about it, too. I think it would be fun and a bit different. What do you all say?" She looked so expectant, J.J. knew no one would dare to pan the idea.

"Great." Evan chimed in first. "You're right—it will be fun adding another element, and I put dibs on a side dish."

"Wow, right in there. We're taking a big leap here, not having a good look at what's offered before claiming a dish, but I'll volunteer for the dessert," Alison said, moving aside some glasses to allow the first two dishes they'd ordered to be set on the table. "Over to you, J.J."

"Hm. Probably another side dish."

"Do we need two of those?" Connor asked. "I see they have a soups and salads section, also."

"I trust your judgment," Beth answered. "You can let me know what you think after taking a closer look at what's there." She glanced around the table. "Thank you. I appreciate you all getting into this. I think it will be memorable and quite delicious."

Evan raised his glass in a toast. "Here's to an evening of mystery!"

CHAPTER 2

J.J. slipped her right foot into the black sandal with the two-inch heel and stood staring at her foot. Maybe she should have opted for a more subtle nail polish at the pedicure she'd treated herself to earlier in the day. She'd hoped a mani-pedi would calm her before tonight's big event. But right now, with her color choice of Mandarin Orange glowing on the floor, she could feel the tension settling right back into her shoulders.

She didn't know why she was so uptight about the casino night. Okay, she did know. It was her first attempt at planning an event for a not-for-profit group, and she knew her reputation depended on its outcome. She also was a strong supporter of the group's mandate so she wanted to make lots of money to help them continue with all their projects, from literacy to music programs for children living in poverty.

Sure, she was great at planning birthday parties, retirement parties, and other social gatherings. But an evening designed to raise money—that was higher stakes, for sure.

She was only partly mollified knowing that Skye had confidence in her. That should have been all she needed to know. After all, Skye owned Make It Happen and it really was her company's reputation on the line.

J.J. shrugged her shoulders and held that position for a count of ten before slowly releasing. And again. Temporary relief at best. Oh well, time to get on with it.

She added the matching sandal and took a close look at herself in the full-length mirror. The black sheath ending a good four inches above her knees looked elegant but also allowed for maximum movement. Her jewelry was discreet but classy. She didn't want to draw attention to herself tonight. She needed to blend in and weave her way through the various stations—the gambling, the food, and the dance areas—keeping an eye on everything, ready to do damage control if necessary.

She double-checked that her trusty satin black hobo bag held her mini-bible, a paper backup copy of critical phone numbers, menus, and playlists for the dance floor, and lists of contacts for everything from technical support to the Coast Guard. She'd never planned anything afloat before, and to ease her own mind, she'd hired some first-aiders. Still, she wanted to make sure there was a backup plan in case someone broke their leg trying to skip down the stairs between decks after too many drinks, for example.

She took a final look in the mirror to make sure her thick, long dark hair was securely fastened in a butterfly clip, checked her teeth for any stray lipstick, and took a deep breath.

Indie, her two-year old Bengal cat, wound his way around her legs, then tried to stretch, using the bed skirt for support. J.J. scooped him up, holding him far enough away so that she wouldn't be covered in cat hairs, kissed his head, and placed him on the bed.

"I'd really appreciate no tears in the bed skirt. Please

and thanks. See you later, baby. I'm off to an evening of fun, frolic, and frivolity."

She made it out the front door before Indie came bounding along the hallway after her. Passing the door of her neighbor Ness Harper, she inhaled deeply, enjoying tonight's main dish. "Hmm, smells like chili. I hope he has leftovers to share tomorrow."

She knew she'd be famished by then. She could never eat the afternoon of an event and relied on a protein drink instead. And she'd never eat at the event, either, although she'd be awfully tempted tonight. She'd hired Epicurial Expressions to cater and had figuratively drooled over every dish on the menu. She'd been thrilled when Chef Henri Rousseau had her sample the cassoulet and the lentil salad with goat cheese and walnuts. A taste of the salted butter caramel-chocolate mousse in small individual servings, one of the choices for the dessert table, had added five hundred calories to her day's total, she was sure.

She left her car in the parking lot at the downtown dock of the Crowder Sightseeing Line and found the skipper of the evening cruise waiting for her in the office.

"I'm Jessica Smith," said the tall fortyish-looking woman in the white nautical uniform complete with a captain's cap in her hand. "I'm happy to meet you. Sorry I couldn't make it in earlier when you were setting up everything, but I've looked it over and I'm sure it will all run very smoothly."

"I'm glad to hear that. You've had a chance to look at the schedule?" J.J. looked around the small room with a view of the harbor. Nice place to work.

Smith nodded. "We'll just set a course north," she explained, tracing a path along a map on her desk, "hugging the shoreline so that people can take in the view while it's still light and hopefully also enjoy some of the sunset. We're lucky that the weather forecast is so cooperative.

Mild temperatures and calm winds are perfect for an evening's cruise. Then we'll head outward and circle until we're heading back toward Burlington. We'll aim to be at the dock by one A.M. Does that sound right?"

"It does sound perfect. Did you get a chance to look at the food and sound equipment that were brought on board today? I hope the placement works out okay and nothing's in the way."

"Not my worry. I leave all that to the Crowder staff. They know what they're doing. You're not the first charity casino cruise, you know."

J.J. felt her cheeks get hot. Of course she wasn't. She was coming across like a real first-timer, which in a way, she was. Time to dial it back a bit and trust others to do their jobs properly. Still . . .

"Well, that's good to know," J.J. said absently, her mind traveling back to earlier in the day when she'd been on board the *Lady of the Lake* for the arrival of the gaming equipment. "Can I get on board right now? I'd just like to take another look around."

"It's all yours." Smith went over to a mirror hanging on the wall and tucked her short blonde hair back behind both ears before donning her cap. J.J. thought it added authority along with a few inches in height to the captain. "You've booked it right through and I'm pretty certain some of your crew are working there right now."

My crew? She must have meant the DJ, the caterers, or People and Causes board members who'd volunteered to be croupiers and the like tonight. J.J. had set up a Saturday workshop for them a couple of weeks earlier so that everyone would know their jobs. She'd also attended the workshop and learned more than she ever wanted to know about gambling. She knew she'd hate losing money too much, so she'd never even tried her hand at any of it. You didn't have to be a player to know that this would probably be a big money-raising event. At least she fervently hoped so.

She excused herself and retraced her steps past the parking lot and over to where the ship was berthed. The boarding gangplank was set up and unattended. That worried her. The security company she'd hired had someone on hand while everything was being loaded on board and was supposed to still be on duty until relieved by the evening guards. Where was he? What if a thief tried to sneak on board and steal some equipment? She hurried her pace and almost tripped stepping onto the walkway. Fortunately, its sides were filled in with navy canvas sporting the name of the cruise line, otherwise she'd have a tough time walking aboard. Heights plus open spaces were a bad combination, making her nervous.

She'd just stepped down onto the deck when a young man in uniform appeared from behind a stack of chairs.

"I'm sorry, this is a private charter," he said, then took a closer look, realizing whom he'd addressed. "Sorry, ma'am. I didn't recognize you at first." His cheeks were beet red. Not a good look for a security officer, J.J. thought.

"No problem. I'm glad you're so vigilant." J.J. stared at the space behind the young man. "Where did those chairs come from?"

"They were just delivered, and the guy didn't know where they were going so he just left them. Is that okay?"

J.J. sighed. It had started. "Not really. We'll have to get them out of the way. I'll just take a quick look around the decks and see where they're best used." She smiled to hide her frustration and went in search of the indoor stairs to the upper deck. The dance deck.

She noticed right away that the groupings of chairs and bistro tables took up all available space around the dance floor. She'd have to find another location for the new additions. She took a closer look around to make sure everything was in place. The DJ had covered his equipment with a cloth tarp before leaving. The floor was a good size. Everything looked set.

Back on the main deck, J.J. walked to the rear—aft, she remembered—and ran a critical eye around the outdoor portion. Half of it was set up with buffet tables for the caterers. The menu she'd chosen was cassoulet and sautéed shrimp, along with three salads and four veggie dishes, plus for dessert, a variety of cheese and fruit, along with the salted butter caramel-chocolate mousse, all served buffet style. There were several round tables and chairs in place; however, she thought they could add the new chairs for intimate tête-à-têtes. She knew guests wouldn't hesitate to rearrange chairs to suit their needs. Inside, the gambling equipment was just as she'd left it a few hours earlier. She glanced at her watch. The volunteers should be arriving in an hour.

She liked this point in the preparations, when most things were in place. Just the food and cash tables to add. She'd gone through her mental checklist and the one on her smartphone and couldn't find anything missing. This was when she felt like she'd done her job. In eight hours she'd find out if she'd accomplished her objectives.

She heard a van pull up on the dock close to the ship, and she hurried to the side, fingers crossed that it was the caterer. The white van displayed the colorful Epicurial Expressions sign on the side. She'd never used them before and she was a bit on edge after an incident she'd had in the spring. This time, she'd reread the contract last night before leaving the office. Nothing had been added after signatures and such. Chef Henri Rousseau had turned out to have some clever suggestions for a menu. All would go well.

She greeted them and then stayed out of their way as they finished unloading. Much to her relief, the DJ for the evening followed them on board.

"You're here early," she said to him.

He tugged at his dark goatee. His closely cropped

brown hair and large glasses gave him an owl-like quality. His white shirt and black tux were a surprise. J.J. was used to seeing him in jeans and a plaid shirt when they'd met to go over his playlist. "I like to be early for a first-time gig in particular. It helps to impress the client." He grinned, and she relaxed, feeling for the first time that all was going to come off without a hitch and it would be a memorable evening.

When she next checked her watch it was six P.M. and time to meet up with Megan Spicer, the board chair of People and Causes. They both approached the cabin that had been designated as the greenroom at the same time.

After a quick air kiss, Megan spoke first. "I'm both excited and nervous about tonight. Does that make sense?"

My sentiments exactly. "You've been thinking and planning for a long time, and tonight it all comes together. Do you have any questions for me?"

"Not really. Oh yes, I guess so. I was wondering if Connor is here yet."

"Not that I know. Both he and Miranda should be here in about fifteen minutes or so to do sound checks before any guests start arriving. You look lovely, by the way. That shade of pink really lights up your face."

J.J. meant it. Megan Spicer moved with an elegance that made it hard to peg her age, even more so tonight, as she was wearing a long, dark pink, almost rose-colored chiffon dress with long sleeves, scooped neck, and low back. She wore her naturally blonde hair in a severe bob swept over to the left side of her face. She didn't need jewelry or anything else. She looked fabulous.

"Why, thank you, J.J. That's so sweet of you to say. Umm, did Connor happen to say anything about doing this event?"

"Only that he felt honored to be asked." Also, quite surprised, J.J. remembered but didn't add. She'd been curious about his response but hadn't asked any questions.

"I'm so pleased to hear that. What about Miranda?"

J.J. wondered where all this was leading but instead answered, "Equally honored and pleased."

Megan nodded as she looked at her watch, a Michael Kors she wore on her right wrist. "Good. Now, I'd better go find Sue. She's one of the most competent executive directors we've had, and I know she has everything from our end under control, but I like to make sure."

"I was just going to find her, too. The volunteers should have all arrived by now, and I'd like to have a few brief words with them."

"We'll find her together." Megan hooked her arm through J.J.'s.

Sue Fischer's brilliant red-orange hair stood out like a beacon that J.J. and Megan homed in on. It also helped that Sue was wearing a lemon yellow silk blouse with a long multicolored skirt. The volunteers had all gathered around her at the dance area on the top level. Sue finished her talk to them, then turned to the new arrivals.

"Everyone is ready and eager. Did either of you have anything to say to them?" Sue asked.

Megan stepped forward. "I'd personally like to thank each and every one of you for taking part tonight, board members and volunteers alike. I really appreciate that you're putting in the extra time and effort for this event and want you all to know that. Also, I hope you'll all enjoy the evening."

After the applause died down, J.J. looked around at all the faces before saying anything. "I, too, want to add my thanks and just remind you that I'll be everywhere at all moments—well, that's my fantasy. But if you need me, I'll be floating around all evening, and you know who your point people are. Those in the red golf shirts." The six people waved their hands. "I'll be in contact with them by walkie-talkie at all times and have the answers to all their questions. Again, another fantasy." She'd hoped for some chuckles and was relieved to hear them. "Have fun tonight."

She waited until Sue was free and then pulled her aside. "Do you have everything you need or is there anything you want to ask me?"

Sue took a deep breath and held it a few seconds. "Not that I can think of. I'm so looking forward to this, and also to the end of the evening when I can put my feet up and enjoy a large glass of wine."

"Gotcha. That's my goal also. Don't worry. All the bases are covered. Nothing will go wrong, so enjoy." J.J. said a quick prayer to let it be so, as she went in search of the two emcees who hopefully had arrived.

She found them on the upper deck talking to the DJ, who told her they'd just completed sound checks on both decks. J.J. gave them each a hug, although she'd met Miranda only once before.

"I'm assuming you know each other, both being media VIPs." J.J. said it with a teasing smile. "Is everything okay? Will this work?" J.J. asked as she swept her arm in a circle, indicating the room.

Its sides were enclosed by windows, and the DJ had set up along the right. Starboard, J.J. remembered as she looked around at the layout. Several groupings of chairs with small round tables had been strategically placed, also along the edges of the dance floor, for those who needed a break or preferred to sip and watch.

Connor slid his arm around J.J.'s shoulders. "It looks cool. You've done a great job of planning this, J.J."

She glanced at Miranda and saw a fleeting look of something. Dismay? Distaste? One of those words.

"Thanks. You both know where the greenroom is? Just walk outside and it's a couple of doors forward behind the wheelhouse. We've put out some refreshments in there for you, so please enjoy. I'll come and get you when it's time to start. You'll also have a pretty good view of the shoreline as we set out. It's supposed to be a spectacular view."

J.J smiled and excused herself, feeling uncomfortable

but not really sure why. She and Connor were very good friends and had been dating, or rather, going out occasionally, ever since she'd joined Culinary Capers several months ago. They'd both agreed at some point that there was nothing more than friendship between them, and she was more than okay with that. It's just the vibes he'd been giving off tonight, maybe suggesting there was a bit more going on. But why? Only Miranda was with them. Had he been trying to make an impression on her? Why? To gain her attention? To make her jealous? J.J. shook her head. She'd think about it later. Right now she needed to be on her game. The guests were arriving.

CHAPTER 3

Hours later, J.J. stood watching the many guests who'd opted to stand at the railing to enjoy this final loop around the southernmost islands as the ship headed back to port. The weather was perfect, a still-mild sixty-eight degrees, just as the evening had been. Only the slight glitch here and there, all of which had been swiftly dealt with. She was certain none of the attendees had even noticed anything amiss. But she wasn't ready to breathe a sigh of relief yet. Not until she was back at home, shoes kicked off, a glass of wine in hand.

She did take a few minutes, though, to enjoy the view. Even at this distance the Burlington skyline was a series of jewels flickering against the dark backdrop. She'd grown to love the city, and especially Half Moon Bay, even though she'd lived there only a couple of years. It had what she wanted—a manageable size so that everything was accessible; an active cultural scene; more nightlife than she'd ever need; and an ever-changing palette through the seasons. She sighed and made herself get back to work.

There were still quite a few ardent gamblers trying their luck at the various games, most seeming to have a good time. She'd been keeping her eye on one man in particular, a stocky blond guy who looked to be in his early twenties and seemed to have had a lot to drink as well as a lot to lose. Although there was a maximum amount set on the number of chips each player could purchase, he didn't seem to be taking his losses in stride. She'd alerted security to this and was relieved to see one of the plainclothes guards hovering close by.

On the upper deck the numbers of dancers were fewer, with more seats taken up at the tables, and laughter filling the air. She looked around for Connor and Miranda. They'd soon be needed to wrap up the evening and thank everyone for attending. They'd been an excellent choice as emcees, very easygoing and humorous when performing, keeping everyone in smiles and much laughter. The initial tension she'd felt between the two emcees at the first meeting was nowhere to be seen.

J.J. walked along the deck to the greenroom. Connor met her at the door and gave her a big hug.

"It's been a terrific event. You've done an amazing job. You must be pumped." He held her close a couple more seconds.

"I am," she mumbled against his chest. "But I'm also exhausted."

She pulled back and looked behind him in the direction of the footsteps running from the wheelhouse. One of the male crew members looked over at her and beckoned. She took one look at his face and rushed to follow him, Connor right behind her, back into the wheelhouse.

They'd just pulled the door closed behind them when Captain Smith said in a low voice, "There's a dead body on the main deck." She pointed out the front window.

J.J. gasped.

Connor moved next to her. "Who is it?" he asked.

"A woman."

Connor rushed out the door and looked over the railing. "It's Miranda," he said with a loud sob. J.J. had followed, but he prevented her from getting a look. "Don't. You won't want to have that image in your head."

"I've alerted the police," Smith, who'd followed, said. "They'll meet us at the dock. I've sent some crew members to contain the area and hopefully prevent anyone from seeing it. We'll head immediately back to shore."

The rest of the trip was a blur to J.J. She managed to find Megan Spicer and Sue Fischer to let them know what had happened. She asked the DJ to explain to everyone that there would be a delay in disembarking once they docked, asking for everyone's patience. Then she went to wait at the gangway. It felt like hours before they finally docked, but she knew that it had probably been about twenty minutes.

Two uniformed police officers were the first to board. One remained at the gangway while the other went to see the body. Within minutes more officers had arrived. J.J. knew something had to be said to the attendees but wasn't quite sure what. Fortunately, one of the officers asked her to explain there'd been an incident, and everyone was asked to stay on board for the time being.

J.J. took a deep breath and made her way to the DJ, asking him to turn down the volume. J.J. did as she was told by the officer, and added that a full explanation would be made soon. She hoped that was so. She asked the DJ to please continue playing music, hoping that would be a distraction.

After making the announcement, she wanted to escape back to the greenroom without having to answer any questions, and had almost made it to the passageway when someone grabbed her arm from behind. She swung around, ready with a *No comment*, until she saw who'd stopped her. Words wouldn't come.

"What's going on, J.J.?"

"Devine. What are you doing here?" J.J. felt totally stupid asking that but couldn't think of anything else to say. He was the last person she'd expected to run into tonight. What was a private investigator doing on board?

Ty Devine smiled, a lopsided grin. "I'm a guest, obviously. Even managed to make a bit at the blackjack table."

A tall, svelte redhead appeared beside him and looped her arm through his. Something nudged J.J.'s memory. The woman from the funeral. It just came back to her. This was the woman Ty Devine had been speaking to at the reception following the funeral several months ago. *A cougar, for sure.*

J.J. turned her attention back to Ty. "Well, thank you for helping to support such a good cause. Now, if you'll excuse me . . ."

He grabbed her arm again. "You haven't answered my question. I saw all the cop cars. It must be something major. What's up?"

She leaned a bit closer to him, keeping her voice low. "Look, I've been told what to say in a statement to the guests, and nothing else. Maybe you'll have to use your cop connections to get more information." She shook her arm free and made her escape.

Back in the greenroom, she stopped and took a deep breath. Connor was pouring wine for those inside, namely Megan, Sue, and two of the board members. J.J. gratefully accepted a glass and took a long drink. She'd never expected to run into Devine tonight. Especially when he had a date with him. Not that it mattered. She jumped at the touch of a hand on her shoulder.

"Sorry," Connor said in a low voice. "I guess we're all jumpy. Why don't you come and sit down?"

She looked around at the others, sitting in comfortable chairs, staring into space, and shook her head. "No, I think I'll try to see if I can get any information or at least help facilitate something."

Connor nodded and went back to the table to pour himself another drink. She wondered just how many he'd already had. He didn't look too steady on his feet. She'd have to make sure he had a ride home.

J.J. dreaded the thought of seeing the body, but she couldn't just stand around. She threaded her way around numerous chairs that had been pulled back along the side of the cabins. *These must be a hazard of some sort. What if you needed to exit quickly?* She stopped behind a tall police officer standing with his broad back to her. She stood on her tiptoes, trying to see over his shoulder when he turned around and stared at her.

"No one is allowed here, ma'am. You'd better go back and wait until the detectives come to talk to you."

She had a thought. "Is Detective Hastings here?"

The officer shrugged. "Don't know who's working it. Now, please." He waved behind her and she took the hint. As she was about to step back into the greenroom, she spotted Devine, talking to a man in blue with a badge.

CHAPTER 4

J.J. could barely turn the key in the lock of her apartment door, she was so tired. Those in the greenroom had been the last to be questioned by the police. When Detective Ozzie Hastings walked into the room, she wasn't sure whether to breathe a sigh of relief or to quiver. Earlier in the year, when she'd gotten involved in a murder investigation, he'd been more than a little annoyed with her by the time an arrest had been made. But she had assurances from Alison, who was a cop herself and should know, that he was one of the good guys. And nice, also. At that point in the evening, or rather morning, she didn't really care.

His questions had been brief, but he had answered one of her own, and it appeared that Miranda had been murdered. J.J. had been asked to appear at the police station later in the morning to give a formal statement. She knew the drill. Fine. But what she needed now was sleep. She was too tired to even take a shower. She stripped off her clothes, shrugged into a shorty nightgown, and fell into bed. A moment later she felt a thump on her back as Indie landed on her. He sniffed her hair and rubbed his head against hers before settling down, flat out against her right side.

When she awoke five hours later, Indie had at some point moved onto her back again. She turned over as gently as she could, murmuring to keep him from digging in his claws. Mission accomplished, she lay staring at the ceiling while Indie relocated to her stomach. Her mind played over all that had happened the night before. She still couldn't believe that Miranda was dead, murdered.

Up to then, she supposed the event had been a success, although she felt slightly guilty for even thinking about that. What she couldn't wrap her head around was who would want to kill the TV host, and, equally worrisome, was that person a guest? She wondered if Hastings had any leads, but it was probably too early unless he'd found someone, weapon in hand, on board. She wondered what that weapon could be. No one last night had mentioned the method of murder.

With a groan, she eased out of bed and walked zombie-like straight into the shower. Hot and long was what she needed. After drying her hair, she felt halfway human and was totally shocked when she looked at the clock in her kitchen. Noon. How had that happened? She thought she'd set the alarm for nine. *Oh well.* First things first. She fed Indie, then fixed herself an espresso and grabbed the phone to call Skye, who answered on the second ring.

"I've been waiting for you to call," she said, almost shrieking. "I didn't want to wake you if you were sleeping, and I was sure that was the only reason you hadn't called. Of course, you might have been in prison, but then you probably would have called for me to come and bail you out."

"How can you even think that? I'm not even a suspect this time. I hope." J.J. felt that knot in her stomach tighten. "I guess you've heard."

"Very little, so shoot. Oops, I hope she wasn't shot."

"I don't know how she died. The police have been very tight-lipped. All I know is that one of the crewmen found her body just as we had made the turn to head back to the dock. And I have to go down to the police station to make a formal statement this morning. Better make that at some point today. Maybe Detective Hastings will fill me in."

"Him again. Let's hope so. How are you feeling?"

"Besides tired, groggy, and totally out of it? Fine, I suppose. It's a shock, and I guess I'm still feeling it. I can't believe this happened at such a wonderful event."

"Is it tacky of me to ask how that part went?"

"I won't tell anyone. I'd say it was a big success. But wow, what a finale." J.J. finished her espresso and leaned back on the couch. "I guess I should call Megan Spicer, the board chair, and see how she's doing. She was the one who suggested I ask Miranda to be a co-emcee in the first place."

"What about Connor? How did he take it?"

"He also looked totally shocked. In fact, he and Megan left together practically supporting each other in standing upright. Of course, they'd had quite a bit to drink by that point. They both took it hard."

"Hm. Is there anything I can or should do? Do you want me to come over? Go to the cop shop with you? Lend you my Xanax?"

J.J. chuckled. "As if you'd take that. No, I'll be all right. Thanks anyway. I will keep you posted. Is it a 'move some more of Nick's stuff into the new condo' day?"

"Yes, in fact I made him start without me. As well he should, since it is his condo. Take care now and let me know if you need me. I'll have my iPhone in my pocket. Ciao."

J.J. smiled as she hung up the phone. Skye always knew how to help. She'd relied on her a lot over the past few years and was always grateful that they'd sat beside each other in Marketing 101 many years back. She heard a knock on her door and hoped it was her next-door neighbor, Ness

Harper. Although she wasn't sure she was up to tasting any of his gourmet dishes today, she could sure use his perspective as a retired cop on what had happened.

She peered through the peephole and sucked in her breath. Connor. She wasn't sure what to say to him, but she did want to find out all the details of what he'd seen last night. She opened the door and caught her breath for a second time. He looked dreadful, like he hadn't been to bed yet. His usually stylishly cut dark hair needed a shampoo or at the very least, a combing. His day-long five-o'clock shadow looked to be an eleven P.M. one. Although he'd changed his clothes, she wondered if he'd just pulled the T-shirt out of the laundry basket, and much the same for the chinos. But more telling was the lack of the usual flirty smile and spark in his eye.

She grabbed his arm, pulled him inside, and hugged him. "Let me get you an espresso," she said, and guided him to the chair at the bar separating her kitchen from the living room.

He still hadn't said a word by the time she set the cup in front of him. She was beginning to get worried. This so wasn't Connor Mac.

"I know it's been a big shock for you, Connor. It has been for us all. Would it help to talk about it?"

He stared at her for a few moments, then down at his espresso, and finished it off before speaking. "It took a while to sink in, but it's just so unbelievable. She can't be dead. She was so . . . alive. So full of energy and fun. So beautiful," he added almost reverently. "And to know she'd been murdered. I can't bear the thought of that."

He shuddered, and J.J. wondered if he'd cry. She reached out to him and squeezed his arm. "I guess being in the media, you two must have met several times before."

"We'd been engaged."

J.J.'s jaw dropped. No one had told her. Well, why would they? It had nothing to do with the fact that she'd asked the two of them to co-emcee the casino night. And she'd done that at the request of Megan Spicer. Had she known? What did it matter anyway?

"I had no idea. Was it very long ago?" At least six months, since that's the amount of time they'd been dating. Friends dating.

"We broke it off three years ago, but lately we've been seeing each other off and on."

While we were dating?

The doorbell prevented her asking the question, which she figured was a good thing. She shook her head to get back to reality and pulled the door open without checking first.

"Good afternoon, missy. I thought it would be a late night for you and you'd be overseeing cleanup in the morning, so here's some lunch, if it's not too late." Her neighbor Ness Harper held out a plate covered in aluminum foil. "Osso buco. My new specialty."

She couldn't think of a thing to say, although the thought that she should have checked on what was happening at the boat floated through her mind.

"What's the matter? J.J., is there anything wrong?"

She nodded. "You might say that." She stepped back and opened the door fully. Ness spotted Connor and looked at J.J., eyebrows raised.

"It's okay. Come in. We have a story to tell you." She stood aside and then closed the door behind Ness.

She busied herself making Ness a cup of coffee in her Keurig, but she could feel him watching her. She was well aware neither guy had said a thing.

She set the mug in front of Ness and then leaned on her folded arms, across the counter from them. "There was a murder at the casino night."

He shook his head. "Not again. You do have a certain knack."

"I'm not a suspect this time. At least I don't think I am, but I am responsible for the victim being there." She glanced at Connor, who was staring at his cup. "Her name is, was, Miranda Myers."

"From TV."

That surprised J.J. "Yes. Did you watch her show?"

Ness shrugged. "The odd time I'd have it on while experimenting with a new recipe. She was what some these days would call *hot*. That's too bad. How did it happen?" He looked at Connor and raised his eyebrows slightly.

J.J. shook her head slightly, then explained, "I don't know. The police haven't said anything yet. A crewman found her lying on the main deck just as we were heading back to shore. Connor confirmed it was her."

"That's pretty hard, finding a body," Ness said softly.

Connor looked at him and nodded. "She was a good friend."

Ness sighed. "Never helps. I suppose you've given your statement?" he asked J.J.

"Not yet. I could hardly drag myself out of bed, so I'm way behind on everything." She stifled a yawn. "Funny, I thought I'd lie awake all night."

No one said anything for a few minutes. Ness finished his coffee and stood. "I should be going. Look, if you need anything, just ask. I can run you down to the station if you want. Or, well, anything. I mean it."

J.J. nodded and followed him to the door. "Thanks, Ness. I can't even get my brain in gear to think of what I'd normally be doing the day after an event. But that's certainly not the worst of what's happened."

He squeezed her arm and pulled the door shut behind himself. J.J. gave a few shoulder shrugs to release the tension before rejoining Connor. He'd moved over to the love seat in front of the window and sat at an angle, staring outside. J.J. had never seen him so down. So not Connor.

She wasn't sure what to say. Certainly none of the mindless platitudes. She'd just sit with him until he was ready to talk.

After about ten minutes, he seemed to come to some sort of decision, took a deep breath, and sat back. "We'd been arguing all night, you know."

"Who had? You and Miranda? It sure didn't look like it."

"We were both careful of how we acted when others were around. In fact, I spent a lot of time walking along the deck just so we wouldn't be alone together in the green-room. That's going to look bad if the cops find out, and I'm sure they will. Nothing's ever kept totally from them."

J.J. knew she was on touchy ground but felt she had to ask. "What did you argue about?"

He looked at her and seemed almost apologetic. "Oh, the past. Why we broke up. That was three years ago. I thought it was all pretty straightforward, but she accused me of not having understood her. Then or now."

"It must have really hurt her if she brought it up after all this time."

"That's what's so silly. We've been dating again, on and off, so you'd think she would have put it to rest by now. Besides, if anyone should have been hurt or holding a grudge, it was me. But I don't, didn't. Then, she asked if I wanted to call it off again. I wasn't quick enough with an answer, and that was the final straw for her. I just hadn't expected her to bring this all up, especially not last night and at a public event. I don't understand what set her off." He spread out his hands, inviting J.J. to comment.

"I'm so sorry, Connor. I don't know what to say."

"Something else must have been bugging her, too. That's all I can put it down to. Plus she'd had a bit more to drink than usual." He shook his head. "I don't know what to think at this point."

He looked at her. "I'm sorry I never told you about her. I guess it just seemed like, I don't know, another part of my life. We're still friends, aren't we?"

"Of course."

"Good." He stood abruptly. "I should go. Thanks for letting me ramble."

At the door, he kissed her forehead and left.

J.J. leaned back against the door. She was surprised at what he'd revealed, but not upset. She'd never expected more from their friendship. And she'd be there for him, as a friend. But she certainly hoped he wasn't going to be on the suspect list.

He was acting so oddly, though. What would the police think?

CHAPTER 5

After giving her statement at the police station, J.J. drove to the dock. The police had told her cleanup could get started, and she had already notified everyone concerned. The prow still remained off-limits, although the body had been removed much earlier, and none of the police technicians in their white outfits remained. To reinforce the point, one burly uniformed cop blocked the way forward.

She'd checked in with the cruise line, and they were quite anxious for the ship to be released back to them. Already the regular Sunday champagne brunch cruise had to be canceled. J.J. had assured them all decorations and traces of the casino night would be promptly removed, however, it was entirely up to the police as to when the cruise line could get back to business.

J.J. was pleased that the DJ had already arrived and was removing his equipment. The catering staff was doing the same. J.J. sent a text to the casino equipment rental guys, who responded that they were on their way. She began taking down the various signs that she and some volunteers from the board had posted, indicating the location of various tables. She'd phoned Megan Spicer and suggested the other board members be let off the hook for coming out and helping with the cleanup, as had been previously planned. She was quite prepared to do it all on her own. At least it would keep her busy.

She shouldn't have been surprised when Megan turned up about an hour into her task.

"You really didn't have to come down," J.J. said, although she was pleased to have helping hands.

"I can't let you do this all on your own. We'd committed to helping, but I agree that the others should stay home and not have to dwell on what happened here last night." She glanced toward the passageway. "Have you heard anything?"

"No. I haven't spoken to the investigating officer since last night, not that he was likely to share any news. I did go down to the station and make a statement earlier, but nobody told me a thing."

Megan joined in taking down signs, removing the double-sided tape, and stacking everything. "I still can't believe what happened." She shook her head. J.J. noticed the fatigue in her face, even though she was much better put together than Connor had been earlier. "If I'd had any idea, I wouldn't have even suggested Miranda for the job."

"Of course you couldn't have known. You have no responsibility in this. We don't even know if she was targeted or was just unlucky to be at the wrong place at the wrong time." *And I was the one who asked her.*

"You mean, like, there was a psycho on board just waiting to prey on a woman?" She shuddered.

"We have no facts at this point. I know it's hard but we're best off not dwelling on it." J.J. looked around the deck. "The cleanup is going quite quickly. I know the cruise line is anxious to get their ship back and on schedule."

"The police aren't ready to allow that, are they?"

"I have no idea," J.J. admitted, however, she highly doubted the *Lady of the Lake* would be sailing at all today. She felt bad for the owners and just hoped the stigma of having a murder on board didn't hurt their future revenue. Of course, she admitted, that was the least of today's worries.

By four, the ship was back to normal, except for the cop who remained, looking stoic and disinterested. J.J. knew he was taking it all in, though. She was happy to be out of there. She parted with Megan on the dock with the promise she'd be in touch real soon with her final report, and drove over to Skye's apartment, hoping she'd be home by now. She badly needed to talk things through.

Skype opened the door with a full glass of red wine in one hand, which she handed to J.J. They sat out on the balcony, taking in another mild fall afternoon.

J.J. took a deep breath and let it out slowly. "I'm glad you're home."

"Nick is on call today at the emergency clinic and unfortunately, he did get called out. We got some work done before he had to leave, though."

J.J. nodded. They sat together in silence for a few minutes until J.J. spoke.

"I feel torn," J.J. admitted. "A part of me is still in shock about the murder and also feeling some guilt, while the other part is fighting off hysteria about the damage this might do to our reputation. Two murders at two of our events. That's bad press in anyone's book."

"Here, read this before you go off on a panic attack." Skye handed her a piece of paper with a press release under the Make It Happen logo. J.J. read it two times before sitting back with a sigh.

"Perfect. It's very professional and yet compassionate. Of course, I don't know if it will do any good, but I'm impressed."

"It's a start. The next thing we have to do is get in touch with all of our current clients tomorrow, especially those next up for events, and explain what's happened. Maybe taking them out to lunch would be a good idea. Are you up for that?"

"Definitely. I wish we could do something for People and Causes, though. I feel bad for them."

"If I might be so crass as to point out, they do have the take from the evening. They haven't lost any money because of this, and by the time next year's fund-raiser rolls around, very few will remember. Except I doubt they'll ask us to plan it."

"I hope you're right—not about us being cut out, of course. But I guess that would be understandable." J.J. stood and stretched, then started pacing. "I still can't believe this has happened."

Skye gave her a hug. "What about Connor Mac?"

J.J. shook her head. "I told you he and Miranda had been engaged?"

"No. I didn't know that."

"I guess I haven't had a chance to tell you. Everything's getting muddled in my head. It turns out they were engaged, then broke it off about three years ago. Only thing is, they've been dating on and off ever since."

"Like during the time you've been dating him?"

"You make it sound like we're an item. I keep telling everyone we're just friends who like to go out together every now and then. I certainly don't change my plans just to go out with him."

Skye glanced at her.

"I don't."

Skye reached out and patted her arm. "But still, even given that, it must have come as a surprise to hear that news."

"It did. I'll admit I had this really tiny, brief moment of being teed off, but when I stopped to think about it, what difference did it make to our friendship? Nothing. We were, and still are, just friends."

"Good. But you'd better hope the cops don't think you knew about all this before."

"You think they'll take it as a motive?"

Skye shrugged. "You know better than I how they think. But put that all out of your mind for now, because Nick should be here any minute for supper. You'll stay, of course."

It sounded more like a command than an invitation. J.J. nodded.

"Good. He's picking up some Thai takeout on the way over. Help me set the table, please, and we'll try to enjoy the evening. We'll have a lot to deal with tomorrow at the office."

CHAPTER 6

J.J. checked her smartphone while standing in line at the Cups 'n' Roses coffee shop on her way to the office the next morning. She'd decided to walk to work, partly because it promised to be a beautiful day, but mainly because she had some thinking to do. She had tried hard to shake the feeling of guilt that had crept into her psyche over the weekend. She knew it was irrational. She wasn't to blame for Miranda's death even though she had done the hiring, which had placed Miranda in that location, at that time. One part of J.J.'s mind knew that if it was a targeted killing, the time and place didn't matter. But what if it was a loony who did it, a random killing, and Miranda died only because she had been there? *Ugh.* She shook her head and then remembered where she was.

She reached the counter and waited until Beth had finished plating a blueberry scone for the customer who'd just paid. Beth's face lit up when she saw J.J.

"How are you, J.J.? I tried phoning you last night. I heard the news of course, and I was worried about you."

Beth ran the back of her hand across her forehead, messing up her bangs, highlighted gray to offset her recently dyed dark auburn hair.

"I know, I got your message. Thanks, Beth. I appreciate it. But it's been even harder on Connor. Has he been by this morning?"

"No, which is unusual. He's usually my first customer on his way to the radio station. How well did he know her? I guess being in broadcasting, they've run into each other a lot."

"They were engaged at one point." J.J. wasn't sure if she should be sharing that information, but Beth was part of the club. They were close friends who shared and cared.

Beth gasped. "I didn't know that. Well, I guess we don't know much about Connor's personal life, when you think about it. The only reason we know you two are dating is because you talk about it."

"Not much."

Beth rang in J.J.'s usual large latte. "No, but it's not a secret. Do you think he'll be okay?"

"Connor? I'm sure he will, but while he's getting there, we're all here for him."

"So true."

J.J. looked around her. "I'd better move along. Your lineup is getting longer by the minute."

"Listen, there's something I wanted to talk to you about, although it's probably really poor timing what with all that's happened. But do you think you could stop by later? Latte on the house."

"Sure." J.J. nodded and moved to the end of the counter where the barista had just placed her order. Walking along the first block after leaving the shop, J.J. wondered what was on Beth's mind. During the second block, she was thinking about Evan Thornton and wondering if he had heard the news. He'd admitted that sometimes he and Michael, his partner, didn't turn on any radio or TV all weekend. They had one of the largest CD collections she'd seen, and that seemed to be all they needed.

She walked up the front steps to the white clapboard house that had started life in the 1920s as a post office. Evan had purchased it and transformed the place into a showroom with his interior design office on the main floor. The upper floor was divided in half with lawyer Tansy Paine occupying one half and Make It Happen, the other. J.J. looked through the glass door to his office and spotted Evan sitting at his desk. She knocked and entered after he looked up and waved her in. She could tell by the stricken look on his face that he'd already heard the news.

He leapt up and scurried toward her. "J.J., OMG, what a weekend you've had. Are you all right?" He did the same "hand on shoulders" routine that Skye had done and then pulled her close for a hug. "What a shock that must have been."

J.J. gently removed herself from his arm. "It was, but you know, it's even harder on Connor. She was his ex."

"His ex?"

"I mean, his ex-fiancée."

"Really? I didn't know that. Did you know that?"

"He told me yesterday."

"Yesterday? You mean you've been dating him all this time and you didn't know he'd been engaged before?" He escorted her over to the white leather club chair and then pulled up a stool for himself from where it had been shoved under his worktable. "What did you talk about? Sorry, scratch that. None of my business."

"Correction, Connor and I have been *friends* all this time, and we occasionally go out together. Everyone is so determined this is a big romance but it's not. Really, Evan. We're just friends."

Evan stiffened, and J.J. worried she'd sounded too brusque.

"I know that, but still," he reassured her, "I also know

how hard you take the bad things that happen to your friends."

J.J. smiled. "Thanks for your concern, but really, I'm all right." *Except for a major case of the guilts.* "Have you heard any details about the murder?" She really didn't expect him to have any news, but he was so well connected in Half Moon Bay, there was little that slipped past his curious ears.

"Nada. None of the facts. Of course the gossipers are out and at it. I did hear something about Connor having murdered her in a fit of passion. That after doing the event with her, he made a pass but she turned him down. So he did whatever. What did he, er, I mean, the murderer do?"

J.J. groaned. "I don't know. The police haven't said. However, I was worried about the stories starting up. Why do people do that? Why not just wait for the police to catch the killer instead of starting all these rumors?"

"They can't wait, that's why. Besides, tomorrow there may be another murder or scandal taking place and they'll have to move on to it, so they're milking this one for all it's worth while it's still front and center."

"That's cynical."

"But true. You think too kindly of people, J.J. You can't relate to their mean, ugly tendencies." He made such a grotesque face that it got a laugh out of her.

"Maybe not, but how unfair to Connor. We've got to do something to help him."

"Like investigate?" Evan looked eager, but J.J. shook her head.

"No. I mean, like take him out to dinner tonight. We don't want him to sit alone at home feeling miserable."

"Excellent idea. I'll bring Michael along, too, if I may."

"Of course. He's an ex officio member of the Culinary Capers. I'll phone the others this morning and hope it works for everyone. Where should we go?"

"How about Bella Luna, or is it too soon?"

She shrugged. "Nope. That would work fine. I'm always happy to treat myself to their delicious food."

"Good. Leave the reservations to me. Now, scat. I have a client coming any minute now."

He walked her to the door and held it for her. "Hang in there."

J.J. heard the front door opening as she reached the top step to the second floor. Probably his client. She glanced at Tansy Paine's law office, but it looked dark. When she turned to the Make It Happen side, it also looked dark. She fumbled for her keys, hiding in the bottom of her purse, and unlocked the door, switching on the light with her left elbow. Only nine A.M. and already stuffy inside. Of course, the office had been locked up all weekend. She deposited her clutter on her desk, switched her computer on, and opened the windows. Then she plopped in her chair and sipped her latte. She'd finished it by the time Skye walked in.

"You're looking much perkier this morning," Skye said as she dropped her purse on her desk, opposite J.J.'s.

"Since when do I look perky? I am, however, feeling a bit more chipper."

"Chipper, perky. Potatoes, tomatoes, etc. Anything new?"

"If you mean about the murder, no. If you mean about anything else, same answer. I haven't done much more than turn on my computer."

"But I see you stopped in at the Cups 'n' Roses. No news from there?"

"Nothing. Beth was concerned about me, and Connor, who didn't show up for his usual early-morning coffee. As is Evan. I stopped by his office, too." She leaned forward and clicked on her e-mail icon. "Oh cripes."

"What?"

"Over five hundred e-mails. What am I going to do?"

"Time for your organizational skills. Flip through them

and eliminate any names you don't know, without opening them—I'll bet a lot are from curious outsiders—then there's your usual spam, and finally, the important ones from clients."

J.J. saluted. "So clever." She watched while Skye turned her computer on and pulled up her own e-mail.

"Oh man," Skye said. "Looks like I'll need to take my own advice. Good thing I don't have any appointments until later this morning. How about you?"

"Nope. I'm planning to prepare my final report on the casino night and will also spend a day or so on the Stantons' fiftieth wedding anniversary party coming up in November, to make sure it's on track. Then I'm looking forward to getting back to work on the conference for the Vermont Primary Teachers Association happening next spring."

"I'll bet you'll have fun with that one."

J.J. grinned. "Right up my alley. But first, I need to make some personal phone calls. I'll get to the client ones we talked about a bit later."

She punched in Alison Manovich's home phone number. It went to the message mode, and J.J. left details of the dinner in case Alison could join them. J.J. had no idea what Alison's shifts were these days. It seemed like they hadn't had time to just sit and talk in a while. Then she tried Connor's cell phone. She knew he always kept it on vibrate, even when on the air, and could usually manage a quick text in acknowledgment. She left a message for him and next tried his home in case he'd taken the day off. *Of course he has. He needs some time.* Still no answer, so either he wasn't at home or he'd opted not to answer calls. Another message.

She decided to leave Beth for an in-person invitation. She'd head over after the lunch crowd eased off and at the same time find out what Beth wanted to talk to her about. She pulled out the blue binder she'd used as the bible for the casino night. She'd already printed out the notes she'd made on Saturday during the setup and on Sunday, after everything had been tucked away. She reread it all and then went to work on a report for People and Causes with an added postmortem section on how to do it better next time. She cringed at that word and the thought that struck her—next time, no murder.

By the time she'd finished, Skye was heading out the door to her appointment. J.J. saved the report, wanting to read it over yet one more time before printing out their own copy and e-mailing it to Megan. She hadn't promised to have it done by any particular date, so one more day wouldn't matter. She did know the group had to have their own report in to the licensing authorities within thirty days, though.

She checked her watch. Two P.M. She tried Connor's cell one more time. Still no answer. She was starving and Beth wanted to talk. Now was the time.

J.J. placed her order for a black bean and avocado salad and made her way to her favorite table, latte in hand. She sat staring out the window until Beth joined her a few minutes later. She placed the salad in front of J.J. and sat across from her, her own coffee mug in hand.

"You go first," Beth ordered after watching J.J. enjoying her first mouthful of salad.

"This is delicious. My compliments to the chef."

Beth grinned and bowed her head. "The chef thanks you. Now, what's up?"

"I was talking to Evan, and we've decided to see who can get together tonight for dinner at Bella Luna, six thirty or whenever you can get there. I'm hoping Connor can make it, because we're doing it for him, but so far I've not been able to reach him. Has he shown up at all today?"

"No, and I'm a bit worried. That's a lot for him to be

going through on his own. I think dinner is a great idea, even if he doesn't show. Maybe we can come up with a casserole chain or something."

"A what?"

"You know, like those things the church ladies used to make and drop off at the home of a congregational member going through difficulties." She laughed. "Okay, maybe not a casserole chain, but we should see what we can do to help out. Will Alison be there? She might have some news about how the police are progressing." She held up her hand. "I know that it's unlikely she'll share, but just saying, you never know."

"I had to leave her a message also. It might end up being just Evan and Michael, and you and me."

"No matter. We can still come up with a plan. I think it's a good idea, by the way. Now, you may not think *this* is such a good idea, but before I tell you, I want you to know I've given it a lot of thought."

Oh no. This sounds ominous.

"I want you to agree to be my mystery diner." She held up her hand to stave off anything J.J. might say, but J.J.'s mind was blank. She had no idea what Beth had in mind.

"I'm hoping you'll have time to come in on a regular basis for lunch every weekday and just sit, eat, and observe. The lunch will be on me, of course."

J.J. could think of a couple of reasons it wouldn't work but asked, "What would I be observing?"

"A thief."

"Are you serious?"

"Yes, unfortunately, I am. Things have been going missing, and you know it's just too busy at lunch for me or my helpers to keep an eye on everyone. But you need to eat, and it doesn't take long to get here, so you won't be using up huge chunks of your time. You just sit over in that other corner"—she pointed to the one farthest from the window—"because we don't have a clear line of sight here. As I said, you eat, observe, and if you see anything suspicious, you tell me, and then I keep an eye on that person until I have solid proof. It might not even take more than a couple of lunch hours to track him down."

"Him?"

"Or her." Beth had a small smile on her face, but her mouth looked rigid. J.J. could tell her answer was important.

"What's being stolen?"

"Nothing major that I can call the cops about. You know, napkin holders, salt and pepper mills, menus."

"Menus? Who'd take those?" J.J. quickly scanned the room.

"That's what I want to know. They may not be big items, but they start to add up even though it's just one item a day."

J.J. did some quick thinking. It would be good if she kept to a regular lunch schedule, and it wouldn't be for long. How many days could it take anyway?

"I will do it, but if something with a client pops up, I'll have to skip lunch."

"Fair enough. Maybe we can bring Evan into the loop for days like that, if it drags on for any amount of time. But I'm sure it won't." She reached across the table and squeezed J.J.'s hand. "I'm so grateful, J.J. I already feel much better."

Well, she couldn't get into trouble doing as Beth requested, and if it would help Beth, then what would be the harm?

CHAPTER 7

J.J. was the first to arrive at the restaurant that night. There was a definite nip in the air, which was bound to be even more so later in the evening. She pushed open the glass door and took her time looking around the room, wondering if the owner, Gina Marcotti, had hired a new hostess yet. Gina had temporarily taken over the task herself, as she tried to adjust to recent changes in her life, but J.J. knew it wouldn't take long for equilibrium to set in again.

The place was crowded, but J.J. spotted Gina talking to a table of six in the far corner. Gina glanced over and gave J.J. a small wave, then pointed to a table quite close to the bar with a Reserved sign on it. J.J. chose a seat that allowed her to see the front door and be able to get the others' attention.

Alison showed up right on the heels of Beth and Evan, who'd met in the parking lot and walked in together. By the time they had been sipping at their drinks and were well past wanting to order their meals, Connor still hadn't shown.

"Connor is coming, isn't he?" Alison asked, looking over her shoulder toward the door.

"I haven't spoken to him, but I left messages at work, on his cell, and at home." J.J. joined the search, which the server took to mean a signal to him.

Evan glanced at his watch. "Let's go ahead and order. He'll just have to catch up."

"No Michael?"

"He sends his regrets. He thought it would be better if it was just us tonight."

Gina Marcotti appeared with a server in tow. She smiled warmly at J.J. "I'm happy to see you all here again." She touched J.J. lightly on the shoulder. *"Buon appetito."*

When the food arrived, J.J. pulled out her smartphone. "I'll just try reaching him again." They all waited and could hear the rings until J.J. gave up. "Should we be worried? He was pretty upset by what happened."

Alison finished chewing the mouthful of seafood lasagna she'd just taken. "I know he was at the station for quite a while with Detective Hashtag, er, Hastings, earlier today."

"Can you just check to see if he might still be there?" J.J. took one look at Alison's face. "Pretty please?"

Alison sighed as she pulled out her cell. "Okay."

After a brief conversation, she filled the others in on what she'd learned. "He left the station around four."

Beth took a sip of her wine. "You know, he's been through a lot and no matter how long ago it was they were engaged, her death had to impact on him. Maybe he just wants some quiet time alone. I think we should allow him that." She pushed her lamb ragout around on her plate with her fork.

The others looked a bit uncertain.

"However," she continued, "it might also be thoughtful of us to go over to his place after dinner and see if he might want to talk. We could take a dessert with us. He needs to keep up his energy, you know."

J.J. felt better that a decision had been made. She took another mouthful of the linguine with clams she'd ordered and found it tasted much more flavorful this time.

J.J. looked around for Gina as they were getting ready to leave, but she was nowhere to be seen. J.J. must come by sometime on her own, or maybe even with Devine. The thought brought a small, wicked smile to her lips.

They'd just finished paying their bill when Beth said, "Did you walk, J.J.? Would you like a ride to Connor's?"

"Yes, thanks." She followed Beth out to her car, and they made arrangements to meet the others there.

By the time they'd reached the lobby of the five-story condo Connor lived in, Beth was starting to second-guess herself. "I hope this is the right thing to do, and I hope Connor agrees. I'd hate to have him think we're butting into his life."

But J.J. was anxious to talk to him. "He won't think that. And if it sounds like he does, we'll just back off."

She punched in the code to number 505. They waited a minute and then she did it again. When there was still no response, Evan volunteered to go around back and check if Connor's red Mazda CX-3 was in the underground parking lot.

"How will you do that?" Beth asked. "You can't get in without a code."

Evan winked. "It may be underground, but it's not fully enclosed. There's a two-foot gap all the way around the building, protected by bars, of course, and I know where his parking space is located. Right across from it and in full view."

He was out the door and along the walkway before anyone could answer. The others waited in silence, shuffling feet and trying to see into the lobby.

"No car," Evan reported. "I guess there's nothing more to do here."

"So, do you prowl around here often?" J.J. couldn't help but ask. She felt uptight and wanted to lighten the mood.

"Only when necessary," he answered with a grin that quickly faded.

J.J. couldn't shake her feeling of anxiety. "I hope everything's all right."

"Of course it is," Alison answered. "He's obviously out for the evening, maybe with close friends. We're not the only ones in his life."

"Point taken. Somehow I feel like we've let him down, though."

CHAPTER 8

J.J. walked briskly down the hill toward the office the next morning. It was a great day to be out getting some fresh air and exercise. She'd meant to get up early and walk all the way down to the lakeshore and back before getting ready for work, but best intentions don't always make things happen.

That was one of the reasons she'd made the move from Montpelier to Burlington. She'd been drawn to the shores of Lake Champlain since the first time she'd visited Skye's home, that first year in college. Of course the primary reason was to leave her old job and two-timing fiancé behind, but she thought the lake was a fine substitute. She also loved the small-village feel of Half Moon Bay and had opted to live close to where she worked, a short walk, rather than in the heart of the city. And when she had the time, a slightly longer walk took her down to the lake. But not this morning.

She'd checked her messages, both phone and e-mail, before leaving the apartment, hoping that Connor had gotten in touch. When she'd picked up her latte on the way to work, Beth had said she'd also not heard from him and was getting worried.

J.J. tried to shake off her unease as she climbed the stairs to Make It Happen. She unlocked the door and flipped on the light switch, then made a beeline to her computer. Skye would be out most of the morning, and J.J. was determined to have most of her long to-do list tackled by the time she started on her new career as a private eye at lunch.

She checked for messages and responded to the work-related ones. By the time she'd finished a second coffee, this one from the Keurig, she'd progressed to proofing the handout sheet she planned on using when teaching the event planning course at the community center, starting later in the fall. When she thought about it, she realized she'd enjoy teaching, which came as a big surprise to her, although she wasn't about to change careers anytime soon.

She glanced up as the door opened. Detective Ozzie Hastings, or Hashtag, as Alison said the others at the station referred to him, filled the doorframe. Despite the fact that his hair was longer and blonder than Ness's, and he had to be at least twenty-plus years younger, he did remind her of her neighbor. Maybe it was that certain cop thing about him, a weary yet alert look in his eyes. All comparisons ended immediately when Hastings opened his mouth. Hard to disguise that British accent.

J.J. tried to keep a friendly look on her face, although her insides had turned to jelly. This could not be a good thing. She'd been through this before.

"Detective Hastings, what can I do for you?"

It took just three steps for him to make it to her desk and hover while looking around the office. "You're on your own today?"

"For the morning, anyway." She tried not to sound defensive. It was an innocuous question, after all.

"Good. I thought you might rather do this in your office than in mine."

She gulped. "More questions?"

He pulled over a chair and sat back in it, looking fairly relaxed.

J.J. felt herself do the same. This might not be so bad after all. She actually felt emboldened to ask, "How did Miranda die?"

Hastings frowned. "I'd really like to be the one asking the questions, Ms. Tanner. But I can tell you that she was stabbed."

J.J. gasped. All of a sudden, she saw knives and dripping blood. *Not again.* "That's dreadful."

"Murder usually is. Now, tell me again why you chose Miranda Myers to be a co-emcee at the casino night."

J.J. shifted in her chair. Funny how uncomfortable it had become. "As I mentioned last time, Megan Spicer, the chair of the board for People and Causes, suggested both Miranda and Connor Mac. I followed through, and they both accepted."

"Did she give you a reason for picking them?"

"Not really. She may have mentioned something about them being so well-known in the community, being media personalities and all."

"How well did you know Ms. Myers?"

"Not at all. Of course, I knew her name because she really is quite the celebrity, but we'd never met before I asked her, which I did in person." There was that twinge of guilt again.

"So, how did you feel about asking the ex-fiancée of your boyfriend to work with him?"

J.J.'s jaw dropped. She felt flustered and tried to gather her thoughts before talking. "For starters, he's not my boyfriend. We're good friends and we go out on occasion, but there's nothing more to the relationship. And I didn't know about their past until that night."

"Mr. Mac hadn't told you before that?"

"No. There was no need to. We weren't serious. We hadn't exchanged dating histories or anything. Ask Connor."

"We're trying, but he seems to have run off." Hastings leaned forward, one elbow propped on her desk, his chin resting in his hand.

"What? I know he wasn't at home last night, but you make it sound almost like he's avoiding the police."

Hastings's smile was not a pleasant one. *Cynical* might be a good description. "That's what I call it when a suspect is told to stay in town and doesn't. Do you have any idea where he might be?"

"No. In fact, a bunch of us—you remember my dinner club, the Culinary Capers—well, we met for dinner at a restaurant last night, and were worried when he didn't turn up. That's not like him. And I know he was really upset about Miranda's death." She chewed on her bottom lip.

Hastings stood and started pacing, stopping to read Skye's collection of certificates and diplomas on the wall beside her desk. He turned back abruptly to J.J.

"What's bothering me right now is that I have only your word that you didn't know about their relationship. And that it was a continuing one. Are you the jealous type?"

J.J. sputtered. "No. Not a jealous bone in my body." She flashed briefly on the scene she'd made when she found her then-fiancé in bed with a client. Maybe she should qualify that statement. "As I told you, we weren't seriously involved, so there was no reason to be jealous, even if I'd known."

"I find it hard to believe. I've never known a woman who wasn't a small bit jealous of previous girlfriends." He sighed.

This was interesting. A personal tidbit? She sat back and folded her arms across her chest. She did not like where this was going. "Like I said, I wasn't jealous. You don't suspect me of murdering her, do you?"

He stared at her a few moments before answering, just long enough for her to start squirming. "Let's just say you're not off the list."

"But that's, that's . . ." she sputtered.

"How it is. If it makes you feel any better, you're not alone on the list." He allowed a small smile.

She perked up. "Can you share some names?"

He shook his head. "Although I would be concerned with us not being able to locate Connor Mac, if I were him. Are you sure you don't know where he is?"

"No, I don't know, but I am sure that he's unavailable because he's upset, not because he's a murderer in hiding." She bit her tongue. She shouldn't even mention those words together. Who knew how Hastings was connecting the dots? She tried for some composure. "Is there anything else I can do for you?"

"No. That takes care of it for today. Just don't go into hiding." Now he did smile. He stood and exited so quickly she didn't have a chance to think of a smart retort. Not that she should make one, she realized.

What a mess. Connor would, of course, be a prime suspect, and it appeared, so was she. How did these things happen? That's two murders to her tally as a suspect. *Me. I don't get it.*

She had just logged into her computer again when the office door opened. *Now what?* Only it wasn't Detective Hastings. Ty Devine stood with the door open, looking at her.

She cleared her throat. "And it continues. Please, come in."

"What continues?"

"I'm guessing this isn't a social call." Not likely, since she'd turned him down for dinner a couple of months ago, and he'd never tried again. Not even called.

He closed the door and sat where Hastings had been. "I have a few questions for you."

"Is it about the murder? Does Detective Hastings know you're doing this?"

Devine grinned. "So, he's grilled you, has he?"

"He just left."

"Did you tell him where Connor Mac is hiding?"

She was sure he could tell how affronted she felt. "I don't know where he is. What business is it of yours anyway? Why are you here?"

"I've been working for the television station, and now they want to make certain Miranda Myers's death isn't part of a plot against them."

"Conspiracy theory? Really? What makes them leap to that conclusion?"

"The fact that another of their employees was almost run down by a vehicle a few nights ago, some attempts at vandalism, and the station has been receiving harassing telephone calls."

"Aren't those calls something that media get on occasion? Like, when they report something wrong. Oops, that never happens."

He shrugged. "Let's just say they like to cover all their bases. Now, do you know where Mac is?"

"No. I really don't. As I keep telling everyone, we're good friends, nothing more. We do go out together once in a while but as good friends. Why is that so hard to believe?"

"Methinks the lady doth protest too much." His face looked somber but his eyes sparkled.

She sighed. "I'm really getting tired of this. Okay, new topic. Who was your date at the casino night?"

She could have given herself a head slap. The last thing she wanted to be asking him was *that*. He just sat there grinning.

"Jealous?"

"I am definitely not. It's just that I think you should be sharing if I'm forced to explain my personal life."

"Nobody is forcing you, but in the interests of fairness, the lady is Candice Edmonds, widow of the late Hunter Edmonds, heir to the Edmonds resorts empire. I did some work for her a while ago and she needed a date for the event. She asked, I said yes. Okay?"

J.J. felt her cheeks doing a slow burn. Best to move on. "Have you discovered anything relevant?"

"Early days. Why did you ask Miranda to be an emcee, especially with Connor Mac, knowing their relationship?"

"I didn't know they had any type of relationship when I asked her." She made a face when he raised his eyebrows. "And they were both requested by Megan Spicer, chairperson of the board of People and Causes. So I asked and they both agreed."

"Why would Megan Spicer want those two specifically?"

"Why don't you talk to her? She was the client. I didn't need an explanation."

"You'd like to know, though, wouldn't you?"

J.J. sighed again. "Yes, I've been wondering the same thing."

"But you're not going to get involved in the investigation this time, are you?" He looked serious again.

She shrugged.

"If I tell you what she says will you promise to stay out of it? You know there's a killer on the loose, and it could get dangerous."

"That's what you said the last time, as I recall."

"And I was right." He stood. "At the very least, think about calling me if you stumble across anything significant. Okay?"

She gave a noncommittal nod. At least that's how she saw it. Why would she share with him? He had a paying client. She had the futures of Connor and herself at stake.

"How about some lunch?" Devine asked.

"What?"

"It's lunchtime. After your harrowing brush with the law, I think you could use a calming lunch at Rocco G's."

Tempting. "I love Rocco G's but I promised Beth I'd eat at Cups 'n' Roses."

"Okay. Let's go."

She shrugged again. Maybe a professional eye would help with her lunch-hour stakeout.

CHAPTER 9

When they walked through the doors of Cups 'n' Roses, J.J. worried they might not find a table with a suitable view of the room. Beth spotted them and dashed over, steering J.J. to a table with a Reserved sign on it.

"I was worried you might not be able to make it, what with everything that's going on," Beth whispered. "And you brought professional reinforcements?"

"He insisted on taking me out to lunch."

"Does this make up for the supper you declined?" she whispered.

"Hardly. It's business," J.J. hissed.

"I can hear you," Devine said.

J.J. grimaced.

Beth smiled as she gave them each a menu. She rattled off the two specials of the day. They both ordered right away, J.J. choosing the pear with brie salad, and Devine, the mixed deli meat panini.

"I'll bring you each some water." She paused and flashed

a somewhat harried smile at J.J. "You know how much I appreciate this. Good luck."

Devine looked at J.J., eyebrows raised. "Why *good luck*?"

"Beth has asked me to have lunch here for a few days and try to spot who's stealing from her."

"Stealing? As in what?" He took a good look around him and then settled back, his gaze focused on her. "Must be awfully small if the thief is doing it right under her watchful eye."

"The items are small. Things like salt and pepper mills, cutlery, even menus. Beth has switched from cotton serviettes to these thicker-weave paper ones, but even these are being taken. It doesn't make any sense."

"You'll find it makes sense to whoever is taking them." He leaned back in his chair. "I think this is a good project for you. Concentrate on catching the thief and leave the murder to the police."

"And you, you mean."

He nodded. "Yeah. Could be because I have a client and I'm trained as a cop, as you remember."

Then he smiled the sexy smile.

J.J. flashed back to the time he'd kissed her quite unexpectedly in the car after trapping a stalker. She struggled to regain her equilibrium. "Well, the TV station may be your client, but I'm a suspect, once again, as is a good friend."

"You should be pleased there are at least two of you on the list."

She couldn't read the deadpan expression on his face. "Are there others?"

"There usually are to begin with."

"Either you don't know who or you're not willing to share. Which is it?"

"This is getting us nowhere." He leaned forward, his

arms crossed on the table. "You know I'm not going to tell you anything, and all I want from you is your word that you'll stay out of it."

Her spirits plummeted but she wasn't sure why. "I'll try. How's that?"

His eyes bored into hers. "It will have to do, but I'd really try my best to stay out of Hastings's way this time, if I were you. And also, the killer's."

"Believe me, I don't want to mess with a killer. Now, any ideas about how to spot what's happening in here?"

"I haven't noticed anyone doing anything suspicious yet."

"But we've been talking. You haven't been watching."

"It's what I do, J.J. I wouldn't get too far if I looked obvious about watching people. Besides, I'm quite good at multitasking." He grinned and J.J. grinned back, for some unnamed reason feeling relieved and happy at the same time.

Their meals arrived, and Beth stood at the table eyeing them both for a few seconds before winking at J.J. and stopping at a number of tables to talk to customers on her way back to the counter.

"Oh man, this is delicious," J.J. said after swallowing her first bite of the salad.

Devine nodded but continued chewing. He washed his food down with some coffee. "She's got a good business going here. How long has she been at it?"

"I think around five years or so, before I moved to town. She retired from teaching and apparently, this is what she's wanted to do for a long time. I first met her because everyone raved about her coffee."

Devine's eyes narrowed, focusing on a spot behind J.J.'s right shoulder.

"What is it?" she demanded. "Someone stealing?"

He shook his head. "No, just looking a bit odd. When I tell you, turn around and look at the woman with light brown hair tied back from her face, in the brown jacket. She's at the table next to the door. Okay, now."

J.J. turned quickly, just in time to see the woman stand and abruptly exit. "You're sure she didn't take anything?"

"Not that I saw, but I think she was spooked. Maybe by Beth talking up the customers. But I'd be on the lookout for her next time you're working this case."

Is that a smirk? J.J.'s lips flatlined. "You may make light of this, Ty Devine, but it's important to Beth. So, I will continue and see if I can find out something to help her out."

They walked back in silence, and when they reached his car, which was parked on the street in front of the building, parted with a quick good-bye. J.J. kept checking behind her as she climbed the stairs to her office. Silly, really. There would be no reason for him to come back in.

Skye sat at her desk, phone tucked between ear and shoulder. J.J. gave her a quick wave, then flicked on her computer and got straight back to work. About an hour later, she surfaced, having finished off a list of possible entertainers for a thirtieth high school reunion she was planning for next June. She'd be meeting with the school grad committee in a couple of weeks and needed them to make many decisions at that point.

She next did a final read of the casino report. She printed a copy for the paper files and checked it over again before e-mailing it to Megan Spicer and Sue Fischer. Then she breathed a sigh of relief. It was always a good feeling to finalize a project, except this one was still far from being closed. There was still a murderer on the loose.

She picked up the phone and tried calling Connor. Just in case. When it went to voice mail, she admitted to herself that she was getting really worried about him. *He had decided to take a drive after visiting her on Sunday, to clear his head. Suddenly his car went out of control as he turned onto a dirt road in some remote location. The car came to rest in a thicket, hidden from the road by trees*

*and underbrush with Connor, trapped inside, unable to
reach his cell phone, unable to call for help. Slowly getting
weaker and weaker.* She shook her head to get rid of the
image. She'd read a book by Frances Itani not too long
ago, with a similar plot. It obviously had stayed with her.

Or, he was on the run from the law. Which would probably mean he was the killer. She didn't know which scenario was the worst. Neither was good news.

"What is wrong with you?" Skye asked. "You look like
you've lost your best friend."

"I may have. Well, not my best. That would be you, but
I'm thinking about Connor and why we haven't heard
from him."

Skye grabbed a Ghirardelli dark chocolate bar from the
desk drawer and tossed it over to J.J. "Here, my treat. This
may help. Or not. I don't know what to say. It's really looking bad for him with the police, isn't it?"

J.J. broke off a hunk of the chocolate and ate it before
answering. "It makes him look guilty, but I really don't
believe he did it."

"Is it because you're stuck on him?"

J.J. looked shocked. "No, I'm not. And you, as my best
friend, should know that."

Skye shrugged. "I thought I did, but it's always good to
check in. I have to admit I wondered if he was the reason
you said no to going out with that private eye."

"You thought that? You were relieved, as I recall, that
I said no to Devine." J.J. glared at her.

"Not the same thing."

"Well, if you must know, the reason I said no was
because I'm afraid of him." She sucked in her breath and
hurried on when she saw the look on Skye's face. "Not that.
I don't think he'd hurt me, well, not physically, that is."

"Ah. All is revealed. You felt this real connection with
him, didn't you? He got you all hot and bothered without
even trying, and you're afraid you'll really fall for him,

right? And, having done that, you're equally afraid he'll dump you."

"Wow. You don't hold back, do you? Of course, that doesn't surprise me." She sighed. "I just didn't think I'd been that obvious."

Skye walked over and gave J.J. a hug. "Honey, you're always that obvious. At least to me. For what it's worth, I think it was the right decision, no matter what the reason."

J.J. appreciated the hug, but she wasn't so sure about the comment. She watched her friend cross back over to her desk and focus on her computer screen. Skye would soon be back in the zone, that place she went when plotting an event. J.J. knew that would be a good place for her also to be but now that she'd been thinking about Connor, she needed to be doing something about finding him.

The television station seemed like the best place to start. Followed by another chat with a certain board chair.

About half an hour later she pulled into the parking lot of the WBVT station and eased into a narrow space between a Porsche and a BMW. She knew neither was likely to add any dents to her car. She'd come up with a game plan, of sorts, during the drive downtown. Start at the top. Surely the station manager could fill her in, at least on the reasons why he'd hired Ty Devine. That could turn out to be a part of a key to this entire scenario. If Miranda's murder was part of some sort of conspiracy against the station, Connor would be off the hook. *Of course, that's it.*

Feeling a bit cheerier, she asked at the reception desk but was told that Donald Cooper, the station manager, was out of town for the day. Bummer. The receptionist might be a good source, though. She peered at the nameplate on the counter.

"Wanda, I'm the event planner from the casino night last weekend. The event where Miranda Myers died."

"Oh." Wanda seemed at a loss for words.

"I'm just trying to set my mind at rest about what happened and was wondering if there was someone in the station you thought might be a good person for me to chat with about Miranda Myers." J.J. added a slight note of pleading to her voice. She needed this woman on her side.

Wanda leaned toward J.J. "That was such a horrific thing, wasn't it? I'll bet you were right there and saw her body and the whole thing, right? I can't imagine how I'd feel if I was there. And I know I'd feel even worse if I'd planned the whole thing. Oh, I don't mean the murder but the other, the event. You know? You must feel so rotten."

Oh, I do. J.J. wanted to shake this woman to get her to stop talking but bit her tongue instead. *Remember your quest.* "Oh, believe me, I do. That's why I need to talk to someone who was maybe close friends with Miranda."

Wanda leaned even closer. "I always say, it's best to talk to the enemies. Now, if I was you, I'd talk to Kathi Jones. She's one of the noon show hosts."

"They were enemies?"

"Wanted to scratch each other's eyes out. Meow." She added a little swipe of her hand. J.J. tried not to associate this woman in her mind with her own even-tempered feline.

J.J. grinned, conspiratorially. "Is Kathi here right now?"

Wanda glanced at her computer. "She's just off the air and should be in the back office. Do you want me to call her?"

"Please. But first, can you tell me why they were enemies?"

"They were both on-air divas, don'tcha know? Kathi was really pissed that Miranda got the evening entertainment show. That has so much more glamour than the noon show. She let everyone, even me, know that she thought Miranda had done some dirty dealings in order to get it. I think she meant that Miranda slept with the boss, but that's real hard to imagine."

"You mean the station manager? What's his name again?"

"Donald Cooper. And no, I mean the program manager,

her immediate boss, who is a woman. Now, doesn't that sound real mean on Kathi's part?"

Who knows? She could be right, though.

J.J. nodded. "Would you mind trying Kathi now?"

"Sure thing." She spoke into her headset and a few seconds later announced, "Kathi's coming out front to see you." She winked, tucking a stray piece of blonde hair back behind her ear, and then tended to an incoming call.

J.J. moved closer to the side wall and scanned the photos of the on-air employees. She'd just spotted Kathi Jones when she heard her name called. She whirled around and faced Kathi in person.

"You wanted to speak to me?" Kathi asked, sounding curious but pleasant.

J.J. put out her hand. "I'm J.J. Tanner, with Make It Happen. I'm the event planner for the casino night, and I was wondering if I could ask you some questions about Miranda Myers."

A look flittered across Kathi's face, but J.J. couldn't peg what it was. Sadness, dislike, relief? Maybe J.J. was projecting what she'd just heard from Wanda.

"I guess that's all right. The police didn't tell me not to talk to anyone."

"The police questioned you?"

"Sure. They spent most of yesterday afternoon here at the station talking to everyone who knew Miranda. Look, I just got off the air and could use a coffee. How about we run next door to the Coffee Pot? We'd get more privacy, too."

J.J. nodded. Kathi signaled Wanda what she was doing and grabbed J.J. by the arm.

At the Coffee Pot, they easily found a table away from the door. J.J. thought if the coffee shop had so few customers all day long, it wouldn't be in business for very long. They went to the counter and ordered their drinks, and J.J. paid for them.

Back at the table, J.J. waited until Kathi seemed settled

and had a couple of sips of her coffee before beginning. J.J. discreetly watched her over the rim of her own cup. Her long blonde hair, pulled back and pinned so that it cascaded around her heart-shaped face, shimmered in a ray of sunlight. J.J. could understand why Kathi was chosen to host a TV show. The camera must love her. "Can you think of anything that might be useful in finding Miranda's killer?"

"Hm. Direct, I see. For starters, I didn't do it, although I know the rumors are flying fast and thick around the station, that Miranda and I were archenemies."

"And were you?"

Kathi gave a small smile. "Not really. We were rivals, that's true, and I would have loved her job, but it wasn't worth killing her to get it. We actually thought the rumors were amusing and agreed it would be fun to ramp things up. So at staff meetings we'd interrupt each other and sit there glaring in between. It doesn't seem so funny now."

"That's an odd thing to do, isn't it?"

"I asked Miranda to go along with it for the ratings. We knew that Wanda would let it slip to the other media outlets around town, and for a while, it did make headline news. Now it's on the back burner and has been for a long time."

"Did it work?"

"We both had pretty good ratings, tops in our time slots, so I'll let you decide." Kathi's smile said it all.

"Okay. Well, can you tell me if she'd had trouble with anyone at the station?"

"Nice of you not to say, 'other than me.' No, I don't think she did. She could be abrupt, especially when close to showtime, but mostly she didn't mingle too much. She'd come in in the late morning and prepare her show with the help of her researcher, so I didn't see her then. She'd take a break midafternoon and then be back a couple of hours before the show aired live. Her office, more a cubbyhole like mine, was two doors away."

"Who is her researcher?"

"Hennie Ferguson. She's just a kid. She did an internship here and Miranda liked her so they hired her. I don't know how close they were, though."

"Is there anyone else at the station I should talk to?" J.J. just hoped she could remember all the names.

"Donald Cooper, the manager, if you can corner him. He's always at meetings, sometimes in the station, other times off-site. And then there's one of the cameramen she hung around with. Nothing romantic. Lonny Chan is his name." Kathi looked at her watch and finished off her coffee. "Look, I've got to get back. Hope this helped."

She was out of her seat before J.J. could answer.

Helped? I'll say. J.J. decided it would be best to think about what she'd learned before leaping into the next question period. She needed to be cleverer than the murderer if she was going to trap a killer.

CHAPTER 10

J.J. paused, pen in hand, debating if she should put Kathi Jones's name on the suspect list or the bystander list. This wasn't how she'd planned to spend her evening, but she couldn't let it go. She'd spent the last half hour trying to sort out whether or not she believed in Kathi's sincerity or whether jealousy over the job had been such an intense emotion that Kathi had plotted to kill Miranda.

She thought back to her job in her previous life, as an account planner at a major advertising agency in Montpelier. Competition was intense between reps wanting to keep their jobs by landing and keeping new clients. The keeping was the part that had always excited J.J., coming up with the creative plan for the successful marketing of the client's product, be it an actual item or a lifestyle, and working with the copywriters to make it happen. She'd probably still be doing it if she hadn't discovered that her fiancé, also a rep at the same firm, had used his masculine wiles to compete and complete the signing of a new wealthy client. A female client, twenty years older but eager to hop into bed with

Patrick. J.J. had confronted him, then resigned from her job of five years. She couldn't stand being in the same company with him anymore nor in the same city.

At the invitation of her old college roommate, Skye Drake, she'd come back to visit Half Moon Bay, part of the north Burlington shoreline on Lake Champlain. She felt that same tug from when she'd last been there, back in her first year of college, and decided that's where she wanted to live. When Skye offered her a job at Make It Happen, her event planning company, J.J. jumped at the change in her life. She'd never looked back.

So, she knew all about jealousy, how it could eat at you and cause you to take drastic steps. But murder had never been anything she'd considered. And she just couldn't believe Kathi Jones would, either. Especially for a job. Although she could be wrong.

She put Kathi on the suspect list but at the bottom.

Next she made a list of who to talk to on her next visit to WBVT. Lonny Chan. Hennie Ferguson. And, of course, the elusive Donald Cooper. She'd better make an appointment with him. Come to think of it, she'd better make appointments with the other two, also. She made a note to do all of that first thing in the morning, refilled Indie's water dish and left some treats beside it, then headed to bed.

J.J. was the first to arrive at Make It Happen the next morning. She flipped on the lights and her computer, had a few more sips of her latte, and got to work. First of all, she checked her e-mail for anything urgent. Nothing needed immediate attention, so she phoned the TV station to make those appointments.

Donald Cooper's assistant said he was in town and had some time available at ten thirty, so she slotted her in, while Hennie Ferguson agreed to see her just before that. She had to settle for leaving a message for Lonny Chan. She left her smartphone number, hoping he'd call while she was there and she could complete her task in one swoop.

Skye kicked at the door with her foot, and when J.J. opened the door, she waltzed in, her hands holding a cardboard tray with two coffee cups and a bag of goodies in the center. Her pride and joy, her Louis Vuitton purse, swung on her arm in time to the clack of her high-heeled suede boots across the floor.

"Thought I'd treat us today. I know, you've already picked up a latte, but a second one will help, I'm sure." She deposited one of the cups on J.J.'s desk and opened the paper bag, waving it under her nose. "Chocolate croissants, anyone?"

"Hmmm. Not that I need one. But thanks." J.J. eagerly stuck a hand in the bag and brought out what she thought must be the largest chocolate croissant in town.

"Need is not the issue here. It's purely want and desire. Plus, it's a good energy boost."

"And why do I need an energy boost?"

"Because I need you to do some brainstorming with me this morning. I'm stuck on the Northanda account. I need some ideas for a highly spectacular, once-in-a-lifetime corporate retreat. Are you in?"

J.J. pushed aside thoughts of her own brainstorming that needed doing. Skye had helped her a lot in the past. Now it was payback time. "I've got half an hour, if that works."

She dragged her chair over to Skye's desk, sat back, and bit into the still-warm croissant. "Yum. Heavenly."

"Agreed. So, here's what I've got so far." Skye flipped open her iPad and found the document, a work in progress. "They're trying to rebuild with a fairly young team after some setbacks and missteps. I'm thinking make it three days, that's according to management, who feels they can't afford to be away any longer. Something in the Middlebury area so it's not too long a drive."

"What does the Northanda group do?"

"Insurance. Haven't you seen their ads on TV? Their

logos on the sides of buildings? Their name in the paper in some very recent high-profile lawsuits? These kids are the go-getters. They're all pretty savvy when it comes to what they're promoting, in their late twenties and early thirties mostly, and game for almost anything. Ideas?"

J.J. leaned back in her chair and gave it some thought. Most ideas that came quickly were the old tried and true ones, but she had a feeling that's the last thing the Northanda group wanted. "I suppose you're thinking at least a half day of physical activity forcing them to rely on one another?"

"Uh-huh. I've been thinking about something involving a zip line, among other things, maybe in Jeffersonville or Bromley."

"Now you're all over the map." She grinned. "You know, I've always wanted to try one of those."

"You have? You, who can't stand heights? That you?" Skye couldn't have look more surprised.

J.J. adjusted her posture. "In theory, yes. What appeals is that you're really securely tied in or up, as the case may be. There's no chance of taking a misstep and falling into a canyon or down a cliff."

"In theory. So, we're agreed. That's day one maybe, in the afternoon after they've had a chance to sign in, grab a coffee, and have a bit of orientation. Day two should be . . . what?"

Skye's phone rang and she glanced at the caller ID. "Nick," she mouthed as she answered the call.

J.J. took the cue and moved back to her own desk. She tried not to eavesdrop on the lovebirds' conversation, as hard at that was to do in the small office. She set aside thoughts of the Northanda issue and found her mind wandering back to the murder. She thought it might be a good time to visit their co-tenant across the hall, Tansy Paine, who seemed to have her fingers on every pulse in the community. Chances were she'd heard something about Miranda Myers or the TV station or both.

Tansy's outer office was empty. Again. J.J. wondered if the assistant was soon to be a former employee. She could hear Tansy's voice coming from behind the door in the inner office. It sounded like she was on the phone. J.J. sat on the side of the desk, waiting, hoping it wouldn't be a long call. When she heard the phone being hung up, she knocked on the door and entered as Tansy called out.

"J.J., great to see you. Business or pleasure? Should I start the clock?"

J.J. gave an exaggerated shudder. "I can't afford your lawyer fees, I'm afraid, so it's purely pleasure."

"Good. I'd hate to think you're in trouble again, although that was a nasty business on the boat."

"I think I'm still in shock. It's almost surreal what happened to Miranda Myers. Did you know her?" Might as well jump right in.

Tansy eyed her a few seconds and then smiled. "I didn't know her, and I know you're trying to get information out of me because you're meddling again, aren't you?"

J.J. bristled. "I wouldn't call it meddling. I feel a certain amount of responsibility. I did organize the event, after all, and asked her to be an emcee. And then there's my friend Connor Mac, who I'm sure is at the top of the suspect list."

"Why would you say that?"

"Because they had history and he's disappeared. Or something."

Tansy whistled. "Oh boy. Not a smart thing on his part. This is the guy you've been dating?"

"Not really 'dating.' We're good friends and go out on occasion."

"So, dating. Define *disappear.*" Tansy pulled a small compact mirror out of her desk drawer and did a quick check of her face and hair. The spiky ends of her short red hair stood at attention and almost matched the shade of her lipstick.

"No one has heard from him for a couple of days."

She looked up at J.J. "I gather, not even the police?"

"As far as I know, no."

She placed the compact back in her drawer and slowly closed it. "Well, I wouldn't get involved if I were you. But I know how you love being told that. So I'll tell you that I have met Miranda Myers on occasion, but it's her brother I know better. We were classmates at UVM and have kept in touch. He's actually running for state attorney, and knowing him, it's just a stepping-stone. He asked me just a couple of weeks ago to work on his campaign, but I declined. As much as I respect and like him, I try to keep out of politics."

"Interesting. Quite a high-profile family, then."

Tansy shrugged. "They're both the types of personalities that are out there. At least, his sister was."

"Do you think I could drop your name if I try to talk to him?"

"Sure, but I'd hold off for a while if I were you. Don't want to appear too crass."

J.J. bit the inside of her cheek to hold in her first response. Then she smiled as she stood, and said, "Of course. I'm not planning on intruding on his grief. Thanks for the information."

Tansy nodded and started flipping through her pile of papers before J.J. even opened the door.

J.J. was still shaking her head as she entered her own office.

"What's up?" Skye asked.

"I think Tansy must believe I'm a total idiot." She outlined their conversation, and Skye laughed.

"I wouldn't take it to heart. You know Tansy. She's dynamite in a courtroom, or so I've heard, but doesn't always apply a filter out in real life. I fully believe you will act tactfully and tastefully."

"Thank you. I'll try to live up to your expectations. Ready to get back to brainstorming?"

"Actually, if you don't mind, I'd like to put it off till a bit later today. I have a Nick errand to deal with first."

"That's perfectly fine. I'll start my search for a caterer for the high school reunion, and then I think I'll try out some of that tact at the TV station."

"You're not planning on using Epicurial Expressions again? I thought you said they did a good job for the casino night."

"They did, but I want to try someone a bit more in tune with the times, that being the '80s. I'll have to do some research and see just what food was popular back then."

"Uh, right. You were too young to remember."

"That's it. What does Nick want you to do?"

"He asked if I could pop by the drapery store and make a final choice between the two sets we've been looking at. He doesn't know when he'll find the time to go back. And here I thought dentists led well-ordered, nine-to-five lives." She chuckled.

"He's lucky he's got you is all I can say." She glanced at the clock hanging on the wall behind the coffee machine. "Whoa, no time for caterers. I'd better take off or I'll miss my chance to talk to the manager at the TV station. Wish me luck."

"You got it."

Hennie Ferguson was waiting at the front desk for J.J. when she walked into the station lobby.

"Hi," Hennie said, sticking her hand out, then introducing herself. "I saw you when you were in yesterday so I thought I'd wait here. I'm sorry but I don't have a lot of time. They're rotating staff in Miranda's slot"—she paused to sniff—"so I'm running at turbo speed. It seems I'm the only one who knows what's going on here."

"The glue."

"Huh?"

"That's what my mom always calls herself. The glue that holds the household together. Guess you're it for the show." J.J. smiled, hoping to put Hennie at ease.

It seemed to work. Hennie's narrow lips relaxed into a small smile, but the blue eyes behind her large, dark-rimmed glasses remained wary. Her dark hair was held back with clips and fell straight, well past her shoulders. She wore a long-sleeved white blouse with a dark green cotton vest overtop, brown slacks, and flat shoes. She reminded J.J. of one of the characters on the TV show *The Big Bang Theory*. She wondered if it ran on WBVT and that's where Hennie found the look.

"Yeah, guess that's right. So let's go to my desk. What do you want to ask me anyway?"

J.J. followed her down the corridor, keeping her eye on the interior "courtyard" that was completely glassed in and held the broadcast studios. The offices were built around this core. Hennie's office was almost directly across from the front door, J.J. guessed. Hennie pushed open the door and pointed to a chair. The office was barely large enough for one desk, a massive file cabinet, and the chair. Posters of classic rock groups covered what wall space wasn't hidden behind furniture. A small window, tiny horizontal shades pulled shut, probably looked out on the alley, or so J.J. imagined.

"Cozy," J.J. said, moving some newspapers off the chair before sitting.

"I don't even notice anymore. I'm usually buried in newspapers. Yes, it's the old-fashioned way, but it complements researching on the computer."

"What are all the file cabinets for?"

Hennie shrugged. "Old stuff. Before my time, in the age of dinosaurs when everything was totally paper. Nobody's gotten around to sorting it or throwing it out. I've forgotten it's there. So, what do you want to know?"

J.J. pretended to be interested in her surroundings, but

she kept Hennie in sight, watching for reactions. "Did Miranda have any enemies here at the station?"

"Right to the point." Hennie sat on the edge of her desk and looked to be pondering the question. "Not really enemies. There's a lot of jealous people in TV, and since she had a prime-time spot, she was the target of a lot of it. But then again, she gave as good as she got."

"Oh, really?"

Hennie nodded. "She wasn't about to be put down by Kathi Jones or anyone else. I admired her for that. She knew what she wanted and set about getting it."

"Do you think Kathi might have tried anything?"

"Like killing her? Not likely. Kathi likes spreading rumors about people. Death by words, that's her style." *Interesting. Maybe.*

"And Miranda's style?"

Hennie straightened up and grabbed a clipboard from her desk. "What's that got to do with it? She is the victim, isn't she?"

"You're so right. What about Miranda's private life?"

"She didn't talk about that very often. I knew when she was planning on meeting someone after the show, of course. She'd leave here dressed to the nines. And, of course, I knew if a guy showed up here to see her, like Connor Mac would the odd time."

"Were they seeing each other?"

"I guess, but like I said, I had no real way of knowing." She glanced at the clock. "Uh-oh. Got to move it. The pre-air meeting starts in five. Let me know if there's anything else I can do."

She nodded at J.J. and went to hold the door open for her. "Miranda was more into innuendos."

J.J. looked at her sharply and got a deadpan look in return. She thanked Hennie and made her way back to the reception area. She watched the goings-on in the studios as she retraced her steps. One large window allowed her to see what looked to be a recording studio. For what, she wasn't sure. One fellow with a large headset on glanced her way, then quickly looked back at the page he was holding.

"Mr. Cooper is waiting for you," the receptionist told J.J. when she approached the desk in the front entry. "Just go down the hall, the other direction. His office is the corner suite at the far end." She answered an incoming call before J.J. could say anything.

Walking around the opposite side of the studio block presented an entirely different view. This was the newsroom side, and J.J. marveled at the number of monitors and TV screens angled around the room. Most people were sitting at their desks, either typing on the computer or talking on the phone. For so many people and so much equipment, J.J. found it surprisingly silent. Talk about soundproofing. She found Cooper's office right where she'd been told. She took a deep breath, trying to ease the knot in her stomach that had started to tighten when she'd first mentioned Miranda's name this morning. *Get a grip. It's not your fault.* She knocked and entered when he called out.

Her first impression was that this was the power place. The window blinds were open and the view was a spectacular one of Lake Champlain. From this level, it was difficult to see the buildings cascading down the hillside below the station.

She pegged Donald Cooper to be in his late fifties, although his closely cropped light hair and freckled face made it hard to be sure. A stocky man, maybe five foot six, close to J.J.'s height. He was wearing a blue dress shirt, with the sleeves rolled up to his elbows, and a red tie. A dark suit jacket hung on a hook behind the door. He rose to shake her hand as she crossed to his desk. When she'd settled in a chair, he offered her a coffee but she declined.

"Okay, right down to business. What can I do for you, Miss Tanner?"

"As I said on the phone to your assistant, I'm the one who hired Miranda Myers to be co-emcee at the casino night, and so I feel some responsibility here. I'm hoping an untrained eye, namely mine, can spot something that the police might not in their investigation."

"Well, as much as I can understand your feelings, I think you're wasting your time. Detective Hastings seems well qualified to do his job, and I've hired a top-notch private detective, Ty Devine, to look into it, as well."

"Why did you do that if you think the police are doing their jobs?" She wanted to hear his version.

He put his hands on the desk in front of him and entwined his fingers, leaning slightly forward at the same time. "He's been on my payroll long before this happened. I believe this death was part of a bigger conspiracy against WBVT. We've had a few other incidents happen in the past several weeks, and I think this lunatic has just escalated things or maybe got carried away and didn't mean to kill Miranda. But she's dead, either way."

"What else has happened?"

He took a few seconds before answering. J.J. wondered if he might decide not to share this information.

He cleared his throat. "First of all, we received a mysterious package at the reception desk, and when Wanda opened it, some white powder fell out. We called the police immediately, and the hazmat team checked it all out. It was nothing lethal, just a powder that would give the person who touched it a slight allergic reaction. Sneezing, itchy eyes. That kind of thing. A real nuisance."

"I remember hearing about that on the news."

"Yes, well, no media station wants to be part of the news it's reporting." He ran a hand across his head as if patting down his hair, which wasn't there. "But there was no return address and no way of tracing the package. We've kept a close eye on everything that's come in after that. Then about two weeks ago, one of our weather specialists was out doing a live segment on the sidewalk right in front of the station. When he'd finished and was walking back to the station, a dark truck, no markings, jumped the curb and went straight for him. The cameraman realized what was happening and pulled our weather guy out of the way, but he was bumped by the car and went down, spraining his ankle."

"That's frightening. No one got the plate or anything from the van?"

"No."

"Anything else?"

"A few acts of vandalism, some minor, others a bit more costly to us."

"I suppose Mr. Devine has looked into disgruntled employees. Anyone recently fired?"

"Of course, and I'll tell you what I told him—all firings were for legitimate reasons and no one seemed overly surprised nor angry at what happened. There were only two."

"Oh? Who were they?"

"I don't think I should be sharing that information with you. Privacy, you know. Ty Devine is in full possession of the details, and I'm confident he'll figure it out. It could be some kook who doesn't like what the station stands for or is upset about the way we covered a story. Or even someone who's hankering for the limelight and won't mind getting caught. That happens, but usually it doesn't get beyond crazy e-mails."

"Did you get any e-mail warnings about these incidents?"

He shook his head. "No. And that's the strange thing. Everyone uses e-mail these days."

The intercom on his desk buzzed and he held his finger in a "just a minute" signal to J.J. The assistant's voice sounded panicky as she told him he was needed in the garage downstairs. Something had happened to the station truck.

Cooper excused himself and quickly left the room. He

didn't seem to realize that J.J. was trailing right behind him. When she slid onto the elevator just as the door was closing, he raised his eyebrows at her but didn't say anything.

The first thing she saw when the doors opened was Ty Devine, looking straight at her.

CHAPTER 11

"I won't even ask what you're doing here," he hissed at her as he directed Cooper to step over to the side, where they spoke in hushed tones.

J.J. looked around the garage. It looked like any other underground concrete lot. She wasn't sure how many levels there were. Most of the parking slots had Reserved signs on the wall, especially those for the management level of employees.

The news department had an entire wall of signs. In the parking slot at the far end, the WBVT van she'd seen at so many live news stories was sporting a new addition to its usual logo. Angry thrusts of red and black paint criss-crossed the sides and back of the van. She slowly walked around it, taking it all in but came to an abrupt halt when Devine stepped in front of her.

"Okay, out with it." His clear blue eyes meant business.

"What? You mean, what I'm doing here? Now? Well, I

had just finished talking to Mr. Cooper when he got the call to come down here." She hoped that would be enough information for him but knew way down deep that it wouldn't be.

"What kind of a talk? You're sticking your nose into this, aren't you? Didn't I tell you I was doing the investigating for the station?"

"I realize that," she said, trying to keep calm. "I wanted to know more about Miranda, not the vandalism and other problems the station is having."

"And you don't think they're tied together?"

She shrugged. "Do you?"

He glared at her a moment and then strode back to Cooper. After a few more minutes of talk, Cooper left, shaking his head. Devine appeared back at her side just as she was doing another pass around the truck.

"We need to have another little talk. Come with me." He grabbed her arm but held on gently, steering her out the open garage door and over to his Acura, parked in a visitors' section of the outdoor lot. He held the passenger door open while she slid in. She remembered one of the last times she'd been in his car and the kiss that had ended that evening, after confronting a murder suspect. She shivered in spite of the warmth in the car, which had been sitting in the sun for what felt like some time.

Devine slid behind the steering wheel and locked the doors.

J.J. made a face. "You didn't have to do that, you know. Really quite juvenile."

His fingers tapped the steering wheel. "Don't push me too far, J.J. I want you to talk. Tell me who you've spoken to and what you've learned so far."

She sighed. Maybe she should tell him. Maybe he had a different take on it all. She started with her talk first with Kathi and then with Hennie and Cooper. Devine listened without comment. When she had finished, she asked, "I don't think it's any of them, do you?"

"That's not something I'm going to discuss with you."

"Well, I told you all. Give me something. Is there anyone connected to the station who might have had it in for Miranda?"

Devine turned in his seat to face her. "You really expect me to tell you that?"

"Well, yes, if you want to keep me from nosing around some more. You know that I will just keep on doing so."

It was his turn to sigh. "You're right. I do know. But that doesn't mean I'm sharing any information. Last time, you almost got killed. Or have you forgotten?"

"Last time you were there for me," she said in a quiet voice.

He reached out as if to touch her cheek but pulled back his hand at the last minute, unlocking the doors instead. "I know it's important for you to clear Connor Mac, but let me handle this."

She didn't know what to say. Did he think she was in love with Connor? It sure sounded like it. But she couldn't just go blurting out again that they were only friends. It would sound like she was interested in Devine and had regretted turning down his dinner invitation. Which she realized, she did regret. *Too late now.*

She swallowed hard, opened the door and got out. "You may not be aware of this, but I am also a suspect and I sure as hell didn't do it. So I do have a vested interest. Just not the one you're thinking."

She shut the door firmly, lifted her chin, and strode to the side of the building, trying not to slow down on the steep incline up the street to the front of the building.

She looked at her car and back at the station. She needed the names of employees recently let go. Who seemed the most sympathetic to her cause? Who had access to the list?

She realized she was too rattled to think it through right
now. Devine still had that effect on her. She cursed silently
as she returned down the slope to where she'd parked her
car and drove back to the office.

The entire building seemed to be empty. Evan had hung a
Closed sign on his office and the showroom doors; the light
in Tansy's office was off; and Skye was nowhere to be seen.
This was all good. She needed to be away from distractions
so that she could double-check all the details for the upcoming Stanton fiftieth wedding anniversary. Just over one
month to go. It took her less than an hour, but when she
glanced at the clock, she'd missed lunch. Beth would not
be pleased.

She closed the office and made her way to Cups 'n'
Roses to apologize.

Beth brushed away her regrets with a swipe of her hand.
"Listen, I know you're busy and have a real job. I'm not
worried. Whatever time you can give me is a gift, so do
not worry about it, please. Now, you can still enjoy something to eat, and since it's not too busy right now, I'll join
you."

J.J. chose a roasted vegetable salad and carried a latte
for her and a regular dark roast coffee for Beth to the table.
Beth joined her a few minutes later with their lunches.
After two mouthfuls, J.J. put down her fork and leaned
forward.

"This is really delicious, Beth. Your menu just keeps
getting more interesting every time I'm in."

Beth grinned. "I love hearing that. I've been so nervous
about branching out into light meals. But dishes like this
are easy to prepare in quantity and seem to be a hit. Now,
tell me, what's the latest with Connor?"

J.J. shook her head. "Not much, I'm afraid. I've been

checking out the TV station, trying to find someone with a motive to murder Miranda."

"And?"

"No motives leap out at me. But tell me, what do you think about someone who's jealous that Miranda got the better program and time slot?"

"You mean, is that a good motive? I wouldn't think so, because there's still no guarantee this person would get the job, even with Miranda gone, is there?"

"You're right. The manager thinks someone's out to get the station and it could have escalated to murder."

"Eww. Do you think she had a stalker?"

J.J. sighed. "That's just it. I don't have a clue."

Beth looked over at the lineup starting to form at the counter. "Looks like my break is over. Thanks for coming by, J.J." She smiled as she grabbed her dishes and went back to work.

J.J. sat finishing the rest of her salad, keeping a watchful eye on the other customers. After all, that was her role here, even if she was late getting at it today. She also gave some more thought to possible suspects. Devine had interrupted her plans for the morning. Maybe she should head back over to the TV station. Maybe he'd still be there. Maybe she didn't care.

She waited while Wanda finished taking a call and then asked to see Kathi Jones. Fifteen minutes later, she appeared in the reception area.

"Are you back to ask me more questions?" She sounded pleasant but J.J. noticed the put-down in her smile.

"As a matter of fact, I think we can help each other."

"Oh, how's that?"

J.J. lowered her voice. "You must realize you're pretty high up on the police suspect list. After all, she did beat you out of that dream job, and there were stories about your arguments." Maybe a little bit of bluffing would help.

A look of panic quickly crossed Kathi's face. "That's silly. I didn't do it." She glanced over at Wanda. "Let's go to my office."

J.J. followed her down the hall to the small office at the back of the building and took the chair Kathi waved her into.

Kathi asked, "Just how can you help me?"

"I don't think you did it, but that doesn't mean anything to the police. But if I find the real killer . . ." She let it hang there.

"Okay. So, what can I do to help *you*?"

J.J. hid her smile. "Donald Cooper told me there were a couple of employees who'd recently been fired. I need their names and contact info."

"You think someone who used to work here killed her out of anger?"

J.J. shrugged. "It's a possibility. Mr. Cooper, however, thinks it's part of the problems plaguing the station recently." She looked closely at Kathi. "What do you think?"

"I hadn't really thought much about it, I guess. I mean, I'm so wrapped up in my own job it doesn't leave me much time for other station stuff. But if that's what's going on, it might have something to do with Mikey Cooper."

"Cooper? Same name as the manager?"

"Dad and son. And Dad fired son a few months ago after Mikey smashed up the station van and, believe me, the van wasn't the only thing that was smashed, if you get my drift." She mimicked taking a drink.

"Wow. But do you think he'd take revenge on the station, even kill Miranda, because of that?"

"You're the one connecting the dots. I just mentioned what had happened. I do know he tried to hit on Miranda, though, and she blew him off. He tried it on me, too, of course, but I let him down a bit more kindly."

I'm sure. "Did you hear if he threatened her?"

"I wasn't here when it happened but Wanda was. And she likes to talk. Now, if I get you the names, will you tell the police I cooperated?"

Does she think I'm working with them? "Uh, sure."

"Okay." She flipped on her computer and started typing. About five minutes later, she printed out the names. She'd looked up their addresses in an old station directory and added the information.

"Thanks, Kathi. This will help," J.J. said as she left the office. That made three people who had been fired. Odd that Donald Cooper hadn't mentioned his son, Mikey. Then again, that was probably why he hadn't.

She glanced out at her car. Uh-oh. Devine was leaning against it.

He pushed off from the car as she approached. "So, I'm assuming you now know the names of everyone who has been fired in the past two years."

She couldn't judge from the tone of his voice how he felt about that, but she was certain he didn't approve.

"I won't get in your way." She pulled her keys out, beeped the car open, and got in.

"It's not me you should be worried about. I'd like to point out, again, that there's a killer on the loose. If you're not going to be smart, at least be cautious." He closed her door for her and walked away.

Her fingers drummed the steering wheel. *Totally annoying man.* But, unfortunately, probably right. Her options seemed few. Find the killer. Find Connor. Or both.

She was acutely aware that the longer Connor was MIA, the worse it looked for him. She pulled out her smartphone and punched in Alison's number. She answered immediately.

"I don't have anything new to tell you. Connor still

hasn't shown, and I'm just heading into my shift. I'll phone you later." Alison hung up without J.J. being able to get a word in. At least she had her answer.

She looked back at the station. She needed to talk to Wanda, and to Hennie again. As Miranda's research assistant, she had to know more than she'd let on. It was just a matter of how to approach her.

CHAPTER 12

At precisely eleven forty-five the next day, J.J. entered the front door of Cups 'n' Roses, placed her order for the special of the day, a mozzarella and veggie panini, along with a latte at the cash register, and chose a chair with the best view of the coffee shop, at a table for two. She pulled out her iPad and clicked on her Kindle app. She'd given it a lot of thought and decided she'd look less obvious in her stakeout if she was doing something like reading. She could prop up her iPad so that it was easy enough, without moving her head, to raise her eyes and scan the other patrons. Or, if she really needed to take a longer look, she could pretend she was contemplating what she'd just read. Although she knew she wouldn't remember a darn thing about the book she'd opened.

Or maybe she'd get lucky and be able to multitask. After all, the next Culinary Capers dinner was only two weeks off, and according to Beth's proclamation, she had to at least attempt to find time to read something written by the mystery author whose recipe she'd chosen. That was Cathy

Pickens, whose Fried Yellow Squash was the dish J.J. intended to make. A totally new author to her. So she'd also gone on Facebook and checked on the author's website to learn a bit more about what kind of read she was getting into. Then online she ordered one of her earlier books, *Southern Fried*.

Beth served her lunch and glanced at what J.J. was reading. "Good on you, girl. I hope everyone gets into this like you are."

"Don't give me any medals just yet, Beth. I'm just getting started, but I thought it would be a good cover, so to speak." J.J. grinned.

Beth chuckled. "Good luck. With everything." She scuttled back to the counter, where yet another lineup was forming.

J.J. was truly pleased that business seemed to be booming for her good friend. Even though Beth had launched Cups 'n' Roses before J.J. had moved to the village, she knew that it had been a risk for Beth. Newly retired from her high school music teacher position and still young enough to keep doing something active, she'd decided to follow her dream of owning a coffee shop. And admittedly, she was the first to agree that she knew nothing about running a business. During summers and the fall colors tourist seasons, Half Moon Bay did a lively business, providing a steady stream of customers. Winter was always the challenge, though, when the chilly weather threatened and tourist season had moved to the ski slopes of Stowe.

In the past few months, Beth had added a limited lunch menu to the baked goods she'd been serving right from the beginning, and it was paying off. The little shop that could! Serving coffee and baked goods was one thing, but having to invest in extra foodstuffs as the menu increased was another. Hopefully, the regulars would continue to be just that. And hopefully the theft problem would be resolved soon.

J.J. bit into her panini, enjoying the warm crust mingled with the melted mozzarella, tomatoes, fennel, and eggplant. She glanced at the iPad and read a couple of pages, managing a quick visual scan of the room from time to time. She'd tried to draw out eating as long as possible, but she'd finally come to the end and her latte was cold. She realized she must have made a face when taking the last sip, because Beth appeared at her table in an instant with a fresh cup.

"Thanks, but I'm afraid I'm not doing much to earn this."

Beth leaned over and whispered in her ear. "Early days." She straightened and went on, "I'm willing to keep on going if you are."

J.J. glanced around the room. "Okay. For now."

She looked at her watch and sipped her latte a bit more quickly than she'd normally do, all the while keeping an eye open to what was going on around her. All pretense of reading had been put aside. When she finished, she walked up to the cash register and explained, "I have a meeting in an hour. I'm sorry but I need to go and do some prep."

"No problem. Thanks again. I do appreciate it," Beth answered. "Now go. Remember, it's on the house."

J.J. thought about the whole thing on her way back to the office. How could she justify the time and the cost of lunches to Beth, if she couldn't catch the thief? How long should she continue? The main problem was she just wasn't the best person for the job. She'd had no training as a private eye. She could ask Devine for suggestions, but she hated to feel indebted to him.

Skye greeted her at the office with a small wave. She was cradling the phone receiver between her shoulder and right ear, busily inputting something into her computer. J.J. sat down and turned hers on. She pulled up the new conference file she was working on and slowly read over all her notes. She knew the salient points by heart but wanted to ensure they'd come to her quickly in this meeting. The Wine Growers Association account was another first for her. First in the wine field, at least. She knew she could handle it but she first had to convince the conference committee. The meeting at two P.M. would either ensure she had the job or have her looking for a new client. Not that she was desperate to find one. Business was good these days.

Skye finished her call with a too-bright sign-off. J.J. looked over at her, eyebrow raised.

"That was my contact at Northanda. They want to go to a classy resort. Can you believe it? After all the explaining I've done? If they put their money into the setting, they won't be able to pay for a first-class trainer and some of the unique experiences I've planned. The employees don't need to feel like it's a spa weekend. They need to dig in, and deep, to rebuild the team. I tried to lay out my plan and at the same time, firmly but kindly discourage theirs. And where does it get me?"

J.J. shrugged. She knew better than to take part in this conversation. It was Skye's usual rant, and by the time it was finished, she would have resolved it, on her own, with no need for J.J. to add any input.

J.J. smiled to herself as Skye wound up the soliloquy and seemed to refocus. "How was your lunch? Did you catch a thief?"

J.J. shook her head. "Not today, but Beth wants to continue with this so I suppose I'll oblige, although I think I'm getting the best of it. Her lunch specials are really tasty."

"I'm glad the meals are working out for her. What's on your afternoon agenda?"

"After my two o'clock meeting with the wine people, and after our brainstorming session if you still want it, I'll do some revamping of the website. We're already into fall, and I had great plans to change the look of the page in keeping with the season. At least, I had planned that our new webmaster would do the revamping. I'll jot down some notes, rewrite some of the sections, have you look it all over, and send it off to him. How's that sound?"

"Like you're on a roll. But you can skip the 'having me check it out' bit. And I'm afraid I'll have to brainstorm on my own at some point later. I'm taking a quick trip to Montpelier overnight to meet with some suppliers of high-end promotional items. They're holding an invitation-only reveal and I'm delighted we're on the guest list. Next time a client wants classy and different, I can do classy and different."

"Oh, I definitely know you can do that." J.J. shook her head and grabbed her things. She was at her client's office in ten minutes.

J.J. settled back in at her computer and pulled up the Make It Happen website on her screen. It had been a good client meeting with no changes made to her plan. So now she was on a roll and looking forward to dealing with that pesky website. She quickly read it through and made notes about what needed to be changed or updated.

Then she started writing the article she'd been planning, "Thinking Outside the Wedding Box." They didn't do many weddings, not wanting to compete with the local wedding planners, but there was always the odd time when a client would expand their original job to include a wedding. It would also be good PR to post something on weddings, along with a list of local planners. J.J. smiled when she'd finished. She printed out the article along with the updated course outline for the night school class on event planning that she and Skye were developing.

They'd debated about doing Wednesday classes for four weeks, dividing the evenings between them, or doing two weekends. Since neither wanted to tie up weekends, the evenings won. Skye would be first up. The two-hour class

was being held at the Grange Bay Community Center on
Grange Road at the edge of the village. They'd discussed
inserting the course into the school board evening curricu-
lum, but the amount of red tape had changed their minds.
But the city's Parks, Recreation, and Waterfront department had fewer hoops. She was looking forward to the
challenge but was also a bit concerned about what kinds
of questions the participants might bring. She so hoped
she could answer them all. *She saw herself fumbling for
the right answer to an overly eager student's question and
having the rest of the class start laughing at her. By that
point, no matter how hard she tried, she couldn't even get
a word out. She stared wildly around the room, hoping to
find a friendly face, but couldn't. She couldn't take it anymore and had run out of the classroom straight into the
arms of Ty Devine.*

Devine! Where had he come from? She shook her head
and realized it was time to go home. The day was over and
she hadn't even tried to talk to Hennie Ferguson at the TV
station again. She glanced at the clock. Five fifteen. Maybe ...

CHAPTER 13

Hennie agreed to meet J.J. at the Olde British Pub, just down the street from the TV station, after the show ended, at seven thirty P.M. She was waiting when J.J. arrived.

"Thanks for agreeing to meet me," J.J. said. "I wasn't sure you'd want to do anything more today after being at the station so long."

"I'm used to it. The job, the hours. I really thrive on it all and I usually do go out after work, to wind down." She looked different today. J.J. thought the low-cut neckline of her pale green satin blouse was more of a glam look. Her dark hair, held back with bobby pins each time J.J. had seen her before, was pulled back and secured with a hair clip. She'd even added had some eye shadow. Did she have a hot date later?

Hm. "Did you and Miranda ever go out together?"

Hennie gave her an odd look.

"I mean, after the show to wind down. That just popped into my head." J.J. grinned apologetically.

"The odd time, if a gang was going out. Miranda didn't

join in too often, though, and it was never just the two of us. We were never that close."

She picked up the menu, obviously wanting some food. J.J. had planned to buy her a drink. *Oh well.* The server had obviously been waiting for that movement and appeared at the table. After they'd given their orders for a glass each of on-tap beer and a plate of spicy sweet potato fries for Hennie, J.J. got down to business.

"I'm sure the last thing you want to talk about on your free time is what's been happening, but I need to know a few more things. I hope you don't mind."

Hennie shrugged. "What makes you think I know the answers?"

"Your job. It is your job to know everything or where to find it, isn't it?"

Hennie's grin was lopsided. J.J. realized she hadn't seen her smile too often. She wondered if Hennie was self-conscious about her smile or her teeth. Maybe she just didn't feel like it most times.

"Got it in one. Most people at the station don't get it. They don't realize how much a research assistant does. If I don't get the info, Miranda or whoever doesn't have a show. Unless they know it all themselves, which is highly doubtful."

J.J. smiled back. This is where she wanted Hennie, feeling very pleased with herself as the keeper of the information. Their beer arrived, and J.J. waited until Hennie had taken a few appreciative gulps.

"Do you think Donald Cooper is right and Miranda's murder is part of a plot against the station?"

Hennie looked like she was giving it serious consideration, then took another drink and shook her head. "No way. I mean, who would be so pissed off with the place that they would kill the entertainment chick? Huh? You go for a news reader or someone who has the power, the influence on the viewers. Not entertainment." Her snort punctuated her disbelief.

"That's very perceptive. I hadn't looked at it that way. So who else might have wanted to kill her? Kathi?"

Hennie shook her head. "As I said, not her style." She sat quietly staring at J.J. as if sizing her up.

"Okay, I may know a bit more about her private life than I let on." She leaned across the table toward J.J. "She was seeing a guy. A married guy. A cop."

"Oh." J.J. wondered if Connor had known. What? And killed her? *Don't go there.*

"Do you know his name?"

She shook her head. "She didn't tell me. I'm pretty sure she met him while working on a feature interview. It never went to air, though. Oh yeah, and she'd broken it off a few months ago, and he was really pissed off about it."

A married cop whom she'd dumped. Maybe when things started getting heated up with Connor? Did that part matter? Was the cop a possible suspect? She made a mental note to call Alison as soon as she got home.

Hennie seemed to have said all she would on the topic. She concentrated on finishing the fries, offering some to J.J., who took a couple since she'd be paying for them.

Hennie sat back and wiped her hands with the paper napkin, then grabbed a lip gloss out of her purse and applied it without aid of a mirror. "I can't really think of anyone else. There are always a lot of things going on at the station, mostly 'under the surface' stuff so it's hard to know who started what rumor or who's sleeping with whom."

"She was sleeping with someone at the station, then? Lonny Chan maybe?"

"Oh, get real. Lonny's gay. He thinks nobody knows but we all do. He's such a great guy, and no one's going to let on because it's not as if we'd treat him any differently. But they were just good friends." She finished off her beer.

"Nope, nada. There's no one at the station I'd put on the killer list."

What about you?

J.J. wanted to ask but she also didn't want to cut off her pipeline. She'd have to ask someone else that question. Maybe Wanda, the receptionist. Surely she'd be aware of all the comings and goings anyway.

"Speaking of Lonny," J.J. said, "I've been trying to talk to him but he seems very elusive. Could he be avoiding me?"

"I doubt it. He's on the road a lot or editing video. We don't even see much of him. Besides, he was Miranda's friend but not her good buddy. You probably won't get much news from him." Hennie glanced at her watch and pointed at the restroom. "I'm heading in there, then I've got to meet some friends."

"Right. I've got the check. Thanks for meeting with me."

Hennie did a swift salute and headed for the back of the room, where she'd pointed.

Indie sat next to the phone on the counter, just staring at it. J.J. glanced at her before walking into the bedroom and changing into something more comfortable, yoga pants and a loose denim shirt. She padded back into the kitchen in bare feet and eyed the phone that Indie still sat watching.

"You are spooking me, Sir Indie. Is there a call for me?"

The cat ignored her but did leap down to the floor and sprint over to his favorite chair, the white wicker chair with the blue-and-white-striped cushions, where he started his usual intricate grooming routine.

J.J. watched for a few minutes, then picked up the receiver. Sure enough, the beeping signaled a message was waiting. She punched in the numbers, then her password, and stood more erect as her mother's voice sounded in her ear.

"I'm coming to Burlington for the weekend, arriving

tomorrow night. I certainly hope you can put me up. The love seat is fine. Or if it's inconvenient, I'll take a hotel room."

J.J. could just picture the sly look that would go with her suggestive tone. June Tanner made no bones about wanting her only daughter to get married and provide more grandchildren, although she never came straight out and told J.J. to get working on it. The implication was there, though. Odd coming from someone who was very much her own woman and had a successful career. J.J. shrugged. She was used to it and also to her mom's abrupt messages. No sign-off. That was the Realtor in her.

J.J. glanced at the love seat and knew her mother would find it less than comfortable for the next night or two. There were two positions to choose from—feet propped up on the arm or curled up, fetal position. She sighed and called her mom back and tried to sound pleased about the upcoming visit. The thing was, she really enjoyed spending time with her mom. As with most teen girls, their relationship had been rocky for a while but when J.J. emerged on the adulthood side of life, they became closer. It was just more convenient for the bonding occasions to take place at the Tanner household in Montpelier.

June Tanner answered on the fourth ring. "I'm sorry for such short notice, Josephine, but I just need to get away for a couple of days."

J.J. cringed, mainly for being called by her first name but also because this didn't sound like her mother. She thrived on the hectic life of a Realtor and the home life of being the wife of a fairly well-known artist. With all the kids moved away, there was little housework to do. J.J.'s oldest brother, Rory, lived in Stowe with his wife and two children. Middle child, Kyle, was a firefighter in Rutland, unmarried, and also getting the regular messages about the grandness of grandmotherhood.

"It's all right, Mom. I don't have anything planned this weekend. When will you arrive?"

"Probably not until around nine or so. That's great. I'll see you then. Bye."

J.J. hadn't gotten a chance to ask if everything was all right. Fine. She had her as a captive roommate for the weekend. She'd get to the bottom of things.

CHAPTER 14

The lineup at the Cups 'n' Roses ended at the front door the next morning. J.J. took one look at it and decided she needed a walk to Rocco G's instead. Besides, she hadn't talked to Rocco in a couple of weeks, which was way too long in her books. He turned around from restocking the olive oil shelves as she entered the bistro. His swarthy, lined face broke out in a broad smile.

"J.J., I am so happy to see you." He walked over and kissed her on both cheeks. "I'm guessing you've been busy, because you haven't been in here much lately."

"I'm sorry, Rocco. That's it exactly. And I guess you heard about what happened on the casino cruise?"

He shook his head. "Another murder. That is not so good for you. Have the police found the killer yet? I don't keep up with the news much these days."

J.J. took a closer look at him. His curly black hair, salted with streaks of gray, just about touched the collar of his purple short-sleeved sport shirt. The longer look gave him an even more dashing quality, she thought. His eyes looked tired, though.

"No, they haven't caught the killer, and that means none of us who were involved with the event are free of suspicion." *Nor free of guilt.*

"I know what that can be like." He shook his head. "Is there anything I can do? After all, you were there for me."

"Thanks, Rocco. But I don't think so." She let her eyes rove over the calorie-laden choices on a pedestal cake plate under a clear glass dome. "I have to find Connor Mac, for starters."

"Your boyfriend, the radio announcer?"

J.J. looked up sharply. "My *friend*, the radio announcer. Yes. He was sharing the emcee role with Miranda Myers the night she died, and he's disappeared."

Rocco made a clicking noise with his mouth. "The police must not be happy. What a foolish thing for him to do." He thought a moment. "You don't think he's in danger or maybe has been kidnapped, do you?"

"I hadn't really thought about it but doubt it. I don't know why his life would be in danger, unless he knows something that might lead to the killer. And I don't know if there have been any ransom demands, because I have no idea who they would go to. In fact, I'm finding that I don't really know much about him at all." She let out a long sigh.

He grimaced. "That is often the way. What if he witnessed the murder or knows the identity of the killer?"

"He didn't say anything to us, and he had plenty of opportunity to do so. No, I don't think that was it." *I hope it wasn't.*

"Well, what if the murderer doesn't know he didn't see anything but still thinks he had? He might have done something to him."

J.J. blanched.

"I'm sorry, *cara*. I did not mean to upset you. Just thinking out loud."

"No, you're right to voice it, Rocco. We need to cover all possible bases. I just hope you're wrong."

Rocco covered her hand with his. "Let me make you my special espresso. Perhaps you can take a few extra minutes and enjoy it here?"

J.J.'s spirits lifted and she smiled. "I'd be delighted." She could spare a few more minutes before getting to the office.

She chose one of the tables next to the window and watched the passersby as she waited. For a typical fall day in Vermont, there were still a lot of people who hadn't let go of summer. Mostly young men. Probably students taking classes at the nearby technical college. J.J. pulled her leopard-print cashmere cardigan around her a bit tighter and smiled as a young woman jogged by, long blonde ponytail whipping around her face, as she pushed a stroller with two fair-haired toddlers in it. Possibly twins. She tried to picture herself as that woman but couldn't. Possibly because she didn't have children, wasn't even married, and had no prospects on the horizon. Not even a good friend to go out with on dates at the moment.

The thought of Connor jolted her back to the present, just in time to enjoy the sight of Rocco presenting the espresso with a flourish.

"It is my special treat for you. Some surprises added to the espresso. *Divertiti!*"

J.J. took a sip and savored the flavor before swallowing. What had he added? Some chili powder? Maybe cayenne? Whatever it was, the brew was indeed very special. She glanced at her watch and realized she couldn't stay all day enjoying a single cup of espresso. When she went to pay at the counter, Rocco told her it was his treat.

"Do you know what I added? Can your taste buds tell you?" He looked mischievous.

J.J. shook her head. "Maybe chili powder?"

"*No, ma sei vicino.*" He looked delighted. "You think

about it and when it comes to you, you will smile again. Then come and tell me."

"Thank you, Rocco. You've made my day." She leaned across the counter and kissed his cheeks.

The first thing J.J. noticed when she entered her office was the large brown envelope sitting on her desk. The second thing was Skye, sitting in J.J.'s chair, staring at the package.

"Are you having fun?"

Skye looked startled. "Oops, sorry. Caught in the act. I'm just trying to decide if it's safe to open, not that I intended on opening it. The envelope is addressed to you, and as you can see, it's padded and thick. And with all your snooping . . ." She stood and walked to the other side of the desk.

J.J. took a look at the return address. "It's from the college student who took photos at the casino night. It's a classroom assignment, so he offered to do them for free. Of course, I hired a professional to do the videos, just in case. Let's see what he's got."

She grabbed her box cutter out of the top drawer and sliced open the package. Skye moved closer and watched as she set the photos out on her desk.

"We'll have to look at them in batches." J.J. looked around the office. "You know, we really could use a long, narrow table in here. We could put it along the side wall, behind me."

"You're right. Just like you were the last time you mentioned it. Why don't I task you with picking it out and up since I've obviously dropped the ball. Again."

J.J. grinned. "Happy to. Is there a budget?"

"Just don't go getting teak." Skye picked up a photo taken on the outer deck at sunset. "Hm. He's actually got a knack for framing a shot."

"He does." J.J. scanned the photos, then replaced them with the next batch. She paused over a group shot of the board of directors taken out on the open deck. She pulled a magnifying glass out of her desk to take a closer look.

"What do you see?" Skye asked, hunching down also.

"If I'm not mistaken, that's Hennie Ferguson in the background, beside the stairs. I wonder what she's doing there."

"Who is she and why can't she be there?"

"She's Miranda's assistant, and I don't recall seeing her name on any lists, although I wouldn't have recognized it at the time. But she didn't let on she'd been there when I spoke to her."

"You think that's suspicious? Is she the killer?"

"It is to me, but it doesn't make her the one. What could her motive be?"

"To be there or to kill Miranda?"

"Both."

Skye shrugged. "I thought you were trying to pare down your questions, not add to them."

J.J. groaned. "You're right. We don't need more suspects, and I'd already vetted her. Guess I need to go back and ask her right out why she was there. Meanwhile, I need to finish going through these and pull the best to add to the package I'm taking over to Megan Spicer. I'd also like to add a couple to our website."

"Great idea. By the way, when's your mom coming?" Skye gave J.J. a wide-eyed look.

"Tonight. Thanks for the reminder."

"Oh, come on, it's not all that bad. Just think, you could have my mom, after all."

J.J. flashed on Portia Drake, glamorous model even at her age, outspoken and classy, like the car. Different spelling, of course. She was fascinated by the woman and knew that Skye idolized her even though they were often at odds.

"No, it's not all bad. It's just highly unusual. In the two years I've lived here, she's visited only once. And that was to try to convince me to move back to Montpelier. She has a reason for coming, but I guess I'll have to wait till tonight to find out what it is."

Skye gave her a quick hug. "It will be fine. Dr. Drake guarantees it."

J.J. gave her a look of doubt but refrained from saying anything. Skye grabbed a coffee from the Keurig on her way back to her desk.

J.J. had pulled a dozen photos by the time she finished looking through the stack. She was impressed. She'd have to keep this guy on her go-to list and pay him an honorarium at the very least, for this effort.

At lunchtime, J.J. headed back to Cups 'n' Roses, slid into a seat near the window, and pondered what to eat. Beth looked frantic, so she left her jacket on the back of the chair and walked to the counter to give her order for a plate of penne with black olives and shaved ham salad.

Beth shot her a quick smile. "You'll enjoy this. I'll bring it over as soon as I can."

J.J. nodded, waited for a latte, and went back to the table. She glanced around the room, trying to appear bored, not like she was on a mission. She thought the woman with long, mousy brown hair tied back into a ponytail looked a bit familiar. Was she the woman Devine had fingered? Could she be the thief? Of course, she realized she'd seen several of these patrons before. The regular noontime crowd. How was she ever to find the thief? If she, or he, had been slick enough not to be noticed up to this point, how could J.J. solve the problem?

Maybe she should invite Devine to meet her each day. The thought gave her slight heart palpitations along with an immediate desire to smack herself.

She'd finished her drink by the time Beth put the salad in front of her. "Sorry it took so long."

"You're swamped here. What happened to your help?"

"Erin is off with a cold today and for the next few, probably. And Abby has a dentist appointment. She should be back soon. I do need to hire another staffer, though. I just can't seem to get around to it. Any news about Connor?"

J.J. shook her head. "Nada. My stomach gets tied up in knots when I think about it. I'm so afraid something bad has happened to him. Like, what if the person who killed Miranda also killed him?" She said the last in a whisper.

Beth sucked in her breath. "Oh, don't even think that. I have a feeling he's just fine. I have no idea what's going on in his head, though. Oops, customer at counter."

J.J. watched her scurry back and then took a bite of the salad. She took a second one and let the flavors roll around in her mouth. She loved the sharp taste of the olives or maybe it was something in the olive oil. She'd have to ask.

She looked around guiltily. She was not here to savor a food experience. She needed to catch herself a thief. J.J. pulled her iPad out of her purse and found the point where she'd left off in the novel. However, she soon found her mind wandering.

She needed a system. She had to first have a suspect before she could properly observe the theft, and so far she hadn't been able to narrow down her search. She watched the mousy-haired woman finish the water she'd had with her panini and leave. J.J. rushed over to the counter and asked Beth to go check the table right away and see if anything was missing. She'd do this with everyone who looked familiar. It was a start.

Beth reported back that nothing had been taken. She gave J.J.'s shoulder a quick squeeze and rushed back to the counter. They repeated the maneuver two more times and each time, no results. That obviously wasn't going to work. Besides, Beth didn't have time to keep running around checking after each customer.

J.J. flipped her iPad closed and was about to stuff it

back into her purse when she set it back on the table and
flipped it open. There was another way. By pretending to
be reading, J.J. could take photos of anyone and everyone,
if need be. She wasn't entirely certain what she'd do with
the photos at this point, aside from maybe comparing them
for frequency of visits and trying to narrow down the pool
of possible suspects. At least she felt she'd be doing something concrete. She glanced around and gave it a try, taking
a couple of pictures at random. The next time she was in,
she'd be focused on anyone looking familiar or antsy. Too
bad she hadn't thought about it before Ms. Mouse had left.

Walking back to the office, J.J. thought that this was a
good approach if they just hung in there. She was so
wrapped in deep thought that she almost walked into Evan
as he was coming down the front stairs.

"Whoa. Earth to J.J. Where are you, darlin'?"

She wasn't sure if Beth had told anyone else about her
problems and didn't want to be the one to do so.

"I've got a lot on my mind. Sorry, Evan." She gave him
a big smile, which widened when she took in the black
with mauve polka-dot V-neck sweater he was wearing over
a white T-shirt. He certainly had a flare.

"Connor?" he asked.

"Well, yes, and also my mother, who's arriving tonight."

Evan pulled a somber face and covered his heart with
his right hand. "Ah, is this good or bad?"

"I have no idea. It's unusual, is what it is. Anyway,
where are you going in such a hurry?"

"A new client. A new house that needs my magic deco-
rating touch. It should be a snap. It's right in the exclusive
Rockvale neighborhood." He rubbed two fingers together.
"You may not see me for days. Which reminds me that
I've gotta go. Must make a good impression by being on
time. Good luck tonight." He gave her a quick hug and
rushed off.

J.J. smiled. She valued Evan's friendship. In fact, she was so pleased with everything about her life right now. Being part of Make It Happen. The Culinary Capers. She had Indie. Life was good.

Yes, it is.

CHAPTER 15

J.J.'s phone rang that evening at seven thirty sharp. She knew it was the apartment intercom and that meant her mom had arrived. When June Tanner walked through the apartment door, J.J. gave her a big hug, trying to read answers to all her questions about what was up into the hug she got in return. Nothing. It was a typical June Tanner hug. Long and strong. Maybe nothing was up. Wouldn't that be great?

"Mom, it's so nice to have you visit me. Let me take your bag. Come on in." She ushered June into the living room and quickly deposited the small suitcase in her own bedroom. "Would you like something? Tea?"

"Do you have any white wine?"

J.J. took a closer look at her mom. An unusual request from her.

'Uh, sure. I'll just get us both a glass." She opened a bottle of pinot grigio and poured some for them both.

They sat across from each other in the living room, and while June took her first sip, J.J. took the opportunity to scrutinize her. She looked normal. Her medium-length auburn hair sported new streaks along with a style that screamed *salon visit!* Her eyes were sparkly, no signs of sad lines around her mouth, although J.J. did think several more creases and crinkles had been added in the months since she'd been home. Was her mom working too hard? Was that all this visit was about, a time-out with her daughter? J.J. couldn't wait any longer.

"Okay, I love having you visit here, but I'm dying of curiosity. What gives?"

"I'm here on business, actually." June leaned toward J.J. as if sharing a secret. "I've been asked to run the Burlington main office."

She looked so pleased with herself that J.J. bit back her first comment and said instead, "How wonderful. Congratulations."

"I'm glad you think that. It could mean you'll be seeing a lot more of me. Of course, I wouldn't stay here." Her hand fluttered in a midair arc. "I'd get an apartment of my own. But the job is a real honor. I'm quite delighted."

"What about Dad?" It slipped out on its own.

June's face fell but she quickly recovered. "He's all for it. I'll commute, of course. Home on weekends, holidays, and all that. And it's only for a year. In that time they'll decide whether or not to continue with this branch or move it elsewhere. Of course, they could also add another one." She gave a small laugh.

J.J. smiled, trying not to show all she was thinking. Like, *I doubt Dad is happy. Oh, sure, you'll have your weekends free to go home.* She knew that weekends were often the busiest times of the week with perspective clients having time to visit houses. *Another branch . . . you mean you want that one, too?*

"More wine?" J.J. asked.

"Sure, why not? We are celebrating, after all."

By the time they were talked out, it was almost eleven.

J.J. insisted she was okay on the love seat as she steered her mom into her bedroom. She'd just finished tucking in the sheets for her makeshift bed when someone knocked on her front door. It could only be Ness at this hour. She looked down at her long-sleeved red cotton nightshirt and its tiny white hearts, a Valentine's gift from her mom last year, and shrugged. He'd seen her in worse before.

She opened the door without checking and almost slammed it shut. Devine stood there. Déjà vu.

"I know it's late," he said, "but I saw that your light was on. And I know you want to talk about the murder." He leaned against the doorframe and held up a bottle of a California red wine. And grinned.

She felt those palpitations again and knew she should tell him it was too late and just shut the door. Instead she said, "My mom's staying overnight." She could have kicked herself.

His grin widened. "How nice for you. We won't disturb her. Unless she's on the couch?"

J.J. looked behind her at the love seat. The sheets folded back, inviting. Devine slipped through the door while she had her back turned and walked to the kitchen. He grabbed the open bottle on the counter. "Maybe we should start with this?"

Start? She quietly closed the door and tried to compose herself. She could handle this. Nightshirt and all. Sure she could.

Devine had already poured them each a drink by the time she found her bathrobe, slipped it on, and flopped on the love seat. In the middle, so that he had to take the wicker chair across from her. He sat back and stared at her, a sly smile on his face.

That flustered her even more, but she was determined not to let it show. "What's on your mind? At eleven at night," she added for good measure.

His smile widened to a grin. "I just wanted to make sure

you're fine. Still alive, actually. And also, I want to know what you've been able to find out so far." His smiled faded.

She straightened her shoulders. She stalled for time, trying to figure out just how much to tell him. What did he already know? What didn't she want to tell him? She wished she hadn't had any wine.

"The still photos taken at the casino night arrived today, and Hennie Ferguson was in one of them."

"And that's important because?"

"Because she didn't tell me she'd been there. She kept it a secret."

"And that's important because?"

"Oh, stop it." She knew he was trying to annoy her. Why did he always do that? "She should have told me when I was asking her about Miranda and everything."

"Did you specifically ask if she'd been there?"

"Well, no but . . ."

"No buts. If you're an investigator, which you're obviously not, you don't assume anything. You figure out the questions and the answers beforehand and then adjust your script according to what you hear. So, maybe now you'll leave the questions to me?"

She shook her head. "Not likely," she said in a soft voice.

He grinned again.

She felt unsettled. He'd tossed the black leather bomber jacket he'd been wearing on a stool at the kitchen bar; the long sleeves on his blue shirt were rolled up to his elbows—the shirt almost matched the love seat, she thought; his jeans were worn to the state of being a good fit; and his short black hair had a windblown look, although J.J. was certain there hadn't been even a breeze all evening. He looked tired, though, despite the occasional wicked flashes in his eyes, and his five-o'clock shadow probably started around three P.M.

He didn't say anything for a few minutes and that made her even more uncomfortable.

"What?" she finally asked.

"You never learn, do you? And, I guess you never will. Why don't you just give in and try getting a PI license? At least you'd have some legitimacy in your snooping and maybe even know how to stay safe. Maybe."

For one tiny, small instant the idea tantalized her. He must have seen it on her face.

"No. Do not even give that suggestion a moment's consideration. I should never have said anything so foolish. I was being sarcastic."

She started laughing, pleased to see him flustered. She decided not to say anything. Let him sweat awhile.

He stood and started pacing. "You know, most people will lie to you when first questioned. They have something to hide or why else would you be even considering them? So, you have to make them think you believe every word they're saying and then, later, sort through it and come up with what they weren't saying. Then hit them with that." He leaned over and poured her some more wine. She hadn't even realized she'd finished it already. This wouldn't do.

"Your turn now. What have you found out?" She raised her eyebrows, settled back, and took a sip.

He sat down beside her when he'd finished talking. She moved over slightly to allow him to do so, although she didn't scoot to the end.

"Not so fast. We're not finished yet. What else have you learned?" he countered.

Fair enough. "I'm pretty sure that Lonny Chan didn't do it, although I haven't yet gotten to speak to him. Everyone likes him and there's no motive. As for the rest of the station staff, I doubt Kathi Jones is the killer. Hennie Ferguson probably didn't do it even though I think she's hiding something since she's being so sneaky about her presence at the event. And, of course, Connor Mac didn't do it." She turned to face Devine. "And yes, I think that because he's my friend and he's not the type to get violent. I don't have any real proof."

"You're just friends?"

"Yes."

He stared at her a few moments, searching her face, then leaned toward her and kissed her. She had known it was coming and returned it with equal intensity.

"I'm so sorry. I hope I'm not intruding, but I need a glass of water," June said as she padded in bare feet toward the kitchen.

J.J. pulled back and gazed at Devine, unable to come up with words. He grinned at her and then stood.

"I'm Ty Devine. You must be Mrs. Tanner."

June changed course and walked over, hand outstretched. "June Tanner. A pleasure to meet you. I thought I heard voices out here."

J.J. jumped up. "Devine is a P.I. working on the murder case, Mom. We were just comparing notes."

"Yes, so I see. Anyway, definitely don't let me stop you. I just need some water." She gave Devine a wide smile and left them.

J.J. felt her face burning. She wanted some water, too, but a cold shower would be better. She wasn't quite sure what to say, which made her all the more uncomfortable.

"I should be going. We'll finish this later," Devine said, his voice soft and promising.

At the door, he turned back to her and said, "I really came to tell you that Connor Mac's car was spotted on South Hero Island this afternoon."

"What?" she almost shrieked. "You didn't think that was the first thing to tell me?"

"I wanted to know where you stood about him."

"As you now know, even though I have stated it all along, he's my friend, and I, along with all his friends, are worried about him. Do you have any other information? Was he found? Is he all right?"

"Apparently, his car was spotted at a gas station by a sheriff's deputy. Do you know if he has any friends around there? Or if he owns any property?"

"I don't know." She looked directly at Devine. "I'm finding out I don't really know a whole lot about him. Just that he isn't a murderer. If the cop recognized the car, why didn't he apprehend him?"

"Apparently, the cop was on his way to an emergency call and made the choice to stick with that. He did call it in, but when the other officer arrived, Connor, if that's who it was, was long gone. I'm going to drive there tomorrow and check it out. Do you want to come with me?"

That surprised her. "Yes. What time?"

"I'll pick you up at nine."

"Okay."

"Okay."

"And, I guess I have more news for you, too."

His eyes narrowed.

"Hennie told me that Miranda was seeing a married cop but had just broken it off."

He looked ready to explode. "You didn't think this was worth mentioning up front?"

"I may have been trying to decide if I'd tell you at all."

He shook his head and left without another word.

I wonder if tomorrow is still on.

CHAPTER 16

J.J. sat at the kitchen counter the next morning, sipping her espresso and eyeing her mom over the rim of the cup. Would June mention what she'd seen the night before? Apparently not. She'd taken J.J.'s news about going to South Hero Island with Devine with interest but no questions. She seemed to be focused on her own appointment, which was at ten, and then she'd head right back to Montpelier.

They hugged at the door and J.J. left, anxious to meet Devine outside and downstairs. Hoping he'd still be picking her up. She was almost at the sidewalk when Ness Harper appeared at her side.

"Good morning, J.J. You're getting an early start." He looked to be going for a walk.

Before she could answer, Devine pulled up at the curb. J.J. thought she could hear a low-pitched growl beside her.

"What does that guy want?" Ness huffed. "Do you want me to get rid of him?"

She put a hand on his arm in case he needed restraining.

"No. It's really quite all right. We're off to see if we can find Connor. His car was spotted on South Hero Island."

"Really? Do the cops know?"

J.J. grinned. "A local cop spotted it, but he was on a call so he couldn't check it out."

"Well, just don't go getting caught sticking your nose in where they've told you not to."

"We'll be careful. See you." She hopped in the car, and Devine gave her an inquiring look.

"Ness just wanted to make sure I'd be safe." She fastened her seat belt. "He doesn't trust you, you know."

Devine grunted. "It's good he's got your back covered. Now, I need some caffeine before we hit the open road." He drove a few blocks to a Starbucks, a short detour on the way to Highway 2 out of town.

J.J. waited in the car. At least he hadn't continued where they'd left off the night before. He must be over it. Thankfully. He was back in a few minutes with an Americano for her and his own caffeinated whatever. They drove in companionable silence, each sipping and watching the passing scenery. She finally broke the silence.

"I didn't ask how you knew about Connor's car. Did the police tell you?"

"Uh-uh. I have civilian eyes in the department." He stopped and waited for a cyclist to cross the road. "I'm hoping we can find someone who knows where he was heading. Someone who may not have wanted to share that information with the police, because I'm certain they were back asking. Someone who isn't worried about talking to civilians." He looked at her and smiled.

Good. He smiled. It was okay.

After about twenty minutes, J.J. spotted the sign for the islands along the side of the road. Connor hadn't been all that far from home. What was he doing there and where was he now? She felt some anxiety and realized she was hoping he was fine but not sure if she was ready to confront him. There were too many questions. Mainly, why had he run? She still didn't believe he was a killer, but what other reason did he have for disappearing?

She looked over at Devine. "I haven't asked you, but do you really think that Connor is the killer?"

Devine kept his eyes on the road. "He's still on the list, but there are a lot of other possibles with motives, too. He's made things a whole lot worse by running. I want to be the first to hear his reasons."

"I think maybe he was really devastated by her death and needed some alone time."

Devine glanced over at that. "Does that bother you?"

She shrugged. "I'm worried because, as I've said, he's a good friend, and you turn to your friends when things are tough, although he didn't." She chewed her bottom lip as she thought about that, then roused herself. "But, and I may have stated this before, we were not romantically involved, so no, it doesn't bother me in that way."

"How about some breakfast?"

"What?"

"Have you eaten?"

"I had an espresso and split a bagel with my mom."

"Okay. I know a little diner just off the road on the island. Makes a trucker-sized breakfast that's hard to beat." He signaled a turn. "Your mom seems nice. Where does she live?"

"Montpelier. And she's headed back there after a meeting this morning. She doesn't often come up to Burlington." *Too much information.*

"Is that where you're from?"

"Yes, but my folks are the only ones who stayed put. My two brothers live elsewhere."

Devine flashed her another smile as he pulled onto the bridge going over to the island.

Way too much information.

Another couple of turns and he pulled into the parking lot at Johnny's Diner. About a dozen cars sat empty in front of the place.

"Looks like a popular spot," she ventured.

"Uh-huh." Devine led the way inside.

After they'd placed their orders, both choosing the traditional breakfast, they sampled their coffees and then both stared out the window. J.J. wondered if he was waiting her out. For what, she wasn't sure. She wanted to get his take on the married cop but didn't want to break the truce. Maybe she'd ask on the way back.

"Do you think we'll find Connor today?"

"I have no idea, but at least we might get a lead. He's too smart to stay out in the open if he doesn't want to be found. Will you be all right with not finding him?"

"Of course. Well, not really, but that's because he's got to stop running, if that's what he's doing. But it isn't, is it? If he were running he'd be long gone, wouldn't he, not within a half hour's drive?"

Devine nodded. Their meals arrived and they ate in silence. They were on their third refill of coffee when Devine asked, "What does J.J. stand for?"

"What?"

His grin was lopsided. "I'm curious."

"I would have thought you'd found that out when you were investigating me way back when."

"I told you, I didn't go into your background. Now, give."

"Only if you tell me what Ty is short for."

"Janice? Joyce? Jennifer?"

"Tyrone? Tyler? Tyrell?" she countered.

Devine shook his head and laughed. He raised his hands in surrender. "It's Tyler. Your turn."

She spoke out of the corner of her mouth and kept her voice low. "Josephine June."

He raised his eyebrows.

"Family names. Now, maybe we should get to business."

Devine steered his Acura into a diagonal parking slot in front of Wheeler's Groceteria on the main highway.

About half a dozen houses flanked both sides of the road, all white clapboard, some bungalows but mainly two storied. All had American flags flanking the front steps. All had comfortable-looking chairs, inviting passersby to stop in for a chat. Those were all empty at the moment, though. She could see the edge of the sign for the municipal building farther up the road. That's where the post office, the police, and the unofficial "mayor" of the island had offices. Several cars were parked in front of the municipal building on the side of the road even though there was a parking lot in the back.

"Where's the gas station?" J.J. asked, looking around her.

Devine followed her gaze. "It's just around that curve, but I figured if he's in hiding somewhere around this area, he has to get groceries at some point." He pointed to the store sign. "Doesn't hurt to ask." He turned off the ignition and slid out of the car. J.J. scrambled out and looked around. "Besides, the cops will have been all over that gas station, and if they'd found out anything significant, Connor Mac would be in jail right now."

J.J. shuddered. She wouldn't let her mind go there. "I've always thought that it looks like a pleasant, small, unassuming village. It's so much smaller than Half Moon Bay. You'd think that if he is around here, someone would have seen him or talked to him. He could have just been passing through."

Devine grunted and headed for the store door. He held it open for J.J., and she smiled her thanks.

Rustic was the description that leapt into J.J.'s mind. The weathered wooden-slat floor even had creaks in it. The main counter looked to be of reclaimed barn board and the shelves behind it were painted a dark hunter green, in keeping with the outdoorsy look. The room was crisscrossed with freestanding shelves filled with various products from dish detergent to elastic bands.

J.J. looked back at the counter and the older woman— somewhere in her sixties, she'd bet—standing behind it, folding what looked like multicolored dishcloths. She glanced up at them as they approached, and a mottled midsized dog ran to meet them.

J.J. bent down to give it a pat. "What a friendly dog. And such wonderful colors." She looked at the woman, who smiled and nodded.

"She's a mongrel but got all the best traits of whatever got together. I thought she deserved a regal name to make up for her parentage so I called her Svetlana Abrisimova."

"That's quite a mouthful," Devine said, joining the conversation.

"I can handle it," answered the woman, folding her arms on the counter and leaning toward them. "My name's almost as tricky, so just call me Gail. So, what can I do for y'all?" The Southern lilt to her voice had a melodic ring that made J.J. think of long hooped skirts and mint juleps.

Gail's eyes wandered over Devine, head to toe, and she leaned forward even farther, a Cheshire-like smile on her face.

Devine's swallow was audible and made J.J. grin. "We're looking for a friend of ours and heard that his car was seen around here yesterday. Maybe the police even asked you about him?" Devine paused, watching for a reaction. "His name is Connor Mac."

Gail stood upright again and went back to folding, but she kept glancing up at Devine. "Oh yeah, they came by and asked. Most excitement we've had here all month.

Maybe all year, though it's not over yet. The year, that is."
She fluffed her short graying hair that had been helped
along by silvery highlights. "You say he's a friend? You
sure you're not more cops?" That idea didn't seem to
appeal to her.

J.J. thought it was her turn. "No, we're not. He's my
boyfriend." She thought she looked suitably upset. "He's
been missing for several days and I'm really worried. I
think he must have had an accident of some sort and maybe
has amnesia or something. I can't understand why else he
wouldn't have been in touch and let me know he's okay."
She dared not glance at Devine. She focused on the
woman, who looked suitably convinced.

"I'm really sorry to hear that, honey. I wish I could
help." She touched a hand to her hair again and smiled at
Devine. "As I told the police, I didn't see the car they were
looking for, but the guy, Connor you say his name is, he
was in here earlier in the week. Stocked up on your basics
like eggs, bread, potatoes, some canned meat. Seemed like
he was planning on staying a bit. That's what I told the
cops."

"He didn't happen to say where he was staying?"

"No. He seemed like a nice guy, though. We talked
mainly about the weather." She tucked a stray hair behind
her left ear and stood up straighter, thrusting her chest
forward.

Devine glanced at J.J. "Do you have a photo of Connor Mac?"

She thought a second. "Yes, on my phone." She pulled
it out and flicked through the photos, stopping at one of
Connor and Evan at the last Culinary Capers dinner.

"Is he one of these guys?" she asked the store clerk.

She squinted and grabbed J.J.'s hand, pulling it and the
phone closer. "Yeah. I think it's the one on the left."

J.J. showed it to Devine. He nodded. "Just wanted to be

sure. Well, thanks for your help." She started to turn away and thought better of it. "Are there many cabins for rent around here?"

"For sure, on both islands, but the ones on North Hero are probably more private in setting. Those folks wanting to rent out at this time of year usually have a sign posted at the end of their drive."

Gail looked at J.J., and her voice softened. "I'm sorry he didn't let you know, honey. Do you think he's in trouble?"

J.J. wasn't sure how to answer. "I guess he just needed some alone time."

"We all need that now and then." She looked straight at Devine, a playful look now on her face. "Come back anytime. Oh, and don't you think I should have your number in case he comes back?"

Devine didn't miss a beat, although J.J. noticed he stiffened.

"Of course, here's my card."

"Hm. A private detective. And I can call anytime? Mrs. Devine won't get upset?"

J.J. turned away to hide her grin.

"Call me if you see him," Devine answered. "Thanks again."

He grabbed J.J.'s elbow and practically pushed her out the door with him right on her heels.

"Do not say a word," Devine said as he audibly exhaled.

J.J. nodded and kept her eyes straight ahead, across the street, and looking at the small restaurant with a vacant lot on each side of it. She was trying her hardest not to burst out laughing.

Devine followed her gaze. "Let's talk this out over a coffee."

They chose one of three booths, in the far corner by the window. J.J. sat back and waited for Devine to say something. He took his time drinking his coffee.

J.J. couldn't wait. "So how do we know if he's still

around or was just passing through and thought he'd pick up some supplies? And how do we know what direction he was going? Was he headed back to Half Moon Bay or up to one of the other islands?"

"I think he's probably still on the islands. If he'd headed back to town, someone would have been on top of it. I'd bet he's continued north. That's a lot of shoreline and also wooded areas. There might be lots of hiding places around."

J.J. shook her head. "He must be staying somewhere. I can't really picture Connor roughing it. He's not a tent type of guy. Do you think he'd chance an inn or a bed-and-breakfast?"

"I doubt he'd want to be spotted or have to talk to too many people. He might have either rented a cabin or borrowed one. I'm sure the police have searched the immediate vicinity looking for his car, but he's hidden it, if he's smart."

"If he's in hiding, you mean. I still don't understand what he's doing. This makes it look really bad, doesn't it?"

"It always was bad. You don't just disappear during a murder investigation." Devine shrugged. "I know it's not what you want to hear."

"But it is possible that he just needed some time away. I'm sure he's not the killer."

Devine covered one of her hands with his. "You are so fiercely loyal. This is the thing with Rocco Gates all over again. While it's admirable that you support your friends, it's foolish that you do so without questioning the possibilities."

"I have thought about the possibilities, believe me, and I still believe he's innocent. So let's just play a game. Say, you believe the same thing. Who would be at the top of your suspect list instead?"

Devine let go of her hand and sat back against the bench. "I'm still on the clock with the TV station, tracking down their supposed vandal or stalker or whatever he is. I haven't given much thought to this."

"What about Mikey Cooper? Could he be a murderer?"

Devine sat up straighter. "What do you know about him?"

"I know he's the station manager's son but was fired for crashing the station van while drunk. There must be a lot more to it, also. You'd think he'd give his son a second chance. I can imagine Mikey is pretty disgruntled, as they say. The perfect person to harass and stalk."

"He's under consideration. But murder is a big jump from threatening letters."

"What about the near miss with the weather guy?"

"Possibly not deliberate."

"What about some of the coworkers as killer? There seems to be a lot of jealousy and rivalry going around."

"Possibilities. But how many of them were at the casino night? You can check those photos again to see if there's someone else we've missed." His eyes narrowed. "Or is there already another person you haven't told me about?"

"No, there isn't." She avoided looking at him and he kept silent.

Finally, she went on. "But I do want to talk to Miranda's assistant, Hennie Ferguson, again. I want to know what she was doing at the casino night."

"Let me handle it."

"No. It's my clue." She leaned forward, arms crossed on the table.

"May I remind you, you are not the professional." He leaned toward her and tapped the tip of her nose with his finger.

"But I'm here with you now. I'll go with you when you talk to her, too."

He glared at her but she held his gaze. He shook his head. "Okay. But I choose when and where."

"Okay."

"So, tell me all about this married cop."

There it was. She searched his face but didn't find any of the anger from the night before. He just wanted information.

"That's all I know. Hennie said Miranda met him while doing an interview."

"That's an even better reason to talk to her again. We need more information on the identity of the cop."

CHAPTER 17

Sunday morning, J.J. lay in bed longer than she'd intended, going over the previous day's happenings in her head. They'd arrived back in town long before supper, and J.J. had to admit she was a tad disappointed when Devine didn't suggest they eat out. He instead dropped her curbside at her apartment with a warning to stay out of trouble.

Oh man, he irritated her.

He could run hot or cold or both at the same time, even. She refused to take her own feelings out for examination. She just didn't like not knowing what was going on. Okay, nothing. Quite right. He hadn't asked her out on a date since she'd turned him down. She wasn't sure if she regretted not accepting. She just knew he was an irritating man.

She flung the duvet off and crawled out of bed. She needed a long walk after being in the car so much of the day before. Indie appeared from under the duvet and followed her to the kitchen, waiting patiently while J.J. filled his wet and dry food cups after putting fresh water in his bowl.

J.J. watched Indie vacuum up the canned food, then ground some espresso beans for her own morning treat. She would take a walk down to the boardwalk. That should clear her thinking.

As soon as she'd savored her first cup of espresso.

She had her hand on the doorknob when the phone rang. She checked caller ID. It was Beth. She'd better take it.

"Good morning, Beth. What can I do for you?"

"Glad you're around, J.J. I'm just trying to get everyone together this afternoon. I'm so worried about Connor since he hasn't shown up yet. I thought we could talk it over some more. Also, I've been trying some recipes in this *Mystery Writers of America Cookbook* and want you all as guinea pigs. I know, it's not the dinner day but this is just for fun. I'm saving Sara Paretsky's Chicken Gabriella for the club dinner."

"Sounds good, and I do have some info on Connor, although he's still missing. What time?"

"Nice thing to leave me hanging with, J.J. How about four P.M.?"

"I'll be there. Can I bring something?"

"How about some sparkling water?"

"Done."

J.J. took a final look out the window before heading out and decided to add a Windbreaker to the hoodie she wore. Her jeans should be warm enough. She was halfway down the slope of Gabor Avenue when she realized what a good idea the Windbreaker had been. The few flags that hung outside the shops were fluttering and a chill crept up the back of her legs. She walked faster.

Several people were walking along the beach, which surprised her. She'd expected to see the numerous dog walkers, but she would have thought the cold wind would put off the others. *That's silly. Look at me.*

She took a couple of deep breaths, then pulled her hood

forward a bit more. Sticking her hands in her pockets, she started walking quickly along the edge of the lake, scanning the shoreline for interesting rocks or driftwood. Her mind was blank as she concentrated on where she was walking and listening to the waves lapping the shoreline. This was just what she needed. Very therapeutic and soothing. By the time she reached the far end of the beach, where it became too overgrown with thicket to walk, she was feeling the cold. She turned back, walking even faster with her head down against the wind, trying to assemble her thoughts.

She did have information to share with the Culinary Capers gang but nothing that got them much closer to finding Connor and getting him to come home. Maybe the group could come up with something once they'd heard all the details. Someone had to know where he'd gone. What was he doing?

J.J. arrived at Beth's first-floor condo at the appointed hour. She rang the doorbell with her elbow, juggling a cloth bag from Walgreens with two bottles of S.Pellegrino in one hand and a box of truffles from Lake Champlain Chocolates in the other. They could always eat more chocolate!

Evan opened the door for her and grabbed the bag after giving her a quick kiss on the cheek. "Come in and be prepared to savor."

J.J. sniffed the air. "Oh, yum. This will be a treat, I'm sure."

The doorbell rang, and Alison was next to arrive. "I guess the gang's all here. All that will be here, anyway."

Beth joined them. "Unfortunately, that's right. Let's grab a coffee and a seat. The meal will be another thirty minutes."

They followed her into the kitchen and helped themselves

to the coffee on their way into the family room. J.J. grabbed the worn club chair next to the sliding patio doors while the others also took their usual places.

"So," Beth started, "let's get right down to business, and I mean Connor. You said you had some news about him, J.J. First of all, though, Alison, is there anything new from the police end of it?"

J.J. hid a smile. She could so imagine Beth as a high school teacher when she was in this mode.

Alison shifted in her club chair. "Why do you all always do this to me? You know I can't share any information with you. However, just musing out loud to myself, I wonder if my sarge has gotten an update on the reported sighting of Connor's car on South Hero."

Beth grinned. "I'm sorry you feel you can't discuss this, Alison, and we do understand. J.J., what's your news?"

"Well, surprisingly enough, Connor's car was spotted on South Hero Island a couple of days ago."

"Do tell." Beth grinned again and sat forward in her chair.

"So, yesterday I drove up there and had a look around."

"Alone?" Alison sounded less than pleased.

"I may have gone with Devine," J.J. said under her breath.

Evan picked up on it. "Devine? As in that PI you were none too pleased with a few months ago? You're seeing him again?"

"I am not *seeing him*. Our paths just happened to cross on this case." She noted out of the corner of her eye that Alison's eyebrows rose ever so slightly. "He was hired by the TV station to determine if Miranda's murder is part of some other attacks on TV personalities and property."

"Wow," Evan said, sounding suitably impressed. "Is it? That would be great. Well, for Connor, anyway."

J.J. shrugged and went to refill her coffee. When she

sat back down, she continued. "So, what we need to figure out is, why was Connor on one of the islands? Is he still there and if so, where? Does he know someone who has a cabin around there?" She glanced around her. "Any ideas?"

Nobody said anything for a few minutes, each lost in thought. Beth was the first to speak. "I'm not much help. I can't think of an answer to any of your questions, except maybe that Connor is somewhere around there and wants to be alone, just to get his head back on straight. He's never been overly effusive when talking about his life. I think even though he is the big media personality, he's a very shy person. And he needs to take this time to himself."

Evan looked at Beth, admiration in his gaze. "Eloquently put, Beth. And I do think you're on the right track. Connor never really talked much about his past or his other friends or even family. When we'd all get together, he'd always be asking what was going on in our lives or talking about the food, right? J.J., what was he like on dates?"

"Well, firstly, we're talking about him in the past tense." She shuddered. "What is he like on a date? He's charming, fun, really knows a lot about the place we're eating and the food itself. But, you know, and I hadn't thought about it until this all started, he hasn't shared many details about his life or his past with me, either. And all of our dates have been out to dinner or lunch. The odd movie. That was the focus of our talks, the food, the movie, or whatever we were doing." She thought about that a few seconds. "I never realized it before, but we didn't go for walks or long drives, activities that would allow for getting to know each other better."

"Introvert," Beth said.

"Secretive," Alison countered.

"Do you think there's something in his past that might be related to what's happened?" Evan asked.

J.J. shook her head. "I don't know and I don't even want to go there. Not unless we have to. I'd hate to intrude on his privacy. There must be a reason he hasn't shared more information about himself, and we should respect that."

"Unless it's made him a murderer," Alison added softly.

"Don't even think that."

A timer went off in the kitchen and Beth excused herself. Nobody said anything, but in a couple of minutes the aroma from the kitchen brought smiles to their faces.

"Dinner is served," Beth called out. "Evan is on wine duty, please and thanks."

The mark of a truly delicious meal, as J.J. was learning, was its being eaten in silence. That equated with true appreciation. J.J. watched as Beth looked from face to face for some sign. Sometimes, it was like they were playing a game. Who would cave first and break the spell by talking? J.J. decided today it would be her.

"Delicious, Beth. I loved everything about it."

Beth's face beamed. "It's from Hank Phillippi Ryan in *The Mystery Writers of America Cookbook*. I love her writing and now, I love her food. She called it Worth-the-Effort Turkey Tetrazzini, and it does take some prep work but lives up to the name. Of course, I didn't have any turkey leftovers at this time of year so I bought a large turkey breast, which I precooked." She looked totally satisfied with herself.

"Not only will I give this one a try sometime," Evan said, "I'll also read one of her books."

"I'll guarantee you'll read more than one," Beth replied as she started clearing the table. "Michael's a big pasta fan, isn't he?"

"He is, and any excuse to use my new pasta machine is appreciated." He refilled everyone's wineglasses.

Alison stood to help clear the table. "I suggest we all put our thinking caps on and try to recall if Connor made mention in any way of someone he knew with a place on one of the islands."

J.J. nodded. "And I think I need to talk to Megan Spicer

again. She's the chair of People and Causes, and the one who suggested I ask both Connor and Miranda to emcee together. I want to know why those two. I should have asked her a long time ago, but she's been ill and off work. I heard she was back near the end of last week, though."

No more excuses.

CHAPTER 18

J.J. phoned Megan's office first thing Monday morning, hoping she was indeed back at work, and was lucky enough to snag an appointment with her right after lunch. Until then, she worked some more on the thirtieth-year class reunion coming up next spring. She'd obviously had one corner of her brain tasked with thinking about it, because she'd woken up with the thought of a blue jeans tea for the women attending while the men would be off at a golf tournament. *Hah!*

At 11:50, she took a seat near the window at Cups 'n' Roses and sipped the latte she'd grabbed while waiting for her food. She glanced around at the other customers. There were a couple she now recognized as being fairly regular. Could one of them be the thief?

Beth brought her ham and Swiss cheese panini to the table and added a side of beet salad. "I'm thinking of adding it to the menu. You can be my guinea pig."

"Looks delicious. Happy as always to oblige. Any shortages reported on the weekend?"

Beth sighed. "I'd like to be able to say 'no' but in fact, one of the small rectangular plates that I use for small side salads disappeared. And it was dirty. Can you imagine? I hope it made a big mess in the perp's purse."

"So, you believe it's a woman, and a 'perp' no less," J.J. couldn't help adding, biting back a smile.

Beth shrugged then wiped her hands on her apron and looked around the room. "I can't really expect my weekend staff to be totally vigilant. But it's annoying. Oh well, one day we'll catch a thief. Male or female. Enjoy your lunch."

"I always do but I feel like I'm eating under false pretenses."

"Not today. Remember, I want a serious rating of the beet salad." Beth winked and went back to work while J.J. enjoyed her lunch, keeping an eye peeled just in case. She also took some more photos, just in case the deed was happening right under her eyes.

As she left, she told Beth, "It's a keeper."

Beth grinned and nodded.

J.J. pulled into the parking lot at Megan's office on Park Street overlooking Battery Park a few minutes before one thirty. She checked a second time to make sure she hadn't spilled any lunch on her black pencil skirt. She liked to look her best for all meetings, especially this one. Megan, always elegantly dressed, stood at the receptionist's desk when she walked in.

"So good to see you again, J.J. I'm sorry I wasn't available sooner, but the flu really knocked me off my feet and then there was just so much work to get caught up on. You know how it is."

J.J. was surprised by the quick hug she received. "I'm glad you're better. Nothing worse than being sidelined."

Once in Megan's office, J.J. took a minute to look at the large picture frame filled with photos from the casino night, hung on the wall next to the door. "These look really great. I'm glad it worked out. The photographer came highly recommended even though he's still in school."

"The board is very pleased with his work as they are with yours. We had a meeting on Friday morning to review your report, and then all hell broke loose, so I didn't get a chance to call you about it. They really were delighted with the overall outcome of the evening, notwithstanding the grisly ending."

J.J. noticed a slight shudder pass through Megan's body as she said this.

J.J. nodded. "I'm glad to hear that. What happened on Friday, if I may ask?"

Megan sighed deeply. She looked tired even though as usual, she was dressed for success in a red suit with a cream-colored blouse. Her blonde hair looked like she'd just left the beauty salon. "We were subjected to another round of police interrogations. Or at least, Sue and I were. They wanted to know if I knew where Connor might be hiding."

Nice lead-in to the reason for her visit. "You? Why would they think you'd know?"

Megan stood and walked over to the window, seeming very intent on what she was looking at. After a couple of minutes she turned back to J.J. "You see, Connor and I were once engaged."

J.J. could feel her jaw drop. "You were? When? And, what happened?"

Megan started pacing and after a few strides, explained. "We met at a basketball game in college and just clicked. After a year of dating, he asked me to marry him. I was the happiest girl on earth."

She sat down in her chair behind the desk and picked up the stapler, just looking at it for a few moments. She cleared her throat and put it down. "Then one night we went to a frat party, and Miranda was there. I didn't know they were seeing each other behind my back until one of Miranda's friends let it slip. I was livid and broke up with him on the spot."

She looked up at J.J. "Over the years, our paths have crossed a few times. It's hard not to with him being in the media and my job with the foundation. Everything has been very cordial. I left all that behind a long time ago, as I told the police."

"But I don't understand why you'd want both Connor and Miranda to cohost the event in that case."

"Well, a board member suggested Miranda, but I wasn't sure I could go through with it. Then I thought, she and Connor had parted on bad terms, or so I'd heard, and I guess I just wanted to rub salt in their wounds by throwing them together. I realized I wasn't as much past all those negative feelings as I had thought." She sat chewing on her bottom lip and, to J.J.'s horror, looked like she might cry.

J.J. cleared her throat. "That was taking quite a chance. What if they started arguing onstage or something and ruined the event?"

"I was pretty certain that wouldn't happen." Megan sighed. "They're both professionals, after all. But I guess a small part of me was hoping for something like that." She covered her face with her hands. "I can't believe I acted in such a mean and petty way. I really did want to be totally over it all."

J.J. took a few minutes to consider what she'd heard. "And what do you feel now?"

"I feel so ashamed, and horrified that Miranda died. And poor Connor. I feel so very sorry for him. If it turns out that he did it and if I pushed him to that point, I'll be mortified."

"You can't believe he did it."

She shook her head. "No, I'm pretty sure he couldn't commit murder. But how well do we really know anyone? Even ourselves?"

J.J. didn't have an answer for that. "Megan, do you

know if he had any friends in the islands area or someone with a cottage there?"

"Why do you ask?"

"Because his car was spotted on South Hero earlier this week."

Megan smiled. "So that's why the police were back. They wouldn't tell me. I guess he's all right, then. I'd also been worried that something had happened to him. But no, it's been a long time since Connor shared anything about his life with me. And I don't recall anyone from the past who lives around there. Sorry."

J.J. drove back to her office almost in a daze. She was trying to process what she'd just learned and wasn't sure what shocked her more. The fact that Megan had once been engaged to Connor or that Megan wasn't totally prepared to believe him innocent.

She hoped Evan was in his office and alone. She needed to talk this out.

He took one look at her face and suggested they have a coffee at the Chatterbox across the street. She headed for a bistro table for two while he grabbed their espressos at the counter. She finished hers before telling Evan what she'd learned.

"Oh boy. This just keeps getting messier," Evan said when she'd finished. "Don't get me wrong. I like Connor a lot. He's a good pal. But, boy, he's just not very clever when it comes to women. Sorry to say that to you."

J.J. nodded. "It's okay. I totally agree. But it still doesn't get us any closer to finding him. I think I'll just head back to South Hero tonight and do some door knocking."

"You can't do that alone, and I don't think you should call that private eye guy in on this. I think he has designs on you, and I'm not so sure that's a good thing. I'm going with you. No ifs, ands, or buts. But you can drive."

"Thanks, Evan. I won't fight you on this." She smiled, relieved. It would be good to have some company. "I'll pick you up at six thirty. Is that okay? We want to get a good start before dark."

"No problem."

She thought about Evan's assessment of Devine on her way up the stairs. And smiled.

J.J. pulled up to the curb in front of Evan's small two-story white clapboard house at the appointed time. The house looked very similar to the one where he set up office and rented out the second floor. Only this one was quite a bit smaller. The front yard looked the same, though—white picket fence, colorful dahlias, mums, and a mixture of short green shrubs lining the porch that wrapped around the house, with a very neat and tidy patch of green lawn out front.

Evan was halfway down the stairs when the front door opened again and Michael Cole, his partner, came out and caught up to Evan.

Evan whispered as he slid into the passenger seat. "We do have a slight problem, after all."

Michael took the backseat. "Hi, J.J. I hope you don't mind if I tag along. I have this feeling that the two of you on your own might just get into a little hot water with this outing."

J.J. turned to face him. "Huh. Thanks for the vote of confidence, but I'm happy to have more helping hands along."

There wasn't much traffic, so the drive seemed to take no time at all. They were on the bridge over to South Hero when Evan asked if she had a plan.

"Uh, not really. I thought we'd just ask a whole lot of people if they've seen Connor or even know him. And if anyone knows him, whether they know if he has a place somewhere close by."

"That's not much of a plan," Michael said from the backseat.

"It is rather hit or miss," Evan commented. "But I also can't see what else we'd do. I had no idea how easy it is for people to just disappear. No wonder so many crimes go unsolved."

"Not a good thought, Evan," Michael said.

J.J. stopped by the side of the road across from the gas station where Connor's car had been seen at least once. "I looked up the area on the Internet, and there are several cottages along the shoreline. Wouldn't you think he'd be hiding out in one of those? In fact, all of the islands have spots that would work equally well. I'm not quite sure where to start."

"He wouldn't just break in. Does he know someone around here or maybe it's a rental?" Evan pulled up Google on his smartphone. "I'll check for any listings. Maybe he found one he knows is vacant and broke in."

"I thought you said he wouldn't break in," Michael pointed out.

"Just covering all bases. Mainly because I can't think of anything else."

J.J. grabbed her purse. "Let's start in the gas station."

The three of them walked in and found a boy, probably in his midteens, sitting at the messy desk. A cash register took up about half the space while the rest was a mixture of office supplies, various sizes of papers, and Twizzlers, none in neat piles.

He looked up when they walked in. "You want gas? My dad's just gone in the back. Shouldn't be more than a minute or so."

They heard a toilet flush, and the kid went back to watching a small TV screen perched on a shelf to the right of the main door. In a few seconds, the door to the back opened and a taller, older version of the boy walked in, adjusting his belt.

"Gas?"

"No. Questions," J.J. said, trying to sound pleasant. And not at all desperate. She pulled out the photo of the group that she'd printed out. She pointed to Connor. "Have you seen this man in here or in the area in the last little while?"

"Are you cops?"

"No."

Evan and Michael both chimed in, too.

'We're friends and we're worried about him," Evan answered.

"Why do you think he's hereabout?"

"His car was spotted in this area a few days ago. We're just wondering if he's staying someplace around here."

"The cops were in asking, but they wouldn't say anything. Is he wanted by the law?"

J.J. crossed her fingers in her pocket and shook her head. "As I said, we're worried about him. He's had a bit of a shock, and we want to make sure he's handling it all right. Please, if you've seen him, tell us."

She knew she sounded like she was pleading, but that might be to their advantage.

"He drives a fairly new red Mazda CX-3, if that helps," Evan added.

The father scratched his balding head and took another look at the photo that lay on the desk. "Like I told them, he looks sort of familiar although I'm not always working here. My brother's part owner, so, like I told the cops, he might have seen the guy."

"Have you heard of any cottages that have been rented out recently?"

He scratched again. "No, nothing around here. You could try the other islands, although there's not another gas station until you get to the upper North." He handed the photo back to J.J. "Sorry."

"That's all right. It was a long shot."

They left but sat in the car several minutes before driving off.

"What now?" Michael asked.

"I really don't know. It's getting dark sooner than I thought, so I guess there's not much more we can do tonight. I thought we'd get to some door knocking. I should have thought this through a bit more before dragging you both out here." She started the car as the father came hurrying up to her window.

"I just remembered where I saw him. Not here but at the gas station on North Hero. I was on my way back from Rouses Point and stopped in. That would have been a week ago, though."

J.J. felt dejected on the way back to Half Moon Bay. Secretly, way down deep, she'd been hoping they'd find Connor and he'd talk to them, his friends. Now she didn't know what her next step should be.

CHAPTER 19

The answer to that question was waiting for her when she arrived home. Hennie Ferguson had left a phone message. Simple and to the point. She'd suggested J.J. talk to Miranda's sister-in-law, Yolande Myers, about the argument they'd had at the TV station the week before the murder. Too bad she hadn't supplied a phone number or, better yet, an address. She went online in search of both but found the Myerses were unlisted. That made sense for someone in politics.

J.J. wondered if Hennie was trying to help or to divert suspicion from herself. Then she wondered when she herself had become so untrusting.

She also had a message from Beth stating that another coffee mug had disappeared that day. *How can I be so blind?* She didn't have an answer to that so she opted for a good night's sleep instead.

She tried phoning Hennie at the station the next morning from the office but was told she'd called in sick. *Another one?*

What J.J. had wanted was some background info on the sister-in-law and maybe a bit more about Miranda's relationship with her. Had there been other arguments? About what? She also needed to know more about the married cop.

She decided to put Hennie on the back burner and drive out to Gary Myers's campaign office. Fortunately, that address was readily available. Surely someone there would have a home address for the Myerses. But would they be likely to give it out? She'd have to come up with a cover story on the way there.

It took her less than twenty minutes to locate the office that had taken over a deserted store on the outskirts of the busy downtown district. There wasn't much commercial activity going on, so that had probably guaranteed a low rental fee, and there was lots of free parking, an encouragement for constituents and volunteers to stop in.

The brightness of the overhead lights in the office startled her, after the shade provided by an umbrella of maple trees outdoors. She'd taken a few seconds to appreciate the foliage that was at its best at this time of year. Only a few leaves had started to fall so the effect had been quite surprising.

She blinked a couple of times and then took in the busy scene before her. Six desks, the type she'd associated with school teachers, hugged both walls in the large room, and a center aisle led toward the back, where a series of offices had been hived off. Those all had half walls of glass. Most desks had a young person, phone receiver to ear, reading from a small recipe-sized card or making notes on a pad. The din from six voices of different volumes was pronounced.

The walls were decorated with a combination of campaign posters for Gary Myers, Vermont tourism posters, the odd campaign cartoon, and a large display of photos taken at various campaign stops. A tall flagpole with the American flag attached stood in one corner and a smaller Vermont state flag in another.

J.J. spotted a couple of teenagers in one of the offices, their attention on whatever was on the desk in front of them. It looked like they were folding paper.

She smiled back at a young woman sitting at the desk nearest the front, on the right side, stuffing envelopes. She looked to be in her early twenties, lean and athletic-looking, her long auburn hair framing her pale face. A welcoming face. J.J. walked over to her.

"That looks like it will take all day." She indicated the box full of folded flyers sitting on the floor beside the table.

"That's okay. That's what I'm here for. Are you a new volunteer?" She looked hopeful.

"Sorry, not today."

"No problem. If you decide you want to help . . ." She waved her hand over the boxes of envelopes and flyers, and smiled.

"I'll remember that. My name is J.J. Tanner."

"I'm Dawn Reese." She stuck out her hand. "Nice to meet you. What can I do for you?"

"I'm the person who hired Miranda Myers as an emcee at the casino night."

A slight gasp escaped Dawn's lips. "OMG, that was so terrible. Gary, Mr. Myers, is so devastated."

"It was very tragic. I'm hoping someone here can give me the Myerses' home address. I'd like to extend my condolences in person and bring them some flowers." She'd realized that not only was it a good cover story, it also made a lot of sense to actually do it.

Dawn looked to be giving it a lot of thought, and then smiled as she reached into the top drawer of the desk. "I'm sure it will be all right to give it to you. That's such a nice thing for you to do." She consulted a laminated sheet of paper and wrote the address down on a telephone message page.

As she handed it over to J.J. she said, "Don't forget, we'd be happy to have your help on the campaign."

J.J. thanked her and quickly left before she'd be cornered into filling out an application or something.

She stopped by a florist and chose a modest bouquet, then headed to the south end of Burlington, just a few notches on the price scale below Forest Grove, where she'd planned a twenty-first birthday party not long ago. That, too, had ended not as planned.

The impressive sprawling brick Tudor home was tucked into a large wooded lot with a circular driveway framing a well-tended lawn. She couldn't help admiring the tasteful lawn ornaments that lined the paving-blocks sidewalk. It looked like someone had been accumulating paving stones from around the world. Or else someone had a very good landscaper.

She rang the doorbell and waited, trying to peer through the stained glass window in the door but appear not to be doing so. She heard footsteps and shifted her gaze to the rhodora bush in the left-hand corner of the house.

"Can I help you?" An attractive tall woman in her midforties was walking toward her from the garage attached to the left side of the house, a Shaw's Supermarket bag in one hand, her purse in the other. Her shoulder-length brown hair was swept back with a headband of crocheted flowers. It spoke of someone confident in her style and contrasted the turquoise sateen long-sleeved blouse over beige skinny ankle-length pants. Her height had been aided by the multicolored fabric platform sandals on her feet.

J.J. hadn't thought to peer in the garage even though the door was open. "I'm looking for Yolande Myers."

"That's me. And you are?" Yolande shifted the cloth bag to her purse hand as she positioned the key.

"J.J. Tanner. I'm an event planner. I organized the charity casino night. We wanted to extend our condolences." She tilted the bouquet toward Yolande.

"Oh." Yolande looked so sad that J.J. wanted to kick

herself for even suspecting her. "That's so kind. Please come in."

J.J. followed her into a formal-looking entry, the dark hardwood floors showing off two large white and black area rugs. J.J. wondered about removing her shoes but noticed her hostess hadn't bothered. On a metal and glass credenza placed near the stairs lay a stack of colorful campaign brochures for Yolande's husband. J.J. waited while Yolande deposited her bags, accepted the flowers, and put them in a vase filled with water.

"I'm sorry," J.J. said as she watched. "I know it's a hard time for you, but I just wanted to ask you a few questions about Miranda, if it's not too difficult."

"Why?"

J.J. squared her shoulders. "Because a good friend of mine, Connor Mac, is a suspect, and he's disappeared. I'm trying to find him and maybe clear him at the same time."

Yolande studied her a few seconds before saying, "I don't mind talking to you, but I'm not sure how much I can help. I didn't really know her friends or much about her personal life. She didn't really share—she was too busy trying to run our lives."

J.J. didn't know what to say to that.

"Have a seat and we'll have some tea."

Yolande indicated the counter and six tall barstools. J.J. sat on the one closest to her. So, it was to be a friendly, casual gab. She wondered what that meant, if anything. J.J. would have preferred coffee at this hour of the morning, but she'd drink anything in order to quiz the lady. She picked up one of the brochures and scanned it. "Is this your husband?"

"Yes. He's a candidate for state attorney in a few months. He could use your vote. Sorry, I'm in campaign mode, even now, and I'd do anything to help his cause. Do you take sugar or milk?"

"Neither."

"A puritan," Yolande said with a chuckle. "Me, too." She set a Spode china mug in front of each of them and a teapot in between. "So, ask me some questions."

"I guess I just wanted to get a feel for Miranda and learn a bit about her friends. But if you can't help me with that, can you suggest who could? Your husband maybe?"

Yolande shook her head vigorously. "I don't want you bothering him with this. Not now. He's pretty torn up, and he has to get his head straight for the campaign. I'll try to answer your questions."

"Okay. Did she have a boyfriend?"

"She hadn't mentioned anyone new lately. But I had a hunch that she had started going out with Connor Mac again. You know about their past history?"

"Not much," J.J. hedged, hoping to get another take on the story.

"Well, they were madly in love with each other at one point, just after college. We thought there'd be a wedding soon. She brought him over to meet us and everything. That was unusual. So, we were hoping. And then, all of a sudden it seemed, it was over and there was a new guy. At least that's what I assumed. She didn't bring this one around. So, how good a friend are you to Connor?"

"We're part of the same dinner club, and we're all a fairly close-knit bunch. None of us believe Connor could be a killer, and we're really worried about him." An idea hit.

"Did they talk about anything in particular that you remember? Maybe someplace special they would get away to?"

Yolande poured their tea before answering. It was far too strong for J.J.'s liking, but she took a sip.

"Oh, I can't remember much of what they talked about. It was too long ago." She looked to be pondering the question, though. "Would you like a cookie?"

Not what J.J. had been hoping she'd been pondering. Yolande walked over to a cupboard and pulled out a plastic container. She found a plate and put two cookies on it, sliding it in front of J.J.

"I just discovered the French Bakery on College Street. Their butter swirl cookies. Delicious. Please try one."

Oh well. Maybe they were bonding.

"You're right. Really delicious," J.J. said, trying to swallow quickly so she could ask some more questions.

Yolande beat her to it. "I actually do remember they'd go away the occasional weekend to a cottage on North Hero Island that belonged to one of their friends." She sat staring ahead as if reading something. "I think it was around the time Connor started that restaurant. The cottage belonged to his business partner. That's it, but I can't remember the guy's name."

Bingo. "That's a real help. Did Miranda mention that she was seeing a married guy?"

Yolande looked surprised. "No, she didn't, but I doubt she would tell me or even Gary. Wouldn't you keep something like that private?" She chose another cookie and took a quick bite.

J.J. nodded. "Just one more question. Can you think of anyone who would want to kill her?"

Yolande chewed slowly and swallowed before answering. "No. No one. She wanted to be an investigative journalist, you know, so was always in practice mode. Always ready to stick her nose into everyone else's business. Or so it seemed. She could be awfully determined and a pain in the butt but none of that leads to murder. Does it?"

Does it?

J.J. drove slowly around the winding streets leading out of the elegantly manicured area, thinking about what she'd just learned. One thing stood out. They had to find Connor's former business partner. He could tell them where his cottage was and better still, whether that's where Connor was at the moment. She hoped. But first she had to head to the office and get some work done.

Skye had been in and out, leaving a note on J.J.'s desk. *Out to check on hotel sites.*

Work, right. Event planning. That was her job. So on with it. J.J. needed to nail down a caterer. She had a feeling that the staff at Epicurial Expressions would not be too delighted to buy into this next gig after the intense grilling they'd undergone after Miranda's murder.

That thought stopped her. She tried to quell the slight feeling of nausea that took her off guard every now and then. She could think about the murder when it was analytical and she was in sleuth mode, but at other times, like now, she felt some guilt that she'd set this all rolling by having Miranda as emcee. She knew it wasn't her fault but she also knew that until the murderer was found, and also, until Connor was cleared, she wouldn't feel totally at ease.

She shook her head and flipped on her computer, going directly to her contacts file and the caterer folder. She scrolled through the list she'd been accumulating since first moving to Half Moon Bay two years ago. Many were suggestions from friends and colleagues; others, she'd found online because of their specialties. She'd already chosen the theme for this event—*Ferris Bueller's Day Off*, after the popular movie. A kid plays hooky for a day—what better for a high school reunion? She grinned, pleased with herself. Now, to find a caterer who could handle a Pac-Man cake and an '80s candy buffet complete with E.T.'s Reese's Pieces, Twizzlers, and Pop Rocks.

She had a short list of two by the time she closed the file. She also had a couple of people she could call for their thoughts about the choices. She spent the rest of the morning pricing decorations online and searching for a florist to do centerpieces. She'd go with her usual DJ.

Her smartphone was set to alert her when it was time to head to Cups 'n' Roses for lunch. She felt today she might get lucky and spot the thief. Today she felt organized. It was a day for getting things done.

"Hi, Beth, how's it going?" she asked eventually, even though she'd had to wait in a long lineup to place her order.

Beth ran the back of her hand across her forehead. "Busy, which is good. And equally good, but also bad, is the fact that I have an order for a dozen panini to be delivered to the law office just up the street for a one o'clock meeting." She glanced at the clock. "I don't know why I do these things to myself. Why not just say no?"

"Because that word is not in your vocabulary. Is there anything I can do to help, aside from the actual making of the food?"

Beth gave her a sharp glance. "Uh, no, but thanks. I think we've got it under control, and if I'm going to continue to do such things, I'll just have to get better organized or hire more staff. Now, it'll be a short wait for your lunch, I'm afraid." She was already looking at the person behind J.J.

"No problem. I'll just grab a latte while I wait so I blend in a bit." She walked to the end of counter, where Abby was taking care of the coffee orders, and eyed the tables while she waited for her mug. She'd left her scarf at the table, also careful to keep an eye on it in case the thief branched out, and after getting her latte, settled back in her chair to wait.

She quickly checked for her "regulars" and mentally ticked them off her list. One person was missing, though, a guy in his twenties who she'd assumed was a student at a nearby campus, from the distressed look of the clothes he regularly wore. She pulled her smartphone out and made a note to follow up on him. How, she wasn't sure.

She looked up when someone slid into the chair across from her. "Devine."

He nodded. "I was pretty sure I'd find you at your noontime job." He grinned. "Having any luck?"

"I don't know. In fact, I feel like I don't have a clue."

"Anything I can do to help?"

What's he up to?

"Is that why you're here, to help me? Not to pump me?"

He nodded. "Maybe a little of both. You see, I have this theory that you didn't go home and spend the rest of the weekend thinking about other things. I'm pretty sure you've got a new theory, at the very least, and possibly a location where Connor Mac is hiding, as the other possibility."

How does he do that?

J.J. busied herself with the menu even though she'd already ordered. She needed some time to think about just how much to share. Nothing, was what came to mind. However, he had included her in the initial search on Saturday. She supposed she owed him something for that. Besides, Connor certainly wasn't the station vandal, so he had to be doing this for other reasons. She looked at Devine, trying to gauge what might be behind this increased interest in Connor. If they were two separate cases, might he get two fees for solving both? Was this nothing more than a money grab? Her eyes narrowed. He sat seemingly oblivious to her perusal of him, his attention focused on the room.

Did it really matter what his motive was? No. She needed his help, and Connor needed her, even if he didn't realize it.

"I found out that Connor and Miranda had on occasion spent some time at a cottage on North Hero Island. The place is owned by Connor's former business partner." That didn't seem quite right now that she'd said it out loud.

Hadn't Connor told her they'd gone their separate ways? But he had said that at times he still ate at the restaurant he'd been a partner in. At least, she thought he'd said that. She'd have to check with Evan.

"What are you thinking?" Devine asked. "Your mind has taken off in some direction. Was it something you said?" He smiled.

She rolled her eyes. "I was trying to remember what Connor had said about the breakup of the partnership. I guess it doesn't matter. We can get the location from the partner and then check it out."

"We?"

"Yes. It is my tip." She was prepared to fight for this one.

"Okay. What's the guy's name?"

"Oh no. After I finish here, we'll both go to the restaurant and ask about the cottage, then head over to find it. Together."

"You can get away?"

"I don't have any appointments this afternoon and there's nothing that can't wait until tomorrow. Besides, I don't know the former partner's name, but I do know the restaurant."

"Okay, then." He stood abruptly. "'Scuse me. I need my caffeine before we do any more plotting."

She watched him work his way around the crowded tables. Crowded tables. And now, catering. Was Beth hurting for money? She'd obviously added more seating to the place. What came first, the crush of people or the need for more customers? Not that it mattered. She was and would continue to worry about Beth's enterprise, though.

Devine returned several minutes later with a mug of coffee and a plate with two chocolate croissants. He slid it over to her. "Help yourself."

"Thanks, but I've ordered lunch." She glanced at the counter and saw the lineup kept getting longer rather than shorter. Who knew when she'd eat?

Devine bit into one of the croissants and made one of those faces signaling his absolute delight. J.J. eyed the other croissant, then looked around the room. *Ignore that croissant.* She was here on business, after all. One of these many patrons could be the thief. She glanced back at Devine, then quickly cut the remaining croissant in two, careful to scoop up the escaping chocolate, and took a bite. Heaven. Devine was grinning when she'd finished wiping the excess off her lips.

"Thanks," she said. "That was yummy."

"So, did you get any more details about the married cop?"

Hah—the croissant had been a way of softening her up. "No. Hennie is out sick, but I will keep trying. Now, do you see my thief?"

Devine took a sip of coffee and eyed the room over the rim of the mug. He set it back on the table and sank back in his chair. "Offhand, no. But it's so crowded in here, anyone could probably walk off with anything and not be spotted."

"No, don't say that. If that's the case, I'm pretty useless as Beth's eyes in a crowd."

Devine shrugged. "It'll probably be a fluke if you do spot the person. Don't give up, though, just don't look too obvious about it. I think you've got a good plan, spending a reasonable amount of time here each day eating. You'll blend in pretty soon, if you haven't already, and that's when the thief will get a bit careless."

"I hope you're right." She glanced at the large clock, a round tin plate with a variety of cutlery attached, hanging on the wall behind the counter. "I guess we could get going. Beth doesn't really need another lunch to make, not with this crowd. I'll try again tomorrow."

She hurriedly explained to Beth and met up with Devine outside the coffee shop. "Your car or mine?"

Devine gently took hold of her elbow and steered her

along the sidewalk to where he'd parked his Acura. He opened the passenger door for her and hopped in behind the wheel. "Where to?"

"Minstrel Street. At the corner of Bay."

"Harry's Haven?" he asked, surprised.

"That's the place. You've eaten there?"

"I've eaten in practically every place in this town."

"You're not a cook?"

He shook his head. "I enjoy cooking but never seem to get around to shopping. Usually it's easier to stop in and eat while out and about."

"You enjoy cooking." *Really?*

"Don't sound so surprised. Some people do ."

"You never said anything when I was talking about the dinner club." *And more important, my lack of skills.*

"It never came up. However, I will someday cook you up a gourmet meal, just to prove it." He pulled away from the curb, and on the drive, she entertained the idea of Devine cooking for her.

"It looks closed," Devine said as he pulled up in front of Harry's Haven. He parked in front and they walked up to the front door.

"The sign says he's on holiday, back in another week." J.J. looked at Devine. "Do you think this has anything to do with Connor's being missing?"

"A bit too much of a coincidence. And I don't usually trust those."

"Well, he hasn't even left a number or anything. I wonder who would know about his cottage. Someone must have contact information. What happens if the restaurant burns down or gets broken into?"

"The police would have a contact number on file for such instances."

"Can you get it?"

"I can try. Did Connor mention any mutual friends they had?"

"I didn't know until recently that he'd been a part of it."
J.J. was still looking for a note or something taped to a
window somewhere that might have a lead. "What about
the town clerk's office or whatever government department
would handle that? Can you get that information from
them?"

"I can ask, and if that doesn't work, I do have other
skills," he said with a totally deadpan face.

CHAPTER 20

Devine dropped J.J. back at her office, promising to let her know when he'd tracked down an address. She had to take him at face value on this, she realized. She also had to organize her life. What better time than now!

By life, she meant the three main components at this point: find the murderer; find a thief; and do her job. Possibly not in that order.

She first checked her e-mail to see if anything related to the Vermont Primary Teachers Association had come in. She should be getting some quotes around now. Plenty of spam—why couldn't she control it?—some comments on a Facebook post—great, but nothing needing a quick reply or action.

Next, Beth's thief. Maybe if she started with the motive, it would make finding the thief a lot easier. But what could that be? She made a list of the stolen items to date: one pair of salt and pepper shakers; one covered sugar bowl with sugar packets and substitutes inside; a stack of paper napkins; two place mats; one set of cutlery—was another due to disappear?; a small ceramic vase with flowers in it; one mug and one dish, both dirty. She looked at the list. It was almost like someone was stocking their own kitchen. Maybe a student needing a few basics for his or her room? It certainly looked like the perp was female, because she couldn't imagine that a male would swipe the vase and flowers. Then she thought about Evan, and decided to retain an open mind. The unknown male was back on the suspect list.

But there really wasn't a suspect list, and that's what bugged her. There was no way she could come up with a plausible candidate based on what had been stolen. But if by any chance her theory was true, she could start watching for the next possible items to disappear. Like what? Cutlery? A plate? Could be. What else did Beth have out in view around the place? She tried to visualize the coffee shop but decided to leave that until lunch the next day and she'd fill in the gaps at that point.

And, if Beth could remember the dates those items had been stolen, J.J. could check the photos she'd taken and try to match the date with a face and maybe, just maybe, find a pattern.

It didn't escape her that photos were playing a major role in both her sleuthing attempts. She wondered if being a food photographer would have been a more appropriate career for her. She could at least indulge her passion for looking at photos of food. Except for the fact that her knowledge of photography began with a Sony Cyber-shot and ended with her iPad. In other words, she'd have even less success with taking pictures than with cooking. She shook her head to clear her thoughts.

There was also another suspect list she'd been compiling. And if she was right, the killer was on it. She just hadn't gotten all the facts to effectively narrow it to that one person. She realized that her list and the one the police had were probably totally different. Theirs had Connor at the top followed by whom? J.J. knew she must still be on it, but since she hadn't had a visit from Hastings in several days, maybe the heat was off.

While the married cop, whatever his name, was at the top of her list, followed by Kathi Jones or maybe Hennie Ferguson. Jealousy was motive enough for Kathi, but she had no idea why Hennie would want Miranda dead. However, it still nagged at J.J. that Hennie had turned up at the casino night and hadn't mentioned it when they were talking. Not even to say how horrifying to be on the boat at the same time the murder took place. *I'd be saying that a lot if it were me.* A thought struck her—did the police know about Hennie? They would have to, since they detained and questioned everyone that night. And if they didn't, that meant she'd slipped off somehow or hidden, and that was solid proof of something sinister going on.

Megan Spicer was certainly on the list. She'd said she was over being dumped by Connor, but was it true? Especially since she'd then admitted that might not be so. And she was the one who had convinced J.J. into, in fact, setting up Miranda for death. J.J. shuddered at the thought. *Now I'm being overly melodramatic.* But, it was true.

Was that it? She looked closely at the list and shook her head. She wanted it to be the cop, someone she didn't know. Was there anyone else?

The sister-in-law, perhaps. Maybe. A slim chance. But why? Because Miranda butted into their lives? She had made a couple of cutting remarks about Miranda. That probably meant nothing more than irritation. Maybe Yolande was unstable and that's all it took, but wouldn't her husband, Miranda's brother, realize the two should be kept apart and do his best to make that happen?

J.J. sighed. This was getting her nowhere. She could follow up with Detective Hastings, though. See if he knew about Hennie and also if he'd had any further word on Connor's whereabouts.

Half an hour later, she was ushered into his cubicle at the main police building on North Avenue in downtown Burlington. Hastings didn't look overjoyed to see her, but she put it down to his being interrupted when he had such a heavy workload.

"I'm sorry to just drop in like this and I won't take much time. I just have a couple of questions for you."

Hastings's mouth twitched. "That's usually my line."

J.J. smiled. "I knew I'd heard it somewhere." She quickly sat down in the only empty chair before he had a chance to throw her out. "I'm curious. Did your men speak to Hennie Ferguson aboard the ship at the casino night?"

Hastings gave her a quizzical look, then tapped his computer keyboard. After a few seconds, he looked back at her. "Yes. She was there."

"Did she say why she'd come?"

"You mean she had to have a reason other than wanting to support a good cause and maybe win some money?" He leaned back in his chair. His white dress shirt stretched to reveal a white T-shirt beneath and under that, the start of a paunch.

J.J. quickly looked elsewhere. At the solid blue baffle behind him, separating his space from the next one. Still no photos or anything. "No," she hedged. "But don't you think it's odd that she didn't mention her being at the event when I was talking to her?"

"No. There's no reason she should feel the need to answer your questions to begin with."

"Except to help catch a killer."

She realized her error by the look on his face. She was sure she could hear a growl.

"You are *not* to interfere in this case, Ms. Tanner."

"I was just . . ."

"Nor go about asking questions. Nor trying to track down any suspects. Do you understand?"

She gulped. "I do, but sometimes people will say things to a civilian they wouldn't to a cop."

"Oh, that worked well last time you were involved in a murder, didn't it?"

J.J. felt her cheeks burn. *Sexy British accent or not, that wasn't very nice.* "Have you heard anything further about Connor?"

He stared at her a few moments before answering. "No. And that's something else you must stay out of. We're quite capable of tracking him down."

"I can see that." She felt like hitting the side of her head as soon as she said it.

Hastings's face was now beet red.

J.J. stood quickly. "Well, I mustn't take up any more of your time. Good luck, Detective Hastings."

"I meant what I said, Ms. Tanner," he said as he stood. "Stay out of police business. For your own sake as well as ours."

She smiled, although it felt a bit strained, and left, walking quickly down the hall, through the sets of doors, and outside. She hadn't dared ask him half the questions she had been planning, like did they know about the married cop? She'd also like to know who was on the entire suspect list, but she couldn't think of a single way to get them to share that.

Of course, there was Ty Devine.

She sat behind the steering wheel in her car, thinking about her next move. Hennie. Maybe she could get an address for her and go visit. No, she'd promised Devine they'd talk to her together. But that was before everything else happened. Surely he'd forgotten. But if she went to the TV station looking for Lonny, for instance, and happened to be talking to the receptionist and asked for an address . . . She should tell Devine, though. He'd be so mad if she didn't. She tried calling him from her smartphone but decided not to leave a message when it went to voice mail. She shrugged. *I tried.*

She had only a slight twinge about Hastings's warning when she reached the TV station. And she managed to ignore it. Unfortunately, Lonny Chan wasn't in but fortunately, J.J. hadn't yet asked about Hennie before Devine appeared by her side.

"I tried calling you," she started to explain.

"Funny, I thought I had the voice mail feature." She couldn't read his glare, how serious he was or just how mad.

"I chose not to use it. But I really came because I have a question for Lonny, however, he's not in. Again. If I didn't know he spent most of his time on the road covering news, I'd think he was trying to avoid me. Maybe we should go talk to Hennie instead."

He shook his head. "Nice save. You weren't planning on getting an address for Hennie Ferguson, were you?"

"Oh, what a good idea."

"Thank you." J.J. winced as Wanda almost melted on the spot when Devine smiled at her.

"We really need to talk to Hennie Ferguson. Could you give me her home address?" J.J. asked.

"I'm sorry, I can't give that out. Station policy." Her smile was strictly for Devine. "But she's in the phone book."

Outside, J.J. pulled out her phone and Googled Hennie's address. J.J. and Devine agreed that would be the next stop, and they'd meet there. Devine made it first, and J.J. was pleased to see he actually waited until she arrived. The apartment turned out to be on the third floor. J.J. made the pretext of searching for her keys in the bottom of her purse, and they managed to slide through the open door as a tenant went in. They tried knocking on Hennie's door and, after a short wait, agreed she was out. Next stop, Harry's Haven, but the Closed sign remained in place.

"Have you found the cottage?" J.J. asked as they stood staring at the windows of the restaurant.

"No. I've been tied up with something else. What's next for you?"

"I actually do have a job so should put in some time there. Let me know when you have a location." She gave him a small wave and felt his eyes on her as she walked to her car.

She parked behind the office and thought about Devine on the climb upstairs. *What was it about him? He ran hot and cold; sharing information, then not; asking for her help, then telling her to back off. But, oh, those eyes. Not a good thing to focus on, not if she wanted to . . . what? Remain aloof? Stay in control? Never go on a date with him? Aagh!* J.J. shook her head, trying to toss aside her thoughts.

She pulled open the office door and grinned when she noticed Skye standing and doing some stretches, reaching to the ceiling, at her desk. The phone rang and Skye sat quickly to answer it. She gave J.J. a thumbs-up as she listened to her caller.

J.J.'s phone rang, surprising her. It was Beth.

"Add another set of cutlery to the missing list."

"Really? While I was there?"

"Uh-uh. The thief came in later, I guess. I wonder if he or she is onto us and trying to avoid detection. This is driving me crazy. I'm about ready to throw in the towel. Except I'd never do that. Don't mind me—I'm just venting."

J.J. could hear Abby in the background talking to a customer.

"I have an idea. Let's have a 'treat Beth' evening and get the gang together for supper at, say, seven at McCreedy's?"

Beth sighed. "That sounds delightful if I can just hold it together until then."

"You do that. It's your task. Mine is to make reservations and gather people. Let's say seven at McCreedy's unless you hear back from me."

"Thank you, J.J."

"Don't mention it." She phoned Evan as soon as she got a dial tone. He agreed that he'd be there with Michael. Next she tried Alison and had to be content with leaving a message. She made the reservation for five people anyway. On a whim she tried Connor but hung up when it went to message.

Evan and Michael were already seated when J.J. arrived. Beth and Alison joined them shortly after. They ordered drinks and appetizers, then Beth filled them in on her woes. She also talked about all that J.J. was doing to help even though it hadn't led to anything conclusive.

"I'm sorry, I can't think of anything else you could do," Alison admitted, "although the cop in me wants to just walk in there and make an arrest. Have you thought of installing cameras?"

Beth shook her head. "I don't really want to go there. I think it would make my customers uncomfortable to know there were cameras. Besides, I can't afford them."

Evan looked thoughtful, then apologetic. "I can't think of a single thing."

"That's okay. Just talking about it with friends makes it seem easier to cope with. Not so much in my head, if you know what I mean, or yet another burden on J.J.'s shoulders," Beth said, and sipped her Manhattan.

J.J. had often wondered about whether Beth had a man in her life or not. She knew about her being widowed way too early in her marriage, but she never mentioned anyone else nor even if she was looking for another Mr. Right. Maybe at some girls' night out. But they'd had those, and although they knew all about J.J.'s failed engagement, Beth had shared little. Oh well, they all had a right to their privacy. But she did wonder.

And look where privacy had gotten Connor. No one knew enough about his life to figure out what had happened to him.

As if reading her mind, Evan suggested, "How about we tackle another unsolvable topic? Is there anything new on Connor's whereabouts?"

Everyone looked at Alison. She shook her head. "Nothing since he was spotted last week. There's not much to go on."

Their attention switched to J.J.

"Well, I was talking to Miranda's sister-in-law, who mentioned that Miranda and Connor had stayed at his ex–business partner's cottage at times. Devine and I went to the restaurant hoping to talk to this guy, but it's closed for a few days. And that makes me wonder if Connor and the ex-partner are at the cottage right now. Devine is trying to track down its exact location."

"I seem to remember something about that cottage, now that you mention it," Evan said, looking stumped. "I'm sure it was on one of the islands near the water, but that's about all I can think of."

"That would make sense seeing as Connor's car was spotted on South Hero. Can't you remember anything else?"

Evan looked like he was trying, but then he shook his head. "Sorry."

"I'll help him try to remember," Michael promised. "He gets so stressed out these days. He just has to relax at night and things settle into place."

J.J. wondered what was stressing Evan besides the usual business woes, but thought she'd save the question for another time when she was alone with him.

"There has been another development. She was having an affair with a married cop. They apparently met when she needed a cop on her show. Do you think you could find out who he is, Alison?" J.J. asked.

"Well, sure. I'll just go in and ask." She shook her head. "Sorry, it's been a long day. I'll need some details, like when this happened, for starters."

"Of course. I'll have to get more details from her assistant, when I find her again."

"Someone else is missing?" Beth asked. "Is that a coincidence?"

J.J. shrugged. "There's no reason to think it has anything

to do with Connor. She might have just taken a few days off, and the station is not giving out any information." That was probably it. She needed to have a heart-to-heart with the receptionist tomorrow.

"I've been wondering," Beth said after their entrées had been served, "if you all figure it's okay to carry on with the Culinary Capers dinner this month."

"Of course it is," Evan said. "Connor would insist on it." The others agreed.

Beth let out a sigh. "I'm happy to hear that. I think it will do us all good. So, how was your visit with your mom, J.J.?"

"Um, good, I guess. I didn't see much of her. She was here for meetings about the company opening a new office, and Mom would be put in charge of it."

"Wow, is this a good thing?" Evan asked. "How's your relationship with your mom?"

J.J. laughed. "It's good, Evan, although I think distance is better. I'm a bit concerned what this might mean to Dad, though. It's just the two of them, you know. My brothers have also moved away."

"Remind me what your dad does," Alison said.

"He's an artist, a painter. He has a studio in the house, and he spends most of the daylight hours in it. But even though Mom's out on a tear all the time, showing houses and whatnot, she's always there to cook his suppers. If she takes this job, she'll go home on weekends, but it can be a long, lonely week for him."

Beth reached over and patted her hand. "Or, it might not. Men are often more resilient than we give them credit for. He's got his work, and I'm sure he can fix himself something to eat. They'll be together on weekends, which should make it that much sweeter. I wouldn't worry about it if I were you."

J.J. couldn't take Beth's advice that easily. She found herself still worrying later that night, so she phoned her older brother, Rory, in Stowe.

"What do you think of the possibility that Mom might move to Burlington?" she asked after they'd caught up on his two young children and their growth spurts.

"Do you mean, how much will she be in your hair? Or how will Dad cope?"

J.J. laughed. "I really am more concerned about Dad. She seems to do everything for him."

"That's the part we see when we visit, but I know for a fact he's much more self-sufficient than that. I think he'll be just fine with it. And, so will she. You know how she has to keep busy, and this new project will be good for her."

"Then you're okay with it all?"

"I am. So is Kyle. We've talked. I was wondering when you'd call about it." He sounded so relaxed and sure about it all that J.J. decided she should stop worrying about the Tanner household. Especially with a murderer still on the loose.

Chapter 21

The first thing J.J. wanted to do the next morning was talk to Hennie. She took a long drink of her tepid latte and then phoned the TV station, asking to be put through to Hennie's extension, hoping she'd be back. The phone just rang and rang. Next she tried phoning Hennie's apartment but got the same response. It was time for action.

She tidied up her desk, left a note for Skye, and then drove to the station, hoping to have a heart-to-heart with Wanda, the receptionist. Maybe she and Hennie were good friends, and her lack of forthrightness may have been a misplaced attempt to shield Hennie. J.J. wanted to reassure her that Hennie wasn't in trouble, yet, and that all she wanted was information.

Wanda was on the phone and in fact took several calls before she was able to spare some time for J.J. She looked expectantly at J.J. and thanked her for the coffee she'd brought.

"I'm really hoping you can help me track down Hennie.

I have to talk to her ASAP. It's very important and really can't wait. Do you have any idea where she might be?"

"Like I said yesterday, I don't have a clue. We're not really close, you know?"

"Does Hennie have any close friends at the station?"

Wanda shrugged. "Not that I know of. I mean, she'd usually eat her lunch at her desk. I guess sometimes she'd go out but never with anyone from the station. Not that I saw, anyway."

"Do you know if she has any family in the city? Had she ever mentioned someone in passing?"

Wanda shook her head. "I tell you, I really don't know anything. Although, I think she has a boyfriend."

"What makes you think that?"

"Well, one day a bunch of us were in the break room kidding around about dating, and she let drop that she's no longer playing the field. That can only mean one thing, right?"

J.J. thought about it. Could be Hennie was just plain tired of the dating game for the moment, but on the other hand, maybe Wanda was right. "Thanks. I think I'll just leave her a note. Okay if I go around?"

Wanda nodded as she answered another call. J.J. took the shorter hallway to the right, past the station manager's door, which happened to be open. She halted at the sound of Devine's voice and quickly backtracked, scurrying past the newsroom, and took the longer way. He was the last person she wanted to talk to this morning. And she knew he wouldn't be too pleased about her being back on Hennie's trail, without him.

She slipped into Hennie's office and left a note asking her to call. She then wandered around to the office shared by the on-air personalities. She found Kathi at one of the desks, making notes on something she was reading. Maybe J.J. didn't have to wait for Hennie.

"Hi, Kathi. Do you have a minute?"

Kathi glanced up and looked surprised. "Sure, I guess. I'm getting ready for my show, so it can't take long." She looked at her watch, almost in emphasis. J.J. couldn't help but notice the black-and-white zigzag design on the wide band, a close match to the dress she wore, and the black, short-sleeved shrug top.

"It won't," J.J. said as she walked closer. "I was just wondering about Miranda's love life. Had she confided in you about who she was dating?"

Kathi shook her head. "No, she wasn't the confiding type, especially to me. But I did know about her broken engagement to Connor Mac and that they were dating again although not a real item. And there was talk that she was seeing some married guy."

J.J. feigned a look of surprise.

"I know, nothing's sacred in this business. Rumors run rampant, and if there are none, someone is sure to make something up." Kathi shrugged. "But I stress, those are rumors. She never told me anything directly."

"Did you hear anything else about the married guy, like where she met him?"

"The word is that he's a cop, and she met him while she was doing a feature for the news department. I don't think it ever went to air, though." Kathi paused for a few seconds. "That's what she wanted, you know, to be an investigative journalist. She probably would have made the jump, too. I just needed to wait her out and her job was mine. So, no reason to kill her, right?" She looked very pleased with herself.

J.J. nodded, then tried to get her back on track. "How long ago was that? The story, I mean."

Another shrug. "I don't know for sure. Maybe a year or so ago. No, more than that. It was around the time of the annual City Marathon, I remember now. So that would be late May of last year. Now, I really have to get back to work or I will make a fool of myself on live TV today."

"I can't imagine that," J.J. said, meaning it, and waving her thanks, but Kathi had already gone back to her reading.

Bingo. That should make it easy to track him down. She pulled out her phone as she wandered back to reception, and called Alison, asking if she was free for coffee.

"I'm on the road, on my own this morning, and due for a break, so yes. I take it this is important."

"I have a lead on that married cop."

"All right! Ten minutes at Beth's?"

"Better make it twenty-five. I'm downtown at the TV station."

"All right. No speeding. I will not fix your ticket."

J.J. grinned as she hurried outside, careful to avoid Devine. She made it to Cups 'n' Roses in twenty-five exactly. Alison sat at a table, sipping her coffee. J.J. greeted Beth, waited for the latte she ordered, and then slid across from Alison.

"Okay, talk fast. I have to make this a short break."

J.J. filled her in on what she'd learned and watched while Alison processed it.

"That's a start, I guess, but you'll have to find out his name. Besides, if it were about something they were trying to hush up, good luck. He might not even have been working with her in an official capacity. In that case, his name probably won't be listed in our files."

J.J. felt her hopes plummet. "I'll keep at my contacts at the station. Maybe someone can track down something more." She'd noticed a woman dressed in a camel-colored jacket, her shoulder-length brown hair partially obscuring her face. She appeared to keep glancing over at the two of them.

"Well, good on you for getting this far. I'm sorry, I really have to get back on the road. We're shorthanded today, and I should be working another sector. Keep me posted." She stood, and with a wave to Beth, left, putting her cap back on as the door closed behind her.

J.J. sat back to enjoy the rest of her coffee and noticed the woman had suddenly gotten busy searching through her purse, her face now obscured. She watched until Beth sat down, sliding a plate with a cranberry scone and butter over to J.J.

"Yum, but totally unnecessary unless you're wanting me to take up jogging again."

Beth laughed. "You're a long way from having to worry about extra calories, my dear. Now, what were you and Alison in such deep conversation about?"

J.J. filled her in, all the while trying to watch the mystery woman without being obvious about it. Beth caught on. "Who or what are you watching? Can I turn around and look?"

"No, but you can look once you're back at the counter. It's the woman in the camel jacket sitting alone at the table next to the milk and sugar stand. She looked like she was getting antsy with Alison in here. I'm just going to take a photo of you with her in the background. Then I'll compare it later to the ones I've taken every day. See if she's been here before." J.J. slid her iPad out of her purse and flipped it open. When she was ready to take the photo, she angled the iPad like she was showing Beth something, then snapped a frame.

"You think she's my thief?"

J.J. shrugged. "I don't know at this point, but what if I come over and we'll compare your list of dates when the items were stolen with the photos I have from those days. If any."

Beth grinned. "Action. That's what I like. I feel like I've had my hands tied all this time. Try for around eight, if that's not too late. Now, I'll surreptitiously have a better look."

Beth quickly made her way back to the counter, but by then, the woman had left. Rather hurriedly, J.J. thought. Oh well, she had her photo.

J.J. had just finished washing her dinner dishes. She looked around her apartment wondering if she needed to give it a quick vacuum before heading to Beth's. A knock on the door put that notion to rest. She spotted Devine through the peephole and pulled open the door.

"How did you get in here again? Nothing has changed. Nobody is supposed to let strangers into the building. Yet you still manage to do it."

Devine grinned. "Nice to see you, too. I guess I don't look like a stranger."

"Must have been a female," J.J. muttered, closing the door behind him. "I have only a short while before going over to Beth's," she told him, ushering him into the living room.

"I hadn't planned on staying long. I just wanted to fill you in on my investigation."

"Really?" She knew her mouth hanging open wasn't very ladylike but she was so surprised.

"Yes, really. I've tracked down the guy who's caused the station so much grief and determined Miranda's murder had nothing to do with it. Two separate cases."

"Who is it? Mikey Cooper?"

"No, not totally. He did feel inspired by the vandal and decided to redecorate the station van, but he swears he didn't try to run down the weather guy nor any of the more serious incidents. And I believe him. In fact, the perp is someone who never made it onto the station employee list. He'd tried twice to get hired as a cameraman but didn't make it, so he thought he'd teach them a lesson. I just handed over all the information to the police, and they're about to make an arrest."

"You're not going to be in on it?"

He shrugged. "It's not important to me. I've done my job. Now, tell me what you found out at the station earlier today."

"How do you do that? I didn't think you'd seen me."

"So, you were trying to avoid me?"

"Always. And if Miranda's death isn't tied in, why do you want to know what I was doing there?"

"Don't try to change the topic. I'm interested in finding the killer, just like you, so even though I don't have the TV station as a client any longer, I've hired myself to do it."

"Seriously?" J.J. started laughing. "Now, that's a rationalization if ever I heard one."

Devine grinned. "So, what did you find out?"

J.J. looked at him and sighed. Oh well, he'd been useful and would continue to be so, if she played it right. While she was filling him in about what she'd learned from Kathi, she had an idea.

"So, since you're all buddy-buddy with Donald Cooper and gang, maybe you can get a look at that video and find out the name of the cop."

"I should be able to do that."

"But you have to share that information. Promise."

"I guess I can manage that. So what's happening at Beth's? Are your Caper pals plotting some more sleuthing tactics?"

"No, I think I may have a suspect in the Cups 'n' Roses thefts. I spotted a woman who was awfully curious about Alison, in uniform, and me having a coffee earlier today. When Alison left, the woman buried her head in her purse. So to speak. Like she was avoiding being spotted by Alison."

"That sounds more like somebody with a warrant out on them, not a cutlery thief."

J.J. sighed. "You could be right, but I did get her photo, and since I've taken photos lately every lunch hour I've been there, I want to check if she's been there before and then cross-check with Beth's list of days there were thefts." She sat back, pleased with her plan but at the same time a bit wary about his reaction. It did sound like a long shot.

"That makes sense. Mind if I tag along?"

She felt her excitement rise. He must think she was onto something. She gave herself a mental pat on the back and agreed.

Beth carried two cups of coffee over to the dining room table, where J.J. and Devine stood sorting through photos. J.J. had printed them out before they left her place. She hadn't realized how many she'd taken. Once they'd been laid out in a timeline according to the date J.J. had written on the back, they all took a good look at the mystery woman and worked through the other photos, trying to spot her.

"There she is," Beth almost shouted. "And there. That's two times."

"Make that three," Devine said, pointing to another photo.

They kept looking, and by the time they'd gone through them all, they'd pulled out four photos.

"Boy, I'm really falling down on my skills," Beth muttered. "You'd think I'd have noticed her after four visits. I pride myself on knowing my regulars."

"Don't beat yourself up, Beth," Devine said. "You'll notice how she's fairly innocuous in each photo. Nothing really stands out. I'm sure she wouldn't have said anything to you when placing her order, because she wouldn't have wanted to stand out, if she's the thief."

"It looks like all she ever got was coffee," J.J. said, taking a closer look. "That means she wouldn't have spent much time at the counter, and you might not have served her."

"I guess you're right. Here's the list of dates and what was taken."

Beth read out the dates while J.J. checked the dates on the back of the photos. When they'd finished, they sat looking at each other, saying nothing.

"The same," Devine said, finally breaking the spell. "That's the thief, I'd say. What do you want to do about it? Call the cops?"

Beth shook her head. "I'm not sure what I'll do, but I don't really want the police involved. They're small items, really. Not big-time."

"But you can't let her get away with this," J.J. said. "She'll just continue unless we've scared her off today."

Beth sat quietly thinking for a few minutes. J.J. and Devine looked at each other. It was Beth's call.

Beth finally said, "If she does come back in, I'll watch her more carefully and then decide what to do. I really want to thank you, J.J., for giving up all that time to do this, and for figuring it out. Thank you also, Ty, for your help."

"It wasn't so much," J.J. said. "And I did get some wonderful lunches on the house. I'll sort of miss those."

"You should have a lifetime of free lunches," Beth said grandly.

"No way. I'm back to being just a regular paying customer. I'm just glad it's resolved, or almost, anyway." She looked at her watch. "We'd better be going. You have an early start tomorrow."

Beth showed them to the door and gave each a hug as they left.

"I feel good about that," J.J. said as Devine held the car door open for her.

"You should. That was good work."

She basked in the praise, and when he pulled up in front of her apartment, still felt pleased enough to invite him in for a nightcap. *A real one.* "It will give us a chance to talk some more about the video and just how reasonable a suspect the cop is."

Devine grinned. "Yes. We really should talk more about that."

He followed her inside and peered down her hallway. "No Mom?"

J.J. chuckled. "Not at the moment. I guess I'll just have to wait and see what the future brings."

"Really? Is she thinking of moving in with you?"

"What? No. But maybe to the city. Would you like coffee or wine?"

"Wine, thanks." He wandered around the living room, glancing at the array of magazines on the side table and the many titles on the bookshelves that ran the length of one wall, while she poured their drinks. "You read a lot, I see."

"I try. And I love looking through magazines. It's very relaxing." She handed him his glass.

He sat on the wicker chair. "You really want the cop to be the bad guy in all this, don't you?"

"I do." J.J. chose to sit on the love seat.

"What's his motive?"

"Motive? They were lovers and she broke it off so he got mad."

"That's awfully weak. There'd be a lot more killings happening if everyone did that when they were ditched."

"Well, what if he wouldn't accept it and kept bothering her, and she warned him to back off or she'd tell his wife? So he killed her. He's certainly proven he's not a trustworthy guy, and he's a cop so he could outsmart the investigation if need be."

"Only if he's a smart cop, which I think he isn't, not if he committed murder. He really has too much to lose." Devine stood, wineglass in hand, walked over to the window, and looked out.

"Yeah, his wife, his job, his reputation, his freedom."

"His life, quite possibly, if he goes to jail. That's not a very healthy place for a cop to be."

"So I've heard. Do you think that's enough of an incentive to stay clean?"

"Maybe not clean, but committing murder? That's something else. Besides, why would he kill Miranda to keep her from talking? What's at stake if he's an adulterer? His wife, most probably. Not his job—you're wrong about that. And his reputation can survive the hit. Therefore, what's his motive?" He sat down beside her.

J.J. sipped her wine and thought about it. He was probably right. "Okay, maybe he wasn't worried that Miranda would tell all, but what if his ego couldn't take it? What if he's a control freak and even the thought of someone else ending it is enough to drive him over the edge?"

"That's a lot of what-ifs. But I've tracked perps who had even less of a motive. If your friend Alison can get some info on him, I'll also try to check him out, and then we'll decide." He lifted his glass toward her. "Fair enough?"

"Yes. Fair enough."

"And that means that you don't go confronting him or anything equally foolish. He does have a gun, and he knows how to use it. If he is the killer, another murder isn't going to bother him much. Understand?"

She nodded. "I guess. I probably couldn't come up with a good enough cover story anyway." She grinned when she saw his face. Just the reaction she was aiming for.

He shook his head and then leaned over and kissed her. She'd been taken off guard but wasn't displeased. She returned the kiss with enthusiasm until the knock on the door. He groaned and she stood, a little shakily, and went to answer it.

Ness Harper walked in without being invited. He looked at Devine, then back at J.J. "I was just wondering how the case was going. I heard you come in so I thought it wouldn't be too late to stop by." He practically glared at Devine, who had stood and was now heading to the door.

"I'll leave you to it, J.J. Maybe Harper here has some ideas we haven't come up with. Thanks for the wine."

He leaned in, and she thought for a moment he might kiss her cheek or something, but he just said in a sultry voice, "Sweet dreams."

She closed the door behind him and tried to clear her head. Ness obviously had something on his mind.

"Can I get you something? A coffee, some wine?" She heard herself echoing her earlier choices.

"Harrumph. I was worried about you when I heard who was with you. I don't trust that guy, and I think he's using this case for his own ends."

J.J. walked over to the love seat and picked up her glass. Ness moved closer but remained standing. "You're what we would have called an attractive package, J.J. You're smart, feisty, and good-looking, and he's a guy on the loose who, having been a cop, has seen and done a hell of a lot more than you can imagine. I just think you have to keep your guard up. Don't invite him in late at night, like, and certainly don't give him a drink."

"You sound like my dad. Sort of." She didn't know whether to feel honored or upset. She chose to go with the former. "I appreciate your concern, but I have been out on my own for quite a few years now and even survived a broken engagement. I think I can take care of myself, Ness."

"Oh boy, I think it's too late."

She looked perplexed.

He plopped down on the wicker chair across from her. "I know you're quite a skilled and independent young woman, and I know you can probably take care of yourself. And I know I'm also overstepping my place, but I just want you to keep your eyes open and be aware of the whole package."

She sighed. "I appreciate that, but what I need help with is the crime-solving part. And he is helping with that. Hindering, too."

"Tell me what you've got."

She went through all the recent details, realizing she hadn't talked to him in at least a week, an unusual occurrence.

"A lot's been happening," he said when she'd finished her spiel.

"I haven't seen you in a while."

"I guess I've been busy. But as for the affair, that wouldn't be the motive I'd place at the top of the list. I've known lots of cops who play fast and loose with their wives and girlfriends but not one of them led to murder. But the case does have a personal feel to it. If it had been part of the strategy against the station, it would probably have been a more visible murder in front of a lot of people, probably at the station itself."

"I hadn't thought of that. Devine has reached that conclusion also. He's found the station culprit and says there's no way he's good for the murder."

"Harrumph. I may not trust the guy, but I do think he has good instincts. Who stands to benefit the most from her death?"

"It has to be someone at the station."

"There's nothing in her personal life that might be a reason?"

"Not that I can find out."

"What about your friend Connor Mac? Is he still

missing? It seems like he has both reason and opportunity. I know"—he held up his hand as she was about to speak—"you're convinced otherwise. But I advise you to take a closer look at their entire relationship. The answer just might be found there, and it might not be that he's the killer." He looked at his watch. "Gotta go. Late night news is starting."

Chapter 22

J.J. made a quick stop at Book Titles on her way in to work the next morning. She'd stopped by for a book she'd read a review about, *Pret-a-Party* by Lela Rose. She thought it might add some inspiration to her planning events. She couldn't resist a quick look in the cookbook section and thumbed through the new *Food52 Genius Recipes* cookbook displayed on a table of new arrivals. She left with two purchases.

Back at the office, she placed the books on her desk, planning to go through each of them after checking her e-mail. She groaned at the number of new ones and had just clicked on the first one when Detective Hastings walked in.

"Miss Tanner, do you have a few minutes? I have a few more questions." He looked over at Skye and nodded in her direction.

Skye looked from one to the other and then grabbed her jacket and purse. "I think I'll go get some coffee. You two can have the run of the office." She threw J.J. an inquiring look as she made her way behind Hastings, to the door.

"What's on your mind, Detective?" J.J. asked, pleased her voice had just the right amount of curiosity and none of the anxiety she felt.

"I have some more questions about the timetable for the casino event. I just wanted to double-check that what you gave me was the final copy, that nothing had been added or changed." He pulled over a chair and sat at the side of her desk.

"You came all the way here just for that?" She wondered what else was on his mind.

"No. I came to Half Moon Bay to visit Zane Anderson at his restaurant, the Harry's Haven, but it seems to be closed." He stared at her. She tried to keep her face neutral. *How did he find out about it?* "So I thought I'd visit you, too."

Hastings looked around the room and then back at J.J., stating in a casual tone, "He's Connor Mac's former business partner, you know."

"Well, I do now. I knew that Connor had been a partner in a restaurant venture but he talked about it only once, and he'd never mentioned the other person's name."

"And you didn't think to bring up the matter of the restaurant when we were asking about Mr. Mac?" His voice had hardened.

She shrugged, trying not to look too flustered. "The restaurant venture happened several years ago. It didn't even come to mind."

He glanced at the cookbook she'd left on the desk. "That's got some great recipes," he said, picking it up.

"So I'm told. I get their daily digests on the internet." *What is he doing? Trying to throw me off-balance?*

"Some nice photos, too." Hastings glanced up at her and smiled, the first really friendly smile she'd seen. Had he heard about her cookbook addiction? Had everyone heard?

"I'm always on the lookout for a cookbook to use for our monthly dinner club meetings. I've mentioned the Culinary Capers before, haven't I?"

He nodded. "And that sounds like my kind of group. I've been looking for a book club and I sure do enjoy cooking."

J.J. felt her mouth hanging open. *Is he asking to join?*

"What? Police officers aren't supposed to read or cook?" His blue eyes twinkled as he asked his question.

She swallowed hard. "I, well, sure. After all, Alison Manovich is a member and a cop. I guess I picture you as solving murders all the time."

He leaned toward her. "I do have a bit of a private life, now and then."

She wasn't sure what to say to that.

He sat back and flipped through the book. "This looks interesting. Maybe I could borrow it sometime."

"Uh, sure."

"Good. Now, about the Harry's Haven and the partnership. You're absolutely certain there's nothing additional you're not telling me?"

"Absolutely."

"Well then, about this timetable. It's definitely the final copy?"

She nodded.

"And, as far as you know, it all happened as laid out? Everyone was where they were supposed to be at any given moment?"

"That's asking a lot. I have no way of knowing the last part, because I couldn't be everywhere at once." She heard the edge in her tone and dialed it back. "As far as I know, they were, and everything went according to plan."

"Except for the murder."

"There is that."

He stood abruptly. "Thanks for your time. Good luck with the cooking."

Skye must have passed him in the hall. "So he was a cheery boy in leaving. What happened?"

"We actually got to talking about books and cooking," she admitted.

"Let me get this right. The cop detective who you've had run-ins with for many moons now, came all the way here to question you, and you end up comparing plots and recipes?" She deposited a latte on J.J.'s desk on the way to her own. "The plot thickens, as they say."

"It did seem a bit unusual, that's for sure. Maybe a technique he's developing to throw the unsuspecting off guard. But I'm also sure he'll be back to his old snarky self the next time I see him."

"Uh-huh. Well, I think he does snarky very well, too. That British accent sends goose bumps up and down my spine, and he's really quite good-looking, when he smiles."

"Am I wrong or are you not hoping for a ring on your finger?"

"A woman can still look and appreciate, maybe even daydream a bit."

Of course he would be back to snarky. Or maybe it was a tactic, trying to be friendly so she'd divulge what she knew. And, she had. Well, as much as she knew about the restaurant partnership, which really was nothing. She hadn't even added the fact that Connor and Miranda had spent some weekends at Zane Anderson's cottage. There was a limit, after all.

"Hey, J.J.," Evan said, leaning around the door and waving at Skye.

"What's up, Evan?"

"I just saw our fine detective leaving. What did he want?" Evan glanced behind himself before walking into the room.

"More questions. What else?" She heard Skye snicker but didn't look over at her.

"Well, he should have asked me, because I just remembered something about the cottage that Connor and Miranda used to slip away to."

"He knows about Zane Anderson, the ex-partner, and had wanted to talk to him, but his restaurant is closed, for now."

"Huh. Well, the cottage actually was owned by Anderson's grandmother, at that time anyway. She's a Redding, as in the Redding family of local fame."

"The Reddings who own the Redding Winery?"

"You got it. And the Redding Resort and Redding Center. Anyway, the last time I saw her was at a Christmas party that a client threw to show off her new décor, and, of course, she'd invited me. Mrs. Wallis Redding may be in her eighties, but she's a real go-getter and a smart businesswoman. She still runs the family business, although she allows her sons to do the day-to-day stuff."

"You are a wealth of information. What made you remember?"

"Funnily enough, a new client who wants a makeover in time for Christmas. I was showing her some of my work, and there was the Redding house, and that reminded me of meeting the grande dame. Did I mention that Zane Anderson was along with her? She introduced him and mentioned the restaurant. We did all that 'small world' talk, and then they did the requisite oohing and aahing. All very friendly-like."

"Sounds delightful, and thank gosh for your memory. I guess we can check the land registry office for the information now that we have the right name."

"We, as in your PI?"

"He's not my anything, but, yes, he's the one to do it. Unless you and I pay a visit to Mrs. Redding and ask her some questions about maybe where her grandson is, like, perhaps at her cottage—and its location?" She raised her eyebrows suggestively, and Evan looked puzzled for a moment.

"Ah, now the 'we' is you and me. Correct?"

"You're my man, Evan. How about it?"

He looked over at Skye. "This sounds like a bad idea to me. What do you think?"

Skye shrugged. "I think all of her investigating is a bad idea, but if it works, why not?"

"Okay. You're on. I think I'd better call first for an appointment. We don't want to go barging in and maybe ruin chances of getting some information."

"Now you're in the spirit," J.J. said eagerly.

"She probably won't remember me, I hate to admit, but I'll give it a try. What do I say if she asks for a reason?"

"The truth. Say it's a matter of utmost personal importance, and if she still wants more, tell her we're trying to get in touch with her grandson or Connor Mac or both and want to talk to her in person."

"All right. I'll call from my office in case she has caller ID. Hopefully she'll recognize the business name. I'll let you know how it goes." He pulled the door shut behind him, and J.J. looked over at Skye.

"Really? You think my investigating is a bad idea?"

"Of course I do. I know the police don't appreciate it, Devine is usually furious at you because of it, and most importantly, it's dangerous. But I also know you do what you think is best, so good luck. I'll be there to bail you out or choose the casket."

"Ouch."

"Well, you did ask and you are my dear friend. And I worry about you. But I suppose it's not so bad if you have a sidekick along at all times. My money is on the PI."

"He should be so lucky," J.J. muttered as she went back to her computer. She checked her e-mail and answered the most pressing, which took all of ten minutes, and at that point, Evan popped back into the office.

"She's cool. In fact, she said we could come over right now. I hope that works, because I really don't want to call her back."

"Why not? What happened?"

"Her assistant happened. I'd forgotten about the old battle-ax. Oh, did I say that? I meant to say, her personal assistant." He made a face and waited while J.J. shut down her computer and grabbed her things.

"Have fun, kiddies," Skye called out.

J.J. wiggled her fingers as they left.

"Multi dollars involved in all this real estate," J.J. muttered as they drove farther into the ultraexclusive historic area of Burlington. "Thanks for driving, Evan. I would have us off the road by now with all this eye candy."

Evan chuckled. "This is where it happens, J.J. If I could get even a couple of more contracts around here, I'd be set for life." He sighed. "Always a dream."

"I'll bet they throw some dynamite parties, too."

"Oh yeah. It's a good place to get some contacts in your line of work, too." He slowed the car. "This should be it, coming up on the right."

J.J. stared and realized she'd better close her mouth before getting out of the car. She should be getting used to opulence, with the number of prestigious houses she'd visited lately. But this won by a rooftop. It was taller, larger, and more of a surprise. Three stories, at least, with maybe a room or two in the attic, judging by the windows. A wraparound porch that added about half a room of outdoor living. And its white clapboard exterior punctuated by bright blue and black trim. The property seemed to go on forever, as did the driveway they'd just driven up, which continued in through the forest behind the house.

"Do you think they have video surveillance?" she asked under her breath as they approached the house.

"Guaranteed." Evan reached out to knock on the door, but it was opened by a butler before his knuckles touched wood.

"Evan Thornton and J.J. Tanner to see Mrs. Redding."

They followed the silent butler to the right, down a hallway immediately off the large foyer. J.J. was getting used to the idea of butlers by now. However, this one didn't fit the stereotype. Nothing *Downton Abbey* about him. The collar and cuffs of a white dress shirt peaked out from underneath a navy V-neck pullover sweater, complete with some sort of crest on the left side of his chest. His navy trousers sported a razor-sharp crease. And his black leather loafers barely sounded along the tiled hallway. The hunter green walls displayed a variety of contemporary art, nothing recognizable to J.J., but certainly a couple of different artists with a penchant for colors.

The butler wordlessly directed them into a small office at the end of the hall. J.J. glanced around the office, admiring the clean lines and blend of shades of gray. Her eyes came to rest on the personal assistant, she assumed, who was busily reading her computer screen. After what she must consider an appropriate amount of time, she looked up at them.

"I'm Natasha, Mrs. Redding's personal secretary. Mrs. Redding will be with you in a few minutes." She pointed to two chairs in the far corner. They looked comfortable but uninviting.

J.J. sat and watched the assistant, who continued to ignore them. She looked to be in her late forties or early fifties, with dark hair pulled back in a knot. She wore a long-sleeved navy cardigan over a white blouse. After ten minutes, the woman stood, revealing she wore a pair of pants similar to the butler's, and gestured to them to follow her. She knocked lightly on the door behind her desk and opened it, staying in her own office.

J.J. followed Evan, who, hand extended, walked over to Mrs. Redding, who was sitting in a chair facing the door. A cane leaned against one arm.

"Thank you so much for seeing us on such short notice."

Wallis Redding nodded and gave them both a close inspection while J.J. did the same. Her name suited her. The short white hair hinted at blonde highlights, she hadn't tried to hide her age with any major surgery, and she wore a plain dark red dress with short sleeves, barely revealed under the dark, multicolored pashmina draped around her shoulders.

When they had passed muster, they were invited to have a seat. This time there were four wing chairs, upholstered in what J.J. thought must be real velvet, grouped around a coffee table.

"Now, tell me what this urgent business is about," she said, directing her request to Evan.

J.J. could see her better in that lighting and noticed the delicate lines around her eyes and mouth, pegging her age in the high seventies.

"We're friends of Connor Mac and we're trying to find him," Evan said, and then nodded to J.J. "Actually, J.J. can better explain it all."

Thanks. "That's basically it. Connor went missing last week and hasn't contacted any of his friends. His car was spotted on South Hero Island, though, and we wondered if he might be using your cottage. I understand he's used it before. We wanted to ask your grandson, but it appears he's on holiday, too."

"And you wonder if they're holed up together at my place."

Clever lady. "We're hoping that's what's happened. Connor was in pretty rough shape last time we saw him, and it would be good if he's with a friend."

"Yes. The Miranda Myers death. Such a tragedy." Mrs. Anderson sat up a bit straighter. "She was such a pretty young thing, but she was hard on men."

"You knew her?"

"Of course I did. She was engaged to my grandson, Zane, for a while."

"She was?" J.J. felt her jaw drop. Again.

"Oh yes. They met when Connor and Zane had the restaurant together. She, of course, was engaged to Connor at that time but when she met Zane, well, it was the pro-verbial sparks flying."

"Did Connor know? Is that what broke them up?"

Wallis Redding gave her an odd look. "Of course he knew. When your fiancée leaves you for another, and it turns out to be your business partner, there's no way to keep your head in the sand."

J.J. let the information settle. She looked at Evan, who looked as shocked as she felt. "Is that what broke up the partnership?"

"Of course." Now J.J. felt she was being addressed like a nitwit. "Connor was furious. Zane did the honorable thing and bought him out and kept the restaurant going. I felt sure there'd be a wedding very shortly, but then she went and broke it off."

"She dumped your grandson after dumping Connor?" Evan sounded truly amazed. "Had she met someone else?"

Wallis shrugged. "I don't really know. Zane was very upset, as you can imagine, and wouldn't talk much about it. He threw himself into work and continues to do so. She did break his heart, and I think it's still not mended."

"How did he take the news of her death?" *And do the police consider him a suspect?*

"How would you expect he'd handle it? He was tormented all over again."

"Do you know if he had contact with Connor?"

"You mean, after the death or after the dissolving of their partnership? The answer to the second is, after a time they started to have contact again. Connor had insisted that a stipulation in the dissolution was that he be entitled to free dinners in perpetuity. I doubt he'd intended to do so, but it was a bit of a dig at Zane. I had heard, though, that he was making use of that clause on occasion." She allowed a slight smile.

"Could they both be at your cottage?"

"I don't know who, if anyone, is at the place. I don't go there anymore. It belongs to Zane, as far as I'm concerned. But I do know that he is in Turks and Caicos. We have a house there and he needed to get away. I spoke to him yesterday. He should be coming home next week sometime."

"Is it possible Connor could access your cottage on his own?"

"I have no idea. I would highly doubt it, but perhaps the two were in contact with each other and in their sorrow, have put aside their feud. It happens." ·

"Could you please tell us where it is?"

She took a few moments before answering, and J.J. felt her hopes plummet. What if she didn't want them poking around her place or in Zane's affairs?

"I'll have Natasha give you a map. It's on North Hero but well off the main road. Now, if there's nothing else?" She reached for her cane, effectively dismissing them.

They had to wait several more minutes while Natasha located the map and printed a copy for them. She handed it over, and the butler appeared magically, leading them back to the front door. Again, no words were spoken.

Once back in the car, J.J. took a deep breath and leaned back against the headrest. "Gloomy."

"Eerie. Don't those people ever speak? Or smile?" Evan shook his head. "I think I'll revise my desire to work here."

"The butler did look out of place, though. I would have thought she'd wanted him in black tails at the very least."

Evan snorted. "She likes to keep the world at large guessing, or so I've heard. I really should be getting back, although I know you're itching to check out the cottage. Do you even think that Connor is there? It doesn't sound too likely. Not with their history."

"You could be right. But it's the only lead we have. But now we also have another suspect."

"You're thinking it's possible Zane killed her even though it's been a while since she dumped him? Maybe he heard she was getting back with Connor and he just lost it. You should check to see if he was at the casino event."

"I will. You can count on it."

"Of course," Evan said, starting the car, "it could also give Connor another motive. Past history showed him she was flighty, so what if, after they got back together, he found out about the cop? Or maybe there was even another someone. What would Connor have done in that case?"

J.J. thought about it for less than a minute. She shook her head. "No, Connor isn't a killer, and that's not even a compelling enough motive to get him to cross the line. No, I think we should operate on the assumption that Connor is at Zane's cottage, and the killer is"—she shrugged—"somewhere, as yet undetected. But we will find him. Or her."

CHAPTER 23

The first thing J.J. did when returning home was feed Indie. Then herself. But she was too keyed up for anything substantial. Fortunately, she had leftovers. The chicken pot pie that Ness had brought over the previous week worked out just fine. Just a zap in the microwave and she was all set. She looked out the window as she slowly ate. There should be enough time to make it to the cottage. If she didn't get lost.

She knew she should leave it until the daylight or even the weekend, but she was anxious to find out if Connor was hiding there. And besides, once she found it, in the dimming daylight, she could easily find her way back home even if it was dark.

She grabbed her purse and a heavy sweater, knowing it cooled down once the sun departed, and had her hand on the doorknob when someone knocked on the door. She thought it might be Ness and maybe she could talk him into going with her. She pulled the door open to find Devine standing there.

"On your way out?" he asked.

"Uh, yes." She slid past him into the hall, pulling her door shut and locking it. She realized she hadn't even given him a thought; she'd just wanted to find that cottage.

"Maybe we can talk on the way to the cottage."

"What?" She bit her tongue. She'd almost asked how he knew. And she knew, that was his ploy. Catch her off guard and she'd say something. Well, she wouldn't. But maybe it meant something else.

"Does that mean you've found it?"

He nodded. "Why don't I drive?"

How had he found out? He must have tracked it down in the county office. No way could he know about all that history between Connor and Zane. Now that it seemed more likely she'd find Conner, she wasn't so sure she wanted Devine along, but since he already knew where it was, she liked the idea of his going on his own even less. She followed him out to his car, glancing up to see Ness standing at his window, watching. She could almost see the dialogue bubble over his head. *Do not go anywhere with that man.*

She slid into the passenger seat and waited for Devine to start the car. When he didn't seem in any rush, she asked, "Is there something you wanted to talk about first?"

"I want the directions on how to get there."

"What? I thought you'd found it. Weren't you checking with the town clerk's office?"

"Yes and no. First of all, I checked on the name of the restaurant owner and got Zane Anderson. Then, I checked on cottages but there was nothing registered in Anderson's name. And then I saw you and Evan Thornton driving off earlier, so on a hunch, I followed. I did a bit of checking and see that Mrs. Wallis Redding is Zane Anderson's grandmother. I'm betting she was very helpful and you now know where the cottage is."

J.J. turned her face to look back at the apartment. She

was furious with herself. She should have known he would pull something like this. But maybe it was a good thing, she reasoned. He might come in handy. Maybe. She sighed.

"Head to North Hero Island."

They rode in silence for about ten minutes, and then Devine asked, "Does she know if they're both there?"

"She doesn't, although she did tell us that Zane is in Turks and Caicos. She has no idea where Connor is, though."

"So, he's still on good terms with this ex-partner."

"It's not 'still.' It appears there may have been a thaw in their relationship lately. And that's even stranger, given the circumstances. Connor's engagement to Miranda was broken when she fell for Zane."

"You're kidding."

"Nope. According to his grandmother, that's what happened."

After another ten minutes or so of silence, J.J. asked, "What are you thinking?"

"That gives Connor Mac even more of a motive, but it doesn't explain why he'd be hiding out at the cabin. Unless . . ."

"Unless, what?"

"He's holding Anderson hostage there. He killed Miranda, and now he's building up to finishing off the other person who ruined his life."

J.J. tried to keep her voice calm. "I think you're being a bit dramatic. Ruined his life? He seems to have a pretty good life. He's a media star, and, if you'll recall, he and Miranda had started dating again. So why go the route of your scenario?"

"We have only his word that's what was happening. Or did I miss something?"

J.J. bit her lower lip. He was right. *No, he wasn't.* "Hennie Ferguson seemed to think they were becoming an item again and so did Kathi Jones. Also, Connor sometimes eats at the Harry's Haven, so he and Zane aren't sworn enemies any longer."

Devine gave a half nod.

A few minutes later, he pulled onto the bridge joining the mainland to the islands. They covered the last part of the drive in silence until Devine said, "Okay. We're on North Hero. Where to now?"

"Keep driving about four miles, and then there's a narrow, unmarked dirt road to the right. It meanders its way through the forest and ends at the cottage, which overlooks the water, by the way, but it's unseen from the water and also from the road. The perfect hideaway."

"Could be. We'd better find it quickly, though; there's not much more daylight left. I'll slow down when we get closer to the cutoff. You keep your eyes peeled."

"Yes, sir." She added a small salute for good measure and was rewarded with a slight smile.

She looked at the woods and got occasional glimpses of the lake as they made their way. She enjoyed this drive and told herself she should do it more often. There weren't any big resorts with beaches, which was fine by her, but Skye had once shown her a great place to go swimming that only the locals knew about. Maybe next summer.

"That must be it," she shrieked, and Devine hit the brakes and backed up a couple of feet, then turned right.

A well-maintained narrow dirt road wound its way deeper into the woods. J.J. hoped they didn't meet another car as they followed it. Someone would have to back down and back up.

Devine slowed as the cottage emerged through the trees. "Let's leave the car here and walk the rest of the way."

J.J. nodded. They got out and shut the doors quietly in unspoken agreement. J.J. let Devine take the lead. She kept her head on swivel, searching for any sign of Connor out for a walk or down by the water.

"I don't see his car," she whispered, feeling disappointed.

Devine gestured to the left. "That looks like a garage. It could be in there."

J.J. could just barely make out the shape of another building. She realized that it was way darker in the forest, and she was suddenly glad that Devine was with her. They reached the main building, a two-story log house much larger than any cabin J.J. had visited. Devine signaled her to be quiet. He snuck up on the porch that ran across the front of the lower level and cautiously peered through the large picture window to the right.

"What's taking so long?" she said in a loud whisper.

"Trying to let my eyes adjust. It's dark inside. I don't think anyone's here unless they're trying to make us believe that." He tried the door. It was locked.

He pulled a small flashlight out of his jacket pocket and shone it through the windows, then gestured her to the side of the house. He caught up and they continued circling the cabin, peering through all the windows on the ground floor.

"It looks empty except for the fact that there are leaves on the kitchen floor near the doorway. Like when someone leaves quickly and doesn't sweep behind themselves. Let's check the garage."

The door opened easily, showing off a large space, empty except for some ladders and other outdoor equipment propped on the walls. Devine knelt down and shone the flashlight on the ground.

"I'd say there's been a car here and very recently."

"You don't think Mrs. Redding would have phoned and tipped him off, do you?"

Devine stood again. "It could have been her grandson after all, and she did warn him. She was under no obligation to tell you the truth, you know. Now, if you had been the police . . ."

"They wouldn't have gotten any information, and you know it. If she's protecting her grandson, she'll continue doing so. But if it was Connor, why would she call him?"

"Same reason? He and Zane have history. She felt some loyalty was in order after everything that had happened. Or some payback after the betrayal Zane was part of." He took his time scanning the property. "I'd say whoever it was has gone, and we'd better get going also while I can still tell where the road is."

They walked back to the car quickly without another word. J.J. almost tripped a couple of times. It was quite dark by now and she couldn't see where she placed her feet. She didn't want to disturb Devine while he found their way back to the main road, but once he turned onto it, she asked, "What does your gut tell you?"

"My gut?"

"Why don't you ever take me seriously?"

He chuckled. "Oh, believe me, I do." The softness of his voice sent a shiver down her spine.

After a few minutes he went on. "It probably was Connor. There's no reason for Zane to be hiding out. He has no reason to believe he's a suspect. The police haven't even tried to question him. So, if he were here just to get away, he would have waited around. My *gut* tells me he's in Turks and Caicos, as advertised."

"Oh, but the police were looking for him to ask some questions."

"How do you know that?"

"Detective Hastings stopped by the office to ask what I knew about the partnership. He said he'd been to the restaurant and it was closed."

"He may have been hoping to find a link to where Connor's hiding. He may not yet know about their history. That should make Hastings a very frustrated detective."

CHAPTER 24

Skye had called in sick the next morning but didn't want to put off the meeting with her newest client. She asked J.J. to handle it since she knew the account. They'd discussed it when Skye had first thought of taking it on and then had brainstormed ideas for hours over several glasses of wine. J.J. checked her outfit. That would do. Skye had e-mailed her the specs and an update, which she read thoroughly, twice, just to be safe. Was there anything else she needed?

She glanced at the clock. Better not be missing anything. Time to go. She drove downtown along North Avenue and decided to park at the Burlington Town Center. First two hours free, and maybe she could squeeze in some shopping time, unless it turned out to be a complicated meeting. She hoped not, more because she liked to be sure she had all the answers before the questions even appeared, and if not, that could lead to more hours on site. And, of course, less shopping time.

∘ ∘ ∘

J.J. drove back to the village and popped into Cups 'n' Roses at the height of the noon rush hour. The meeting had ended just short of two hours, and J.J. had opted to do her lunch hour vigil rather than stay downtown and shop. She stood in line for about three minutes and finally made it to the counter and a harried Beth.

"Wait when you pick up your coffee. I have to talk to you," she whispered. J.J. nodded and made her way to the other lineup at the coffee pick-up spot. She had to wait another few minutes after getting her latte for Beth to slide over.

"When you walk over to your table," Beth said, her voice barely audible, "check out the woman at the table in the far corner wearing a pale blue jacket and sunglasses. I think she looks a lot like the woman from the other day. I think she's the one."

"Why, because she's wearing sunglasses and it's cloudy out? Never mind, there's no sun inside." J.J. smiled to show she was kidding.

Beth gave her head a slight shake. "Oh, you. I'm pretty sure I saw her pocket a sugar bowl. I can't be one hundred percent sure, though, so I'm not about to confront her. Just keep tabs on her, okay?"

"Sure." J.J. had to use strict discipline not to turn and stare while they were talking, but when she wandered to a free table with a good sight line of the woman, she swept the room with her eyes, trying to appear like she wasn't singling anyone out.

When she took her first sip of the latte, she was able to eye the woman for a longer period of time. She did look nervous. But she didn't look anything like the person they'd decided was the number one suspect. *Bummer.* Although, it could be the same woman, only today she had her hair pulled back, not half covering her face. And she was wearing sunglasses. Maybe as a disguise?

Beth brought J.J.'s panini over just as the woman stood to leave. "Follow her, please. I'll keep your lunch warm." She grabbed back the plate and watched the woman's receding back while J.J. grabbed her things.

J.J. had just started down the street when Beth appeared at her side. "I need to follow this through for myself. You can go back and eat if you want, although I'd like a witness."

"No way am I missing out," J.J. said. "After all the hours I've been waiting for this. Not that they haven't been delicious hours."

She glanced at Beth, who'd added a scarf around her head and her own set of sunglasses. "Disguised?"

Beth nodded. "She sees me every day but not in my jacket. And she shouldn't recognize you. I hope."

After a couple of blocks, Beth started breathing harder. "I didn't realize I was so out of shape."

"Maybe she's training for a marathon. I wonder if she knows she's being followed."

"She hasn't tried to shake us, just outwalk us."

"No. Look, she's turning left onto Jefferson Street."

They scuttled up to the corner and cautiously peered around just in time to see the woman enter a parking lot on the left. By the time they got to that point, she was sliding into the backseat of an older model silver Buick Century. So far, she hadn't looked back at them and appeared to be lost in checking something, head down. They strolled over to the car next to her, pretending to be getting into it, then peered in the Buick through the back window.

Beth signaled to J.J. to get over on the other side. "She's taking my stuff out of her purse," she whispered as she met J.J. at the trunk of the second car. "It's her. She is the thief."

"What do you want to do? Call the cops?"

"No. I want an explanation first." She marched over to the car door and rapped on the window.

The woman looked up in surprise, which changed to

horror as Beth removed her scarf and sunglasses. She moved as if to lock the door, but J.J. had already jumped into the front seat, searching for the power lock, as Beth moved quickly to the other side and slid into the back next to the woman, who looked about to cry.

Beth stared hard at her, then glanced down at the cardboard box in the woman's lap. She pulled it over and began sorting through the items inside. "These are all from my shop."

The woman cringed but said nothing. She looked defeated, shoulders slightly hunched over, wringing her hands. Her shoulder-length light brown hair hung loosely, lacking body and shine. It had been a while since she'd been to a stylist, J.J. bet. Up close, her pale blue jacket looked to be of good quality, as was the brown blouse peeking out from it. J.J. guessed she was in her late forties or so.

"I'd like to know what you think you're doing. This is theft. You could go to jail for this," Beth continued, her voice sharp.

J.J. didn't know if that was true but it sure sounded scary. Surely the woman would explain, but would she tell the truth?

Between sobs, the woman explained, "You're right, it is yours. Please, I'll give it all back, and I promise not to go to your coffee shop anymore. Only please, please, don't call the police. I can't take that."

"Why shouldn't I get them involved? I know these are small items, but they belong to the shop and I did pay for them."

"I know."

"What's your name?"

"Ilsa Grimes." She'd stopped crying but her eyes were puffy and red.

"Why, Ilsa? Why did you take them?"

Ilsa looked out the car window, and it seemed like she'd

finished talking. J.J. glanced at Beth, wondering what she'd do next. Then Ilsa blew her nose and cleared her throat.

"My husband left me a few months ago. And then he actually kicked me out of the house because he wants to sell it. All I got to take were my clothes and some personal belongings. And my car."

"He can't do that," J.J. said. "How can he throw you out of your own house?"

"The house was in his name. I lived with him for a few years before we got married. We never changed over anything, so it was all in his name alone. And I haven't had a job since we've been together. He's sort of old-school. He said that my working made him look like he couldn't support a wife."

What century is he from?

"What have you been doing since you left?" Beth asked.

Ilsa shrugged. "I've sold most of my good clothes and jewelry, and I've been living out of my car. The bit of money I'd saved, which he didn't know about, goes to gas and food. I've looked for a job, but no one wants me. I don't have any real skills, and I'm not so young anymore." She hiccupped.

"I love your shop. It makes me feel so cozy and safe, and I love the colors. The serviettes jump off the table. I started with taking the serviettes and placing them around the backseat for color. Then I thought I could save even more money and picnic in the car, but I needed utensils and other stuff."

"Like salt and pepper. Cream and sugar." Beth didn't bother to ask the question. She knew the answer.

Ilsa's shoulders heaved as she sighed. "I'm so sorry. I wasn't thinking straight about what I was doing or what it would mean to you and your profits. I'll make it up to you. I'll do anything you want."

J.J. signaled Beth out of the car. Beth patted Ilsa's arm, then climbed out.

"It sounds sad, but what if it's not true?" J.J. asked. "What if she's a really gifted liar?"

"I think I believe her. What I haven't been able to figure out is why someone would steal these specific items. It makes some kind of sense to hear her tell it. Why else would anyone take only these small items?"

"There is that."

Beth was silent for a few minutes. J.J. could almost see the wheels in her head turning. "I've made a decision."

She knocked on the car window again and signaled Ilsa to get out. She looked very timid and small when she joined them beside the car.

"I believe you," Beth said. "So, here's the deal. You can keep this stuff, but you have to work it off. Have you had any experience in retail or restaurants?"

"I was a waitress at summer camp for a few years as a teenager."

J.J. thought that probably wasn't such a good reference. She looked at Beth and saw the determination in her face. Although J.J. wondered how smart a move this was on Beth's part, she knew when to keep out of it.

"Okay, you can serve, and when it's slow, clean up and wash dishes. I'll take half a day of free labor to cover the cost of what you've stolen and the frustration it's caused me, then I'll pay minimum wage after that. We'll adjust your hours according to how busy it is. Does that sound fair?"

Ilsa began to cry again. "You can't know how much this means to me, especially after I was so deceitful."

"You're on probation, so you'll have to act sharp. I want you there at seven A.M. tomorrow morning. Deal?"

"Deal." Ilsa looked quite lovely with a huge smile lighting her face.

J.J. knew the probation bit was probably said just to keep her on her toes, and she also was fairly certain that the woman would get close to eight hours a day, busy or not. That was just Beth's style.

As the two of them walked back to Cups 'n' Roses, J.J. said, "That was a nice thing you did. I wonder why they broke up, although his attitude to her working could explain a lot about him."

"It's not really our concern, but I hate to see anyone treated so shabbily, no matter what the reason. I'll have to figure out where she can get a room, too."

"You're not thinking of taking her in?"

"Since downsizing a couple of years ago, I don't even have room for overnight guests. But I know some people who do."

J.J. just hoped Beth wouldn't end up being disappointed in Ilsa Grimes. After all, they didn't know very much about her.

CHAPTER 25

J.J. had just made it back to the office, ditched her purse, and taken off her jacket when her phone rang. She hadn't even had time to sit down at her desk.

"Make It Happen. J.J. speaking. How may I help you?"

"By joining me at the TV station in about twenty minutes."

She looked at the phone receiver. It sounded like Devine's voice. She was sure it was Devine's voice, but for him to be actually asking her to join in something case related? That would be twice in one month. What was coming over the guy?

"Can you give me a hint as to what it's about?"

"Hennie is back at work."

"I hate to look a gift horse in the mouth, as they say, but why are you wanting me there?"

"I figure you're going to talk to her at some point anyway, and maybe by doing it this way, I can keep you alive and out of jail." She could almost hear the chuckle in his voice.

"So kind. All right. I'll be there shortly."

J.J. checked to make sure Skye hadn't called in and left a

message, then she grabbed her stuff. She was slipping into her jacket, going down the stairs, when she met Tansy coming up.

"Are you in that much of a hurry that you can't stop to put your jacket on before leaving your office?"

J.J. paused on the step and slid her arm into the sleeve. "Got it in one, Tansy. How's your day going?"

"Well, besides wasting my time at the courthouse waiting for a hearing that never happened, just fine." Her voice was tight and J.J. pitied whoever's fault this was. She could almost guarantee that Tansy's next stop was her desk and the phone. Someone would get an earful.

"Good luck with that," J.J. said brightly, not wanting to spend too much time talking to a grumpy Tansy. She'd been there, done that.

Tansy continued up the stairs. "Luck has nothing to do with it, kiddo."

J.J. made good time getting over to the TV station. Devine stood at the reception desk, talking to Wanda, who sure looked perky, J.J. thought.

Devine noticed J.J. and motioned her to follow him along the right corridor to the back. Hennie must have known they were coming. She sat in her desk looking rigid and unsmiling as they entered after knocking first.

"What's it about this time?" she asked before either of them had a chance to talk.

"We just have a few more questions," Devine stated, oozing charm.

J.J. watched as Hennie started to thaw. Devine looked at J.J. She took that as an invitation to start asking.

"We need some more information about that married cop you'd mentioned. A name would be great."

Hennie looked from one to the other. "I told you, his name might not even be listed in the files, and it will take some looking to find the exact date. But I'll try."

"Good. Thank you." J.J. was just about to ask about Yolande when Devine took over.

"So, let's talk more about what's been going on around the station." Devine perched on the edge of the desk across from Hennie. "Miranda Myers wasn't the only one with secrets, was she?"

J.J. watched in amazement as Hennie's face turned various shades of red. What did this have to do with anything anyway?

"I don't know what you mean."

"I'll bet Mikey Cooper knows what I mean. In fact, you and he are quite an item. Isn't that so?"

J.J. stared at Hennie. She and Mikey Cooper were dating? But why hadn't she mentioned it before? What was the big secret? The dots started connecting. Was Hennie a part of Mikey's campaign to cause some havoc at the station? J.J. looked at Devine, who had Hennie as his visual target.

"Who told you that?" Her voice was barely a whisper.

"Nothing goes on in the station without someone knowing about it, I've found. Which is good, because it would have been very hard tracking the vandal otherwise."

Hennie stood up abruptly. "It's not Mikey. I heard the guy's been caught." She plopped right back into her chair.

"One vandal is in police custody, but we know that defacing the station van was a separate incident, don't we, Hennie?"

"What makes you think he's involved?" Hennie asked Devine. J.J. could tell she was struggling to control her voice.

"Let's just say, I'm good at my job. Besides, Mikey confessed. So tell me, how are you involved in it?"

Hennie swallowed hard. "We've been dating for quite a while now. I didn't think anyone knew. We didn't want it going around the station since his Dad's the GM." She closed her eyes briefly. "When Mikey got fired, he was livid. He has quite a temper, you know. Anyway, he started making all sorts of threats, when we were alone, that is. So I tried calming him down. We talked about it, and I figured that if he did something that hit the station but didn't hurt anyone that would get it out of his system. And it did."

"Are you sure about that, Hennie? What about killing Miranda? That would certainly be payback."

Hennie jumped up again. "He didn't kill her, I swear. I told you, nothing he planned involved anyone getting hurt."

"But he was on board at the casino night, wasn't he?" J.J. jumped in. It was a guess, but probably a good one. "I saw you were there, so I'm sure he must have been."

She nodded, tears in her eyes, and sat back down. "We were just going to embarrass Miranda a little if we got the chance. If not, he planned to set off a bunch of firecrackers when she did the wrap-up. That's all."

"But none of that happened."

"No. He seemed to have calmed down by that evening, and we were having a lot of fun together. I think he just decided to ditch the plan."

"Was he with you the entire evening?" Devine asked.

"Yes, he was. He really was. I swear."

J.J. and Devine looked at each other. Could she be believed?

"What are you going to do?" Hennie asked in a quiet voice.

"It's already been done. Mikey's father already knows what he's been up to. He's got my report. And for all his poor judgment, I doubt that Mikey is a murderer." He glanced at J.J., who frowned.

"Will he go to jail?" Hennie squeaked.

"That depends on whether he did commit the murder after all," J.J. answered. "I still need to be convinced, even if Mr. Devine has reached another conclusion." She didn't totally trust Hennie. Not yet.

"But I told you, he didn't."

J.J. narrowed her eyes. "How can we believe you, Hennie?"

"Try looking elsewhere for the real killer." She pulled a tissue out of her desk drawer and blew her nose. "Have you talked to the sister-in-law? Did she explain about the big argument?"

"I talked to her, but she dismissed it as something inconsequential," J.J. answered.

Hennie snorted. "And you believe her and not me? There were others around that day—ask them."

"Like who?"

"Lonny Chan, for one. Even the station manager."

"Thanks. I will check with them. You know, it's kind of hard to believe you, though, after what you've admitted trying to do to Miranda."

Hennie stopped chewing on her bottom lip. "I know. I'm really sorry. I truly liked her and wouldn't have done anything to harm her. It was what she represented. It was the station that was our focus."

"Why are you still working here if that's your attitude to WBVT?"

"I like the folks and my job. I like being behind the scenes. It's Mikey who has the issues and I was just helping him. Will you tell the boss about me?" She looked at Devine and either was able to dredge up fake tears easily or she was getting emotional.

He sighed. "I may not have to, but if it comes up, I won't lie to my client."

She nodded and reached into her drawer for another tissue.

J.J. and Devine walked back to the reception area in silence. When they reached it, they were greeted by a group of noisy schoolchildren, probably fifth or sixth graders, J.J. thought, so she and Devine stepped outside to talk.

"What now?" J.J. asked.

"I'm done here unless you think I should be doing something further?"

She heard the sarcasm in his voice.

"You could talk to Donald Cooper and ask him about what he heard of the argument between Miranda and Yolande Myers. That is, now that you don't have to get details about the married cop from him. And I'll see if I can track down Lonny and find out what he remembers."

"You're not planning on heading over to confront Yolande Myers again, I trust."

J.J. shook her head. "Not until I know what the argument was about. I don't want to be caught off guard this time."

"That's smart, but even smarter would be not going to see her on your own. We'll go together."

"Why? Your case was the stalker. You've solved that, so why keep on the murder? I know, you are your own client. But why?"

"Because it's a murder, and because someone has to keep you from getting into trouble."

"That's your task now, is it?" She grinned.

"What?"

"I was just thinking how much we sound like partners. You are actually asking me, not reaming me out."

He smiled back. "How does it feel?"

"Awesome. I'm not really an adversarial person, you know."

"So I'd noticed." He tried to keep a straight face.

She punched him lightly on the arm and walked back into the station in search of Lonny Chan.

She found Lonny in the staff room, dunking a glazed donut into a mug of coffee. *Finally.* "Hi, Lonny. My name is J.J. Tanner. I'm sorry to barge in on your break, but I need to ask a few questions about Miranda Myers, if you don't mind."

He looked surprised but quickly recovered. "That's okay by me. There's freshly made coffee if you want some."

J.J. nodded. "Yeah. That would be great."

He jumped out of his chair and filled a mug for her. *Beanpole.* That's what came to mind, something they'd called a kid named Fred in grade school. Not kind but accurate. Lonny was also tall and thin. In fact, she wondered how he could possibly heft that huge camera she'd seen them use out on location. He must have muscles of iron or shoulders with steel plates in them. His straight black hair reminded her of the bowl haircut her younger brother Kyle had sported for an entire summer until in despair, he'd tried shaving it off, only to be taken to the barber for a proper buzz cut. She liked Lonny immediately.

"Do you take anything?" he asked, bringing her back to reality.

"Nope. Black is the way I like it." She took a sip after he'd set it down in front of her. Hot.

He pushed the box of donuts over to her but she shook her head.

After J.J. brought him up to speed on her involvement and what she'd been doing, she said, "I understand you witnessed an argument between Miranda and her sister-in-law a few weeks back. Did you hear any of it? I'm trying to find out what it was about."

He looked up at the ceiling, scrunching the corner of his mouth, and after a few seconds answered. "I heard a bit. They were in her office, but the door wasn't shut tight. I'd already given it a little push, thinking Miranda was alone, and they were standing there, glaring at each other. I excused myself as I pulled the door shut, but I could hear them launch into it again. The sis-in-law warned Miranda to stay out of her business or else."

That shocked J.J. "She actually said 'or else'?"

Lonny nodded. "I did hear those words and then I got out of there. I didn't want them opening the door and thinking I was eavesdropping."

"Is there any chance Donald Cooper could have heard them also? Was he in the hall?"

"Cooper? Not that I saw, but of course, Miranda had just come off the set, so who knows where they started arguing."

"Hm. Is there anything else?"

"Nope. Can't think of anything. Like I said, I got out of there pretty fast at that point, and when I saw Miranda later, she didn't mention anything about it or my barging in on them. So I didn't bring it up. Is it important?"

"I have no idea. Now that I've got you here, is there anything you can think of that might point to Miranda's murderer?"

He looked surprised, then appeared to be giving it some thought.

"No. Nothing. I wish I could be of help. We were friends and all, but she wasn't one to talk much about her private life. It was mainly work, and, as far as I knew, everything was going just fine. Of course, I'm not hanging around the station often, so I'm not much of a part of what happens here. You know, she had everything. Looks, personality, a spectacular job, and then this happens. It's not really fair, is it?"

"No, it's not fair. Not by a long shot."

Devine was waiting outside, leaning against his car, soaking in some rays when she left the station.

"So, what did you find out?" he asked, not bothering to turn to look at her.

"There was an argument in Miranda's office, but all Lonny could hear was Yolande saying to stay out of her business or else."

"Sounds much like what Cooper said."

"But Lonny said Cooper wasn't in the hall at the time of the argument."

He pushed off the car and straightened. "No, but it sounds like it started in the studio area. Yolande barged in after the taping of the show and confronted Miranda. She didn't say what Miranda had done but did tell her the same thing, to stay out of her business. Miranda told her to lower her voice, and they left, presumably to go to Miranda's office."

"What could she have done that got Yolande so upset?"

"Maybe it had something to do with the upcoming election."

J.J. thought about it a few seconds. "I can't picture Yolande referring to that as 'her' business."

"She does have a vested interest in her husband getting elected, I'd say. I think it's time to pay a visit to the campaign office. If we're lucky, the campaign manager will be in and maybe help clear a few things up. If not, there's still the staff and volunteers. And in my experience, everyone wants to be in the know, so they pay attention to what's being said and done."

J.J. wondered if this might be a good time to tell Devine about her earlier visit to the office.

CHAPTER 26

Devine pulled out of the station parking lot. "Want a caffeine stop along the way?"

"Always. Any thoughts on what we'll find at the office? You'd think his staff would be loyal."

"Not if they've been passed up for a promotion or given lots of extra menial work. Maybe they haven't been thanked since the campaign began. There are a lot of things that set people off. Let's grab a coffee at a place I know just around this corner. It's small but they serve their own freshly roasted beans."

He pulled in front of a small two-story older redbrick house that had been converted for retail use. They went inside, and J.J. breathed in the smell of fresh coffee beans. "Smells amazing."

Devine nodded and gave his order to the young man behind the counter. He asked J.J. what she wanted.

"Medium-sized dark roast, please."

Devine paid for the coffees and they headed back to the car. The next time he stopped was in the large parking lot next door to the campaign office. They finished their drinks, tossed the cups into a trash can on the sidewalk, and then went inside.

"Now, how about I do the talking in here." It wasn't a question. J.J. rolled her eyes and followed him partway through the room to the door of the campaign manager. She glanced around the larger room while he knocked on the glass door.

Fletcher Kane looked up from his desk and waved them in. He was standing by the time they reached his desk. The sleeves on his plaid shirt were rolled up above his elbows, his black tie loosened and askew. He had black-rimmed glasses propped on top of his head. A gap between his front teeth was apparent when he smiled, even though he barely opened his mouth.

Devine spoke first. "I hope you don't mind our just stopping in without an appointment. I'm sure you're a very busy man these days."

Kane had looked a bit put out, but his demeanor changed. "I can spare a few minutes. What's this about? Are you media?"

"No. It's about Miranda Myers." Devine left it at that. J.J. watched for a reaction.

Kane shook his head. "That was so tragic. Gary is devastated. They were close, you know. The only siblings and their folks are gone. It's really too bad it happened so late in the campaign. He has to be at the top of his game at this stage."

J.J. couldn't hold back. "It's too bad it happened, period."

Kane looked only slightly mollified. "Of course. That didn't come out right. Now, what is your interest in this?" He looked from one to the other.

Devine pulled out his ID. "I'm a private investigator, and Ms. Tanner was the one who organized the casino night where the murder happened."

J.J. cringed. It still unsettled her to hear her name linked to the murder.

Kane shrugged. "What can I do to help?"

"How did Ms. Myers feel about her brother's campaign?" Devine asked.

Kane's initial look of surprise was quickly replaced with a folksy smile. "She was excited for him. In fact, she would come in and volunteer, making phone calls, stuffing envelopes, that kind of thing whenever she had the time."

"Was she still doing that at the time of her death?"

"What do you mean? She was a strong supporter."

"I understand that she had stopped coming into the campaign office, and that it had been at least a couple of weeks." J.J. glanced at Devine. How did he know that?

"Well, she was busy. That was all. Gary understood. Celebrities aren't always in charge of the demands on their time."

"But he's her brother." J.J. felt the need to get into the conversation. "Surely she could have made time for him."

"I don't know what you're getting at. Of course she would have if it had been necessary. But as you can see, we have plenty of volunteers available."

"Whose idea was it that she pull back?" Devine took up the thread again.

Kane shrugged. "I don't really know for sure. Now, I'm sorry, but I've run out of time. Gary has a press conference in a couple of hours, so there's lots to do."

"One last question," Devine said as they were turning to leave. "How was Miranda's relationship with her sister-in-law?"

Kane looked startled. "Yolande? Fine, I guess. I didn't see them together too much, but they always seemed to get along just fine. Why?"

"Just trying to get an overall picture of her life."

"One last from me, too," J.J. interjected. "Were you at

the casino night fund-raiser? Or maybe Miranda's brother went?"

"No. Gary definitely wasn't there. He had a speaking engagement at the Kiwanis club, and his wife went with him."

"Okay," Devine answered for them both. "Thanks for your time."

"No problem, and please, feel free to contact me anytime you have further questions." Somehow, he didn't sound like he meant it. He closed the door behind them.

"Oops, sorry," J.J. said as she'd walked right into a staff member. Time to pay attention to the surroundings.

"No problem." The woman continued on her way to the back of the office.

"You know, I did have more questions," J.J. muttered as they headed back through the outer office to the sidewalk. "What did you think of all that?"

Devine shrugged. "We could take it all at face value. What he said makes sense."

J.J. shrugged. "I guess it could. By the way, we didn't talk to the office staff."

"Another day, when Kane isn't in. I'll call first."

"You don't trust him?"

"He has a lot invested in his candidate, so that may be coloring his answers. It's good to have others to compare with."

"Whatever you say. Now what?"

"Now I drop you off at your office so you can do your real work, and I'll go do mine."

"Is it to do with the murder?"

"No. It's to do with insurance fraud. I told you, I run several cases at once. Just like you have events to plan in between solving murders." He grinned.

"You are so right."

CHAPTER 27

J.J. had tried to put aside all thoughts of the murder, and of work, for the weekend. She knew she needed a break. So that meant doing only housework—a necessity, reading—a pleasure, and taking walks down to the lake, so that she could enjoy the fabulous fall weather. But good intentions last only so long, and by Sunday afternoon, she was keying in Fletcher Kane's name on her computer. She hadn't liked the guy, maybe because he came across too sincere, almost a sticking point with her. She'd run across a lot of similar guys in her past life. Overly sincere translated into *slick* in her book, translated into *untrustworthy*, so he must be hiding something. Probably something to do with the campaign, but would that have anything to do with the murder? Probably not.

She'd bet Devine had already done the exact same thing. When he wasn't busy. *Doing what?* Did he have a steady girlfriend and, unlike J.J., was spending the weekend actually doing fun things? On the other hand, what did she care? She'd enjoyed dinner on Saturday night with

Skye and Nick. Again. Several phone calls with friends. And she had Indie. What more did she need? Certainly not any complications.

She pulled her thoughts back to Fletcher Kane. Quite a few hits, all singing his praises, plus a Facebook site with over three thousand friends. Who had that many friends? She didn't want to become one no matter how much information his page was hiding. Surely nothing incriminating, anyway. She gave up after about ten minutes, feeling she knew enough about him to know she didn't really want to get to know him any better.

She decided to thumb through the casino night photos again. Now that she'd seen some more of the people involved in some way, no matter how small, with Miranda's life, it was time for another look. After about a half hour of checking slowly and thoroughly, she sat back and sighed.

There were a couple of possibilities, but unfortunately, the images were too blurry. Also, she'd have to wait until Monday to actually follow up on it.

She stood and stretched, then stared out the window. She felt restless but wasn't quite sure what to do about it. She spotted a magazine from the local school board listing night school classes. Maybe that's what she needed. Food. More specifically, a cooking course. She'd been toying with the idea for some time now, ever since she and Skye started working on their own night school course on event planning, but so far she'd done nothing about it.

She thumbed through the index and flipped to the page outlining the cooking courses. She had proven to herself that she was more than just a cookbook groupie. She had actually presented a few highly edible main courses, but she knew she still was way behind the others in the club when it came to skills. Her main problem was she stuck too closely to the recipes and varied ingredients only after checking with others that it was an okay thing to do. She readily admitted she was afraid to test her own creativity. If she had any. She totally lacked confidence—and terminology. She felt like she was still in kindergarten when it came to discussing and describing the dishes they all prepared. And right now, she wanted to be a high school senior.

Her mom hadn't encouraged her cooking talents nor instilled in her any inquisitiveness when it came to coming up with menus, combining tastes and ingredients, and doing the actual cooking. Of course, she couldn't totally blame her mom, because she'd treated all the kids the same, as she'd rushed in and out of the house between client meetings and house showings, and the family was left to its own devices many nights. J.J. soon found out there were many pizza and Chinese food takeouts in their end of the city.

On the rare occasion when her dad would take over in the kitchen, the family was guaranteed there'd be a culinary treat. But he didn't encourage the kids to get involved, either. So, neither of her brothers cooked. And J.J. didn't cook. Until now.

She slowly read the descriptions of two courses she'd been considering. Only one would be the winner. Cook Like a Chef promised she'd be slicing and dicing her way to a bevy of techniques and recipes. While Cook the French Way promised she would be able to do just that. While the second one sounded magical, the first sounded practical, and she knew that's precisely what she needed. She checked the dates, six Tuesday evenings, seven to nine P.M., starting the second week in January. The cost was manageable also.

She flipped her computer on, found the website, and entered her information. Five minutes later she sat back and smiled. *Hello, culinary world.*

Her phone rang while she was busy congratulating herself. It was Alison calling from downstairs, asking to be buzzed in. A minute later, she knocked at J.J.'s door, opening it at the same time.

"This is a surprise. Not working tonight? Do you actually have the weekend off?"

Alison dropped her red puffy jacket on a chair. "I'm on days so I won't stay late, but I thought I'd deliver my news in person." She glanced toward the kitchen.

"Would you like coffee or wine?"

"Mm, wine, please, and thanks." Alison waited at the eating bar while J.J. poured two glasses of red.

"It's a California cab. Hope that's okay."

"Beggars can't be choosers, and you know, I'll drink anything." She took a sip. "This is quite nice."

"Great. Now, spill the beans, not the wine."

Alison pulled her down on the love seat beside her. "I spent my lunch hour in the station going through old files, and this time found a memo outlining Miranda's request to interview a police officer for a story she was working on."

"Great. What was the topic?"

"Do the movies and TV shows get it right? She outlined the questions she planned to ask—things like, how much of the police part in popular shows is fact and how much is fiction? Standard questions. A fluff piece. I wonder if the cop was on the clock or volunteered. Does he even watch the show?"

"Does he have a name?"

"His name is Sergeant Beau Watts."

"Do you know him?"

"Oh yeah. It wouldn't surprise me at all if he had an affair with her. He's got quite the reputation around the station, even though he's married. Fortunately, no kids."

"So, you know for certain it was him? There were no switches at the last minute?"

Alison shook her head and her straight long blonde hair gently swirled. Although she always wore it in a ponytail or totally pinned up for work, she usually preferred to let it hang loose in off hours. J.J. thought it softened her look. "Doesn't seem to be."

"You're a rock star, Detective Alison. So, what's the next step?"

"Well, I can't really go and ask him. For one thing, he's a higher rank, and for another, there's no proof they were having an affair. It's all hearsay. And furthermore, it's not my case." She took another sip.

J.J. stood and started pacing. "I hear what you're saying, but I think hearsay trumps caution. It's a lead, isn't it? If you really were a detective, wouldn't you be following it?"

"Yes, but when confronting a cop, you need more than gossip. And it's pretty dicey for someone in my position to be asking those kinds of questions."

"Well, I'll do it, in that case."

"And you think a seasoned cop is going to admit to you that he was having an affair with a murder victim?" Alison's face said far more than her tone of voice.

"Well, okay, maybe not when you put it that way, but he might just blurt out something incriminating anyway, thinking, *what could I possibly do to hurt him?*"

Alison shrugged. "Doubt it. He's good."

"Fine. Well, so is Devine, so it's obviously got to be his task. I'll call him and maybe you can fill him in on the sergeant's schedule or something?"

"Go for it."

J.J. tried calling, but got his voice mail. *Bummer.* "He seems to be unavailable. I'll let him know when I talk to him. Do you think our guy could be a murderer?"

Alison looked a bit startled. She gave it some thought. "I'd like to say no, but I have no idea. I don't know him well enough, and as much as I'd like to think a cop wouldn't do anything illegal, I lost my naïveté a long time ago."

J.J. nodded. Not much that could be said to that.

After Alison left, J.J. sat flipping through *The French Market* by Joanne Harris and Fran Warde, one of her go-to cookbooks when she wanted to be soothed. She loved the photos of the produce in the outdoor markets, the scenery, and, of course, the finished dishes. Indie jumped up on her lap when she was partway through, and she had to shift the large hardcover to lean it on the arm of the love seat. After the necessary kneading session, Indie settled and kept up the purring for a while. He was not happy when J.J. eventually shifted him off her lap and onto the warm spot where she'd been sitting.

She was just climbing into bed when the phone rang. Devine.

"I see you called."

She felt caught off guard. Of course he would check his calls even though she hadn't left a message. "I have some information I wanted to share; however, I'm just going to bed. It will have to wait till tomorrow."

"You sure I shouldn't come over now?" She could hear the teasing in his voice.

She looked down at the nightshirt. *There's nothing like a good book in bed!* it read. *No way.*

"Tomorrow will be fine. Do you want to stop by the office or should we meet at Cups 'n' Roses for coffee?"

"Cups 'n' Roses at nine."

"Fine. See you then."

"Sweet dreams, J.J."

Oh, sure.

CHAPTER 28

Devine sat in J.J.'s favorite booth, facing the door as she entered. She gave him a small wave and then felt like chopping off her hand. *How cutesy.* She queued in line for her order and in no time had her large latte, and after a brief chat with Beth, joined him.

"So, you caught your noontime thief?" Devine asked. "And you didn't think to tell me last Friday?"

"I guess I got so caught up in the other stuff. How did you know? I know, you're a private eye. And besides, Beth told you."

"She did." He saluted her with his mug. "But she didn't have an ending to the story. What happened to the woman?"

J.J. shrugged. "Beth decided not to call the cops and instead, gave her a job."

"She what?"

"Yeah. Apparently the woman had been living in her car since her divorce from the jerk husband. Now she has a job, a place to stay, and no reason to steal. It's so Beth."

"I hope she knows what she's doing."

"I'm sure she does." J.J. took a long drink. She didn't really want to go into any more detail about Beth's business, although she supposed Devine had a right to ask. He had tried to help.

He sat looking at her for a few seconds before asking, "So, what's the information you have for me?"

"I have the name of the police officer who was having an affair with Miranda."

Devine looked suitably impressed. "How and who?"

"Alison has been checking whenever possible, and she came across a memo from Miranda asking to interview him. I'm guessing that's how it started."

"Probably. So is she going to confront him?"

"She doesn't want to partly because he's a higher rank. And, it's not even her case."

"I can understand that." His eyebrows knit together. "You're not planning to jump in and tackle him, are you?"

J.J. leaned back. "As much as I'd like to, I realize he won't tell me a thing. Why would he? I could tell Detective Hastings, but then we'd be cut out of it completely."

"We."

J.J. nodded.

"You're thinking I should confront him."

"Of course. Who better to do it?"

"I'm not disputing that. In fact, I would insist on doing it. I'm just surprised you're caving so easily. Why are you caving so easily?"

She shrugged. "If I tried anything, he'd be alerted, and being a cop, he'd know how to divert suspicion. In fact, it's probably because he's a cop that his name hasn't entered into this sooner, don't you think?"

"Not many people have mentioned she was having an affair. She kept it well hidden. I think that's the real reason. Everyone was focused on Connor Mac as being the main person in her life."

"Hm. I wonder if he knew?"

"And did what, killed her because she was two-timing him?"

J.J. squeaked. "I didn't mean that. Besides, I think Connor must be the reason she broke off her engagement to Zane Anderson. She never really forgot him. That's why they were back together. So, what if Zane gets angry because he's not used to rejection, and he starts following her, sees her with Connor at the casino night, and kills her in a jealous rage."

"You've got it all figured out."

"Well, it could have happened that way."

"Did you see him at the event? And was there a fast flight to Turks and Caicos the next day?"

"We don't even know when he left. It might have been after the event. And I don't know what he looks like, so I wouldn't be able to spot him. But, that reminds me, I was looking through the shots again last night, and I spotted Fletcher Kane there. He definitely said he wasn't there."

"No, as I recall, he talked about his candidate's alibi."

"But, he could have said, *Gary Myers wasn't there blah, blah, but I was.*"

"If you'll recall, he wasn't too thrilled about having to keep talking to us at that point." Devine sighed. "You're all over the map. We'll eliminate the males in this picture one at a time."

"Okay. But I want to check through the photos and see if Sergeant Beau Watts was at the event. Do you think you can get me a picture of him so that I can compare it to the others?"

"Maybe your friend Alison has some group shot or something with him in it. If not, I'll do my best. Let's go back to Fletcher Kane. You're thinking he could be the killer? But if so, what's his motive?"

"I really don't have a clue. And there are none that point

to him. I wasn't specifically looking for him, but there he was, and after just telling us he wasn't, or so it seemed." She sat staring at her empty mug. This was getting confusing.

Devine put his hand over hers. "You're thinking about it too much. Go do your real work and let this simmer on a back burner for today. I'll take care of the Sergeant Beau Watts angle and let you know when I've got something."

"Fine," she said, sighing.

"And by the way, I checked on Anderson's movements, and he really had left on his holiday the week before the event."

"Hm. He was a long shot anyway."

J.J. knocked on Evan's office door before going upstairs to her own office. He called out to her and she entered.

"Hope I'm not disturbing you," she said, looking around at the empty office. Not with a client, anyway.

"Not at all. I'm just trying to narrow down the choice of kitchen sinks and faucets for my client. She has such a tough time making up her mind, so leaves it to me to narrow it down to a few that will absolutely work and then attempts to make the final choice." He waved his hand over the worktable where he was sitting, placed in the far corner of the room next to the natural light coming in through the side window. "What's on your mind?"

"Connor. I can't believe we have nothing more to go on."

Evan shook his head. "He should write a book on how not to be found. What if he's moved on, as in out of the state? Maybe he realized he'd been spotted or something."

"That's possible. But where would he go next? We haven't heard of any other friends. In fact, don't you think that's strange? I never realized before how little I know about his life, and it sounds like no one in Culinary Capers is any more tuned in, either. Why don't we know more about his life? Has he been deliberately keeping it private?"

"That's a pretty safe guess. He's a good media person, able to get the information out of someone without giving much away. I hadn't thought about it, either. I've known him for a couple of years, but I don't know any of his other friends. I'm pretty sure his parents both passed a long time ago, though, and he never mentions any siblings." Evan leaned back against the worktable, crossed his arms, and stared at the ceiling. "Do you think there's a reason?"

"What? Like he's hiding out in plain sight in Half Moon Bay?"

Evan grinned. "Maybe he's in witness protection."

"Not likely he'd have his own radio show in that case. That does sort of point out something else, though."

"What's that?"

"How easy it is to let our imaginations run away with us." She grinned.

"Right. Connor is just . . . Connor." Evan walked over to J.J. and placed a hand on each of her arms. "I don't think there's anything else we can do to help him until he wants us to. Are there any other leads on the killer's identity?"

"Devine and I have come up with one more suspect. Don't give me that look. Devine is turning out to be a big help."

"All right. Teasing time is over. Who is this mystery person?"

"Well, Alison found out the name of the cop Miranda had an affair with, so Devine's looking into him. And we also visited the campaign office of her brother, Gary Myers, and spoke to his campaign manager."

"You don't think the brother did it?" Evan sounded shocked.

J.J. shook her head. "No, but Fletcher Kane, his campaign manager, gave off some strange vibes. We want to talk to some of the other staff, too, so we'll try to get to that in the next day or so."

"When do you have time to work?" Evan asked with a wicked grin.

"Huh. I happen to be a very organized person and manage to fit it all in. And if you believe that," J.J. added, opening the door, "I'd like to organize a party for you."

CHAPTER 29

She was still thinking about Connor as she checked through her e-mails. A few minutes later, Skye walked in with a big smile on her face and two large lattes in her hands. "I took a chance you'd be still thirsty," she said as she set one cup in front of J.J.

"Yum. Thanks. You look happy. Eventful lunch?"

"Yes, but not in that way. I had a delightful breakfast meeting with Nick and the president of the dental association, and we now have a contract to do their Christmas party."

"As in three months."

"That would be Christmas."

"This may be Make It Happen, but it can't happen. That's only three months of planning. But you agreed, didn't you?"

"Of course I did. We don't have to come up with original ideas, just be original in how we combine them. And the group is about one hundred and fifty, so it shouldn't be too hard to find a venue. It's the smaller ones that get booked up first. It can be done, but I'm going to need your help. Are you in?"

"Of course. It will be over and done with before I hit any of my major deadlines. I'm assuming you've already chosen the place."

"I have, but I do have to check if it's available." She sat at her desk and started her computer. "Thanks."

"Don't mention it. Do you want to start talking about it?"

"Give me a bit of time to formulate something and then we can bash it all around."

"You got it."

A couple of hours later, J.J. stood and stretched. She usually moved around more when spending long stretches at her computer, but she'd been lost in expanding the bible about the VPTA conference. But she'd been vaguely aware of Skye working away at the whiteboard. When J.J. looked over, Skye was fleshing out the details for the dental association Christmas party, with bullet points of ideas listed.

"What do you think?" she asked J.J. "I've tossed out some ideas and welcome any comments and additional brain waves." She walked back to her desk and leaned against it, arms folded across her chest.

J.J. walked over to take a closer look. Then she went back to her chair and sat, still looking at the board, keeping her face totally noncommittal. She sat forward and propped her chin on her hand, eyes scanning the board.

Finally Skye made an exasperated sound. "All right. You're torturing me. Just tell me what you think."

J.J. started laughing. "I wanted you to know that I take this all quite seriously."

"Duly noted. And, your thoughts?"

"My first reaction is, thank God there's no Santa, at this party, anyway. And I love the idea of most of the decorations being live plants that can be raffled off at the end of the evening. Thanks for thinking of People and Causes. The money will be appreciated."

"I thought so."

"It's a brilliant idea to cross-pollinate our accounts, so to speak."

"I can handle brilliant." Skye beamed. "So, the rest looks like it will work? The cocktail stations, the food stations, the menu? Do you think they'd prefer a sit-down dinner?"

"I'll bet they're used to a sit-down dinner, so this will be a dynamite alternative. I never asked—have you been to one of these before?"

"A couple of times."

"And, sit-down dinner?"

Skye nodded.

"Boring," they said in unison.

Still laughing, J.J. nodded. "This sounds like it will be a wonderful evening. And you didn't even need my help."

"Oh, but you did help," Skye objected. "You approved, and that's what I needed to hear. I'm out of the office for the rest of the day. See you tomorrow."

"Of course," J.J. answered just as her phone rang.

"Meet me for dinner?" Devine asked without even saying *hi*. "I've had a visit with Sergeant Beau Watts."

J.J. glanced at the clock. "All right. Where and when?"

"Do you know the Battered Boathouse?"

"I know it's new and I know where it is, but I've never eaten there."

"How about at six?"

"See you."

She tried to analyze his tone. Was this an aha moment? Was the sergeant the killer? *Was this a date?*

She shook her head. Devine's voice never gave away anything.

What a pity.

She studied the menu with more concentration than necessary. She didn't want to look up at Devine. There was

something about him tonight, maybe the sparkling blue
eyes that challenged her equilibrium, more than usual.
She'd rise above it with a little food in front of her.

"I'm impressed by their menu. I've never even heard of
calamari *fritti*. Oh man, grilled octopus." She made a face
and looked at Devine. He grinned. "I love seafood but
pictures would have been good," she added with a small
laugh. Nerves.

"I've heard that about you." He joined in her laughter.
"Well, I can highly recommend the steelhead trout with
navy bean succotash." He lowered his menu and closed it.

"You've decided already? I know, you have been here
before. So are you going with what you've had before or
are you trying something new? How about the braised
goat? What's that doing on the menu? I thought it was
seafood." *What am I doing? Stop this inane chatter.*

He laughed a bit louder, sounding seriously amused this
time. "They have one non-fish special each day. Hm,
braised goat. Might be an idea."

She glanced at him to see how serious he was. She
couldn't tell. *Still not able to read him.*

By the time the server arrived with their drinks, a glass
of merlot for her, scotch neat for him, they were ready to
order.

She took a sip of her wine. "So, give."

He looked at her over the rim of his glass. "So, I tracked
Watts to where he was having lunch. Actually, it wasn't that
difficult. He ate at the diner a few blocks over from the
police station. It's usually the local lunch spot for cops, but
he was alone so I grabbed a coffee, slid into the booth, and
introduced myself. We talked shop a bit, and then I said we
had someone in common. When I mentioned Miranda
Myers, we weren't best buddies any longer. He wouldn't
say anything about her, except that she'd interviewed him
once, and he'd read she was dead, but that was it. He finished off his sandwich and left, hastily, if you ask me."

"So you didn't really get anything except maybe listed in his bad books."

Devine grinned. "I got under his skin, and he knows that I know. I'll let him stew overnight and then stop by the police station. He might want to keep me quiet in that setting and agree to tell me what he knows."

"Great." She let out a pent-up sigh. "I wish we had a major clue that had the killer's name written all over it. I also wish this didn't feel so much like that proverbial needle in a haystack."

"I've learned over time that sometimes what you're looking for is right in front of you, J.J."

CHAPTER 30

J.J.'s stop on the way home from the office the next day was at Connor's apartment. She'd been thinking about what Devine had said last night. Could Connor be right in front of them, perhaps? Back in his own apartment? She'd run out of other possibilities.

She started at the garage and peeked in as they'd done what seemed like a long time ago, but was really only a couple of weeks, she realized. No car. But that might not mean anything. Connor wouldn't park it there and announce he was back if he was avoiding the police and everyone else, for that matter. Nor would he let anyone into the building, she realized.

She went to the front door and hung around, waiting for someone to go through it. To seem a little less sinister, she took out her phone and pretended to be talking on it, possibly waiting for a friend. She hoped that's what she looked like.

Finally, a preppy guy in his midtwenties, possibly heading to the college, came out and gallantly held the door open for her. She smiled her thanks and kept on talking, wanting to avoid any questions or explanations. She paused outside of Connor's condo. She knew that putting her ear to the door was unlikely to enlighten her. These units were usually soundproof. She did it anyway.

After a couple of minutes, she knocked on the door, standing in front of the peephole. She could only hope that if he were in there, he'd not feel threatened by seeing it was her. She tried again, debating how long she should stand there. One more try and then she turned to walk away. *Where is he?*

She made it to the elevator a couple of units over, when she heard a door open and looked back. Connor stood in the hallway outside his door. He didn't make any motions, but J.J. took that to be a welcome of some form. She hurried back and stood looking at him, not sure what to say.

He opened the door wider and she walked in.

"You don't know how relieved I am to find you here, and in one piece," she said, trying to keep an even voice. She walked straight into the living room without an invitation and turned to watch him following her. "We've all been frantic. And the police have been furious."

Connor looked embarrassed but determined. "I had some thinking to do."

"And you didn't think to let any of us know that you were just getting away for *a few days*? We wondered if you'd been in a car accident and injured. The police thought you'd run away, a sure sign of guilt."

He motioned her to sit down. She plunked herself in the nearest chair and watched as he sat in the matching leather club chair on the other side of the ottoman. She was trying to read him but couldn't. All of a sudden he wasn't the Connor she knew. She waited for an answer.

He leaned forward, elbows on his knees. "I'm sorry, J.J. I just wasn't thinking. I felt like my guts had been pulled out, and all I wanted to do was run away from it all. I don't expect you or anyone to understand."

J.J. took a deep breath. "I know this hit you hard. I do understand that. It's just that we're your friends and want to help in any way we can. Instead, you've shut us out." She wondered if a little levity would help. "And, you've missed some good dinners with the gang."

That earned a small smile. He sighed. "I'm sorry. I just wasn't thinking, but I'm back and I'm staying."

"Good. I'm glad to hear that, but you've got to call Detective Hastings and set it straight with the police before they find you. That would make it much worse."

"You're right. But I don't know what else I can tell them. I've been trying to puzzle it through. I still can't think of anyone who would want to hurt Miranda." He sighed. Such a lonely sound.

J.J. thought it best not to mention anything she'd learned. Instead, she said, "I'm pretty sure they've got other suspects on their list by now, but disappearing put you near the top. So, just call him. First thing tomorrow, please."

Connor nodded.

"I hate to ask you anything that's upsetting, but did Miranda talk about anything that was bothering her in particular lately?"

"I tried to go over all that had happened lately. She did mention something about her sister-in-law one time. It had something to do with her brother's campaign manager."

J.J. gasped. "Do you know what she meant by that?"

"I have no idea, but it wasn't really any of my business. She didn't volunteer anything more. We were out at dinner, and she said it just because I asked what was on her mind. I didn't think anything more about it. Why, do you think it's tied to her death?" He winced when he said the last word.

She shrugged. "I don't know. You didn't ask her anything more about it?"

"I didn't know she'd soon be dead. Had I known that, there're a lot of things I would have done differently.

Believe me. I didn't really pay attention. I guess I didn't pay attention to a lot of things over the years."

J.J. could figure out where the conversation was heading. He confirmed it with his next statement.

"Look, J.J. I'm sorry if I might have given you the wrong impression. I wasn't trying to lead you on. I thought we were good friends."

"We *are* good friends, Connor. I didn't expect or want anything more than that. Believe me. Now the only thing that's important is to figure out who the killer is and get you off the hook. Promise me you'll talk to Detective Hastings tomorrow."

He nodded. "I will."

She gave him a big hug and a small kiss on the cheek, and left.

CHAPTER 31

It took J.J. a long time to fall asleep. She sat up for hours while going over everything Connor had said. It had reinforced her belief in his innocence. She had to trust that he would indeed follow through and call Detective Hastings in the morning. She hoped he would, because that was a call she didn't want to make.

She also stewed about not having heard all day from Devine. Surely he'd been back to talk to Watts. She was itching to know what had happened. Was he now cutting her out of the scene? *That man!*

Indie wasn't happy with her restlessness. He kept jumping on the bed and snuggling down only to jump off when she would turn over. Finally, after a check on the time—three A.M.—they both fell asleep.

Her clock radio went on at its usual six thirty, and J.J. struggled to open her eyes. She knew she had to get out of bed right away or she was doomed. If she fell back asleep, bad dreams and a day of sloth would follow.

She fumbled her way to the kitchen and got an espresso going, then backtracked to the bathroom. Her eyes eventually stayed open, and she headed back to the espresso machine. Indie demanded his breakfast, so she tended to that first and then sat at the counter, sipping her elixir.

She needed to call Devine. He might not be too pleased that she waited until morning to fill him in. Of course, Hastings would be upset, also. But that wasn't her call to make.

She punched in Devine's number and was surprised when he answered on the first ring. She explained her talk with Connor, and he told her he'd be over in half an hour, before she left for work. That woke her up. She let out a small shriek, which startled Indie and sent him running toward her bedroom. She followed, and less than fifteen minutes later had showered, played with her hair, and dressed in a navy business suit with a navy and white polka-dot blouse. She had a meeting with her client later in the afternoon, and she wanted the extra confidence the suit gave her when meeting with Devine.

Devine had two lattes in hand when he arrived. She gratefully accepted one and drank nearly half before acknowledging that he was sitting at her counter, waiting to hear her story. When she told it, she waited while he had an equally long drink before talking.

"What made you think to check out his apartment?"

"What you said about something being right in front of you." She was mortified to feel her cheeks getting hotter. She hoped he'd put it down to the coffee.

"Well, it was good detecting. Do you believe him about talking to Hastings?"

She nodded with more assurance than she actually felt. "He just needed some time alone. He wasn't running. He's innocent and knows the real killer will be found."

Devine snorted. "Okay, let's see what we can do to help

move this along. What was the first thing that came to mind when he talked about Miranda's concerns?"

"I thought that something hinky might be going on between Yolande Myers and the campaign manager."

"Hinky?" His eyebrows rose in amusement. "As in having an affair?"

"No, I didn't go straight there. I was thinking something to do with the campaign, but I'm not sure what." She paused and gave it some thought. "But it could be an affair, couldn't it?"

She looked at Devine, who didn't comment. He seemed to be encouraging her to keep going.

"Okay," she said, getting more into the idea, "but that doesn't make a whole lot of sense. He doesn't seem her type at all. I can't imagine them together."

He chuckled. "You could be right, but sometimes the oddest couples get together."

"But if it's true, what would Miranda have done about it? It's right in the middle of her brother's campaign. It would be quite a scandal, wouldn't it? If it got out?" She drew in a quick breath. "You don't think Miranda threatened to expose it, do you? No, she wouldn't do that and hurt her brother's campaign. But she might tell her brother. He would fire his campaign manager, but there must be other people around qualified to step in. He may have been devastated, though, and not able to carry on. Or, being a political being, he could have taken it in stride. And maybe he would agree to stay with his wife until after the election. So, why kill Miranda over it?"

Devine sat there grinning.

"What?"

"You realize you've just had an entire conversation with yourself and come to the conclusion that it wouldn't be a motive for murder?"

J.J. grimaced. "I could be wrong. What do you think?"

"I think you could be right or wrong. We don't know how the brother would react to that news, and once one person knows, it's hard to keep it secret. All it would take is someone to overhear something or any number of possibilities."

"So, one—are they having an affair? And two—is Yolande Myers or Fletcher Kane the killer?"

Devine thought for a few minutes. "I don't know any of those answers. Not enough information. But it's worth digging into, that's for sure. We need to hit that campaign office this morning, if Kane is out, especially now that we have something more specific to be asking. I'll make the call to check on his whereabouts as soon as it opens."

"And do you plan on telling me what happens this time?"

Devine looked confused.

"You didn't get back to me about Sergeant Watts. You did meet up with him again, didn't you?"

Devine hit his forehead with the heel of his hand and looked to be in the throes of remorse. "Oh my God, I'm so sorry. How could I have forgotten to put a hold on my investigating an insurance fraud that was about to be solved and call you about a meeting that yielded nothing?"

She didn't know what urge was stronger—to smack him or laugh. "Forget the dramatics. What happened?"

"I stopped in at the station. He saw me coming and walked the other way, so I walked into Hastings's office and we had a chat. I don't know what happened after that. Really, that's it. Now, are you on your way to work?"

"As you've pointed out on occasion, I do have a job, so, yes."

"I sort of thought that you looked dressed to persuade rather than to sit alone at home." He grinned.

J.J. sat eyeing the clock that hung above the filing cabinet in her office. It was getting close to noon and Devine still hadn't called. He wouldn't have gone to the campaign headquarters by himself, would he have? She didn't really know the answer to that. She didn't entirely trust him; that much was for sure. Maybe she should just go over on her own. If they left it too much longer, it would be time for her client meeting. She hated not knowing.

Devine wouldn't like it, but she had a life, too. She grabbed her jacket and purse and practically sprinted down the stairs to the parking lot. What would she do if Fletcher Kane were in his office? She didn't want to see him just yet. She was really hoping that Dawn, the friendly volunteer, would be the one who was working at that moment. Maybe she could help fold and stuff envelopes for a couple of hours and slide in the questions along the way. But what would she ask? *Do you know if your candidate's wife is having an affair with your candidate's campaign manager?* Not likely. Something would come to her.

She pulled into the only empty spot in the lot next to the headquarters. She took a good look at the street for any signs of Devine, but his car wasn't to be seen. Maybe she should have waited. Or maybe he'd already been and gone. This was not a time to be indecisive.

She walked in and immediately spotted Dawn at the same moment as the volunteer saw her. Dawn waved her over, and J.J. obliged, glancing toward Kane's office. He wasn't in there but he could be lurking in a back room or something. She'd have to be cautious about what she said.

"How's the pile of paper going?" J.J. asked as she sat in a chair across the desk from Dawn.

Dawn grinned. "I finished it that day." She waved her hand over her desk. "And now I have a new pile."

"Do you know if Fletcher Kane is in?" She glanced in the direction of his office. "I want to ask him a few things."

"He'll be out of the office most of the day, but if you

have any spare time, we could sure use your help doing some stuffing," Dawn pleaded, a grin on her face.

Hah! As I'd hoped. "Well, I can spare a half hour if that helps. I wouldn't want this to be a wasted trip."

"That's great. All we're doing is stuffing from that box to that stack of envelopes."

"I can manage that," J.J. acknowledged, and removed her suit jacket, hanging it on the back of the chair.

"You look very businesslike today." Dawn looked down at her own copper-colored textured pullover. J.J.'s eyes followed along, admiring how it offset her auburn hair.

"You're the second person who's told me that. And here I always thought I looked like I meant business." She smiled.

"Oops. I'm sure you do," Dawn said, giggling. She glanced over at the door. "Hey, isn't that your friend?"

J.J. followed her gaze to an unhappy-looking Devine. She knew a forced smile when she saw one.

"Hi," he said as he looked at the name tag and added, "Dawn." That smile was genuine.

J.J. wasn't quite sure what to say without pandering or giving things away to Dawn. So she said nothing.

"I'm glad you've found a way to be useful. Don't let me disturb anything," Devine said, then wandered to a table at the back of the room where two young blondes were taking a coffee break. They broke into wide smiles as he approached, and J.J. quickly shifted her attention back to the flyers.

"Are you two an item?" Dawn asked.

"What?"

"Well, it's just that you seem mad at each other, and the way you looked at each other when he came in. Seems like something's going on. Or am I sticking my nose into it? Everyone's always telling me I do that, but I'm, like, interested. Okay, nosy."

"No. It's all right." She tried to gauge Dawn. Could she just ask her straight out? "You know I'm an event coordinator and I organized the casino night where Miranda Myers was murdered."

Dawn nodded.

"Well, I'm trying to figure out what happened."

"What about the police? Wait, none of my business. It's just so freaky and sad. Gary hasn't shown up here much since it happened, and when he does, you can tell how hard it is for him to hold it together. We all feel so bad for him."

"Do you know his wife?"

"Yolande? Of course. She helps here sometimes. She's pretty upset, too."

That wasn't the impression J.J. had, but she tried to keep from showing her surprise. "And Miranda. I know she helped out here sometimes."

"Oh yeah. She was real cool. A big TV personality like that. And the dynamite clothes with that fab figure. I know the guys in here were drooling."

"So, everyone liked her? She didn't have any arguments with anyone?"

"No way."

"Ouch." J.J. looked embarrassed. "Sorry, I just got a paper cut. I shouldn't make such a big deal of it."

"I get those all the time and they hurt. Go ahead and swear if you want."

J.J. laughed. "Maybe not out loud. Do you have a bandage? I don't want to muck up the flyers."

Dawn pulled a box out of the drawer and handed it to J.J. "You know, I think she did get into it one day with Fletcher."

J.J. finished covering the cut and then looked at Dawn. "What do you mean? An argument?"

"Well, I'm not too sure, but it sort of looked like it. She looked mad when she walked in, and she went straight to his office. She didn't even stop to say hi to any of us, and that wasn't like her. I couldn't hear anything of course, but it did look like she was arguing. He just stood there in that controlled way of his, but he didn't look too happy."

"When was that?"

"Oh, I'm not sure, a month ago maybe."

"What about Yolande? Did she ever get mad at Fletcher?"

Dawn scrunched her face, like she was thinking it over. "Not like that. She was in his office with the door closed one day, and he did all the talking. When she walked out, her face was beet red and she left right away. You know, I'm not being nosy all the time. My desk does face his office."

J.J. smiled. "Being observant is always a good thing." She glanced over at the back table. "I think I'll grab some coffee. Is that all right? Can I get some for you?"

"Oh, sure. Just help yourself. Yeah, I'd like some. One sugar, lots of milk. Thanks."

J.J. went straight to the coffee machine on the table, trying to listen at the same time to what Devine was saying to the two blondes who were still there. There was a lot of laughing going on. *Humph.*

She didn't hear him come up behind her, and she almost dropped the milk she was pouring into Dawn's coffee.

"How's it going?"

"Just fine. Dawn is very observant. How about your friends?"

"I think we should compare notes. Are you about ready to leave?"

"After I finish this coffee. I don't want to be too abrupt about it, but I have that client meeting in an hour."

"How about we meet at McCreedy's for a drink around five? Or are you planning on coming back here to do some more nosing around?"

She made a face but knew he couldn't see it. "McCreedy's it is."

J.J. drank her coffee quickly as she finished her pile of flyers and listened with half an ear to Dawn as she continued talking about the campaign itself. Part of her brain was trying to figure out what all the arguing meant.

And was it a motive for murder?

CHAPTER 32

Devine was waiting for her when she walked through the front door of McCreedy's. Her meeting had been delayed and then went longer than expected because of continuous interruptions. Her client apologized but explained they were on a deadline. J.J. decided it was better to keep her thoughts to herself.

"What would you like?" he asked as she sat across from him.

"A glass of wine, thanks. The house red is fine."

"Busy afternoon?"

She grimaced. "Let's not go there."

"Okay. Let's go back to the campaign office, then." He sat looking at her.

She shrugged and raised her palms. "I gave up waiting. I thought you'd gone on your own, and I had this meeting coming up, so I just drove over."

"What if Fletcher Kane had been there?"

"I would have thought of something. Maybe signed up as a volunteer."

"It looked like that's what you'd done."

"I thought if we were working together, she'd be more willing to talk."

"And?" He took a sip of his scotch while J.J. filled him in.

"So is that suspicious or what?"

"It could mean anything. Or it could be that Miranda knew about an affair, and he tried to convince her not to talk."

"And his confrontation with Yolande?"

"Lovers' spat?" Devine's eyebrows shot up in a question mark.

"Hmm. What about you? Did you learn anything from those staffers, aside from their phone numbers?"

"Ouch. You really don't have a very high opinion of me, do you?"

J.J. felt immediately chastised. "I'm sorry. That was sort of catty."

"You think? Anyway, I did learn something. There's gossip that the manager is having an affair, not with Yolande Myers, but with someone in the office. Nobody has a clue who it is, though, so it could be pure conjecture. There are no rumblings whatsoever about him and Yolande, so either they're extremely careful or it's not happening."

"I sort of hate to see that theory get thrown out."

"It seems to me I've heard that before. As an investigator, you can't get too attached to any theory. It's just that until you have proof."

"Ah, so now you think of me as an investigator." She smiled, Cheshire-like.

"That's not at all how I think about you." Her spine tingled at the suggestive tone of his voice. But it disappeared at his next words. "But that's how you seem to see yourself, so I'm just saying."

J.J. tried to hide her confusion. "I haven't tried calling Connor today to see how it went."

"Why don't you give him a call right now? I'm also curious as to what the police said."

She nodded and pulled out her smartphone. It went to voice. "You don't think they locked him up, do you?"

He shrugged. "It depends on what parts of his story they believe. Or if they have another suspect in their sights. They also might lock him up because he ran away."

"I'm calling Alison. She might know." She ended up leaving another message and heaving a sigh. "I feel there's too much going on. We need to narrow this down and focus. Who do you think are the most likely suspects?"

"Connor Mac. Sorry, but it's true. And, yes, Mikey Cooper. He swears he was mad at his dad, not at Miranda. But you never know—it could have gotten out of control."

"What about Hennie Ferguson?"

He shrugged. "Could be, but highly unlikely. She doesn't really have one strong motive, unless she did it to help Mikey. She could be an accomplice, in that case."

J.J. nodded. "What about the cop?"

"Still a possibility, but I bet Hastings is all over him right about now."

"Okay. That leaves the campaign manager. Or the sister-in-law. Or both. But I don't think we know enough yet. It's a lot of supposition."

"I'm glad you admit that, but that doesn't give you carte blanche to go back and do some more snooping. Word will get back to Kane, and if he is involved, it could get dangerous."

"Maybe that's what we need in order to draw him out."

Devine leaned forward, his voice strong but low. "Haven't you had enough of being in danger? If you'll recall, it was just some months ago that someone tried to run you down when you got too close to the truth. And that was before being tied up and threatened."

J.J. shuddered. "I know. I try not to think about it. But you're involved here. You'll take care of me."

He grinned. "I'm trying. Believe me. It would be a hell of a lot easier if you just stayed removed from danger to start with."

"So far, so good."

"Or so you think. The killer might already have you in his or her sights. You've been asking enough questions."

"Not if it's the cop. He knows nothing about me. I think." She crossed her fingers.

"And I think maybe you've done enough. It's obvious the police are closing in on the killer."

"How is that obvious? Have you asked them?"

He shook his head, and she could tell he was getting a bit impatient with her. "I've been there, remember? I'm sure they've checked all the bases that we have and even more. They can dig deeper. Just find out what happened to Connor Mac. If he's not in jail, then I'd say they have their sights on the killer. And it's just a matter of time until they make their move."

CHAPTER 33

J.J. wished she could believe Devine. She'd tried to convince herself as she got ready for bed the night before and was still doing so in the morning when she got ready for work. She'd even had a heart-to-heart with Indie over breakfast, hoping that saying it out loud would make it so. But to no avail.

Now, sitting at her computer in the office, she tried to keep her mind on her work and the fiftieth wedding anniversary coming up. Time to double-check that all the arrangements would happen as planned. But she knew the thought was hovering there, ready to take over at any moment. So, she reasoned, the best thing to do was to confront it head-on and either make her peace with it or do something about it. That last thought brought an image of an upset Devine to mind, and she grabbed the phone immediately when it rang.

She was relieved to hear Connor's voice. "How did it go? Where are you?"

"I'm not in jail, if that's what you mean. Look, I'm sorry

I didn't return any of your calls yesterday. I was feeling pretty bummed out after spending a good chunk of the day at the police station."

"What happened?"

"Well, Detective Hastings is still really upset that I left town and has warned me not to do that again, but he admitted they were looking in another direction for the killer."

"Did they mention any names?"

"No, and I didn't ask. Right now, I just want to try to put this all out of my mind. I'm not going back to work until next week, and I'm going to spend the next few days trying to get my life back to normal. I just wanted to thank you for believing in me, J.J."

"Of course I believe in you. We're friends and that's what friends do."

"Thanks."

She was sort of surprised that he hung up without a formal good-bye, but she had what she needed from him. She knew he was all right and he was not in jail. She also knew it would probably take quite some time for Connor to be back to his old self, if ever. He had the Culinary Capers members to help, if he needed any, but other than that, they'd just be there for him.

She was a bit annoyed that he hadn't pressed Hastings for any details, though. Maybe that's the action she needed to be taking. She quickly finished off the e-mail, printed a copy for their files, saved a copy, and hit Send.

She was just about to leave the office when her phone rang again. This time is was her mom.

"Honey, I'm sorry to bother you, but I wanted to ask if you're able to come home not this weekend but the following one?"

"Why, Mom? What's up?" *You're not making an announcement, are you? About a separation?* "Sure, I can do that. Any special reason?"

"I'll save that for when the family is together. So, come

up either Friday night or Saturday morning, whichever works best for you. Love you."

"Yes, love you, too." She hung up and flopped back into her chair.

Skye had been watching her. "What's up?"

"I have no idea and I don't want to speculate. Either it's my worst nightmare and the folks are splitting, or Mom's got some new ingenious plan, or possibly a new guy for me."

Skye chortled. "She'll never give up, you know. A mom is always a mom. It's her task—no, her duty—to interfere with your love life. Maybe you should ask Ty Devine to go with you."

"What?" J.J. shrieked.

"It would certainly throw her off that particular track."

"You forget, she's met Devine, and if I even mention his name, she'll get the wrong impression. Asking him to go with me would be tantamount to declaring an engagement." She shuddered. "It would be safer to take Evan. Better yet, no one at all. Besides, I have no idea what's on her mind. I'll call Rory tonight. As firstborn, he usually gets let in on all the happenings. Anyway, got to go. See you after lunch."

She thought about her mother's call all the way to the police station, wondering what it could mean. When she pulled into a parking spot, she told herself that was it, no more speculating. About anything.

Detective Hastings met her in the front reception area. "I'll bet this has something to do with Connor Mac's reappearance," he said by way of greeting.

"Nice to see you also, Detective. And, it does. I'd like to ask you just a couple of things. Is that okay?"

"Fire away. I may not answer them, though."

He didn't invite her back to his office, but he hadn't shoved her out the front door, either. *Here goes.* "I take it Connor is no longer your prime suspect."

"That's not a question, it's a statement, but it is true."

"Can I ask why?"

He gave her a speculative look and then eventually answered. "He was in conversation with Megan Spicer, the board chair, at the time of the murder."

He was? Nobody told me. "How can you be so sure?"

He raised his eyebrows. "Do you now think he should be the prime suspect?"

"Oh no. I mean, how did you establish that?"

"We have a precise time of death from the autopsy, and Ms. Spicer says at that time they were talking."

"So, that gives her an alibi also." Should she have moved Megan higher on the suspect list? Apparently not.

"And you think she needs one? Maybe is manufacturing one for her own benefit?"

J.J. shrugged. "It happens, I'll bet. Not that I'm accusing her of murder."

"Good, because we aren't, either. There was a witness to this talk."

"But you do know about their former connection?"

"Indeed." He watched her a little more closely. "Maybe you should join me in my office. I may have been remiss in keeping track of your activities these last weeks."

He punched in the code and held the door for her when it opened. She wondered if it had been such a wise decision to come down after all. Instead of his office, he steered her into a small cafeteria and offered her a coffee. "It's actually quite good coffee."

"All right. Black, please."

There were two women in civilian dress sitting at one end of the small room. Hastings motioned her to the opposite end. When they'd taken their first sips, he demanded, "All right now, tell me who you've been talking to about this case."

Where to start? "I guess, mainly the people at the TV station, Hennie Ferguson, Lonny Chan, and Kathi Jones. For a while I thought the vandal might have done it, but

Ty Devine seems to have trounced that theory. Then there's the sister-in-law, who was overheard in argument with Miranda. And her brother's campaign manager, Fletcher Kane. And I guess you know about the cop?"

Hastings lips flatlined and he nodded.

"So, are any of the above your chief suspect these days?"

Hastings let out a noise that could have been anything from an expletive to a puff of air. "That's not something I'm about to share with you. But I will give you some advice. Once again you're playing a dangerous game here. You're not telling me anything I don't already know, so will you just go back to your office and stay out of my investigation? I assure you, we have covered all bases and will no doubt make an arrest soon."

She leaned forward. "Soon, like in the next few days?"

He rolled his eyes. Then stood. "Thank you for stopping by, Ms. Tanner. Always a pleasure to see you."

J.J. didn't want to head back to the office just yet. She wanted one more shot at Yolande, and if that didn't work out, then Fletcher Kane. She knew that Devine would be angry, but that was his problem.

She tried to formulate some questions and her approach as she drove out to the Myerses' south-end address. She was pleased to see Yolande's car parked in the driveway. She just hoped that she was in a good mood.

She didn't really look to be when she opened the door. In fact, the look on Yolande's face turned to a less welcoming one at the sight of J.J. "What do you want?"

Uh-oh. Not a good start. "I'm sorry to bother you again, but this is really important. It won't take long, and, depending on how honest you are with me, may be the last time I come by."

Yolande gazed at her, a speculative look on her face,

then opened the door and stepped back, inviting J.J. to enter.

"Thank you. It really won't take long."

"We'll just pop in here, in that case." She indicated the living room to the left, off the hall.

J.J. chose to sit in a wing chair facing the sofa. She hoped Yolande would take the hint and sit across from her, at a slightly lower level. She did.

"Now, what do you want?"

"I just need to clarify a couple of things. How well do you know Fletcher Kane?"

Yolande looked surprised. "I know him very well. As my husband's campaign manager, he drops by all the time. He stays for dinner sometimes. And I see him at most events. Why? What has he got to do with Miranda?"

"That's what I'm wondering. Apparently, they had an argument at the campaign office."

She shrugged. "So, that's not strange. And she was helping whenever she could. I suppose they clashed over one thing or the other. Miranda had a volatile personality. In fact, they both like to be in charge. That's probably all it was."

"Your name came up in it. In fact, the person who overheard it thought the argument was totally about you." J.J. held her breath, waiting for a reaction.

Yolande looked flustered. "Are you sure? You're not just saying that, are you?"

"No. Why would I do that?"

"To get me to confide in you."

J.J. shook her head. "I don't operate that way. Look, all I'm trying to do is find out who killed Miranda, and to do that, I need to eliminate what pops up as being suspicious. I'm sure the police have already asked you the same questions."

She noticed Yolande blanch at the mention of law enforcement. Was she trying to hide something illegal?

"I know you wouldn't be involved in anything illegal, but you have to understand how this looks to an outsider. Something's going on and it involves you. Both Miranda and Fletcher Kane were concerned or mad or both, and that means it has to do with your husband's campaign."

J.J. paused for effect. *Just ask.* "Are you having an affair?"

Yolande looked like she'd pass out.

"I'm sorry," J.J. said, rushing over to her. "I really didn't mean to upset you." She touched her arm, hoping that some connection might open a direct line to the truth.

The gush of tears seemed to appear out of nowhere. Yolande fumbled in her pocket and brought out a tissue, dabbing at her eyes and eventually blowing her nose. When she'd regained some composure, she said, "No, of course not. How could you think something like that?"

After a fresh bout of tears, she sniffled. "Okay, yes. And you're right, that's what the arguments were about. They both wanted me to break it off and not tell Gary. But I couldn't." Her eyes were pleading as she turned slightly to face J.J.

"We're in love, deeply in love. This isn't just a tawdry affair. My marriage hasn't been working for a long time. We both know that, but we also know that Gary's chances at winning are better if the public thinks we're a happy couple. Gary doesn't know about my affair, but he does know my feelings about the marriage. And I have told him I'll work hard at giving the world a happy couple image for him. For now."

"So, how did Miranda and Fletcher find out?"

"Fletcher has been suspicious for a while. He totally wants me in the picture all the time as the loving house-wife, but I've chosen to not always oblige him. If Fletcher asks, I'm in, but I don't want to be paraded around as the loving spouse all the time. So he hired a private detective to follow me, and now he knows. I can only guess that he told Miranda, hoping she'd talk me into changing my mind."

Private detective? Devine? No, he would have said something, wouldn't he?

"What happened after those arguments?"

"I did some soul searching and decided not to see my lover until after the election. He does understand—that's the kind of guy he is."

"Did Miranda and Fletcher know this?" J.J.'s mind was racing. Where was this leading?

"No. I didn't get a chance to tell Miranda. She was killed the next day. I did tell Fletcher, and he said, as tragic as Miranda's death was, it may have worked out for the best for my husband."

"Really? How so?"

"He thought that Miranda might use the story as a way to break into investigative journalism. That's what she always wanted to do. This TV gig was to help her build a reputation and name, but she was always on the lookout for that big story."

"Do you think she would have done that?"

"No. I know she loved her brother deeply. She would not do anything to jeopardize his future. Fletcher had it all wrong, but then again, that's what he might have done in her position. He's a shark, and while that works as a campaign manager, I wouldn't want to be his friend."

"Do you think he might resort to murdering Miranda if he truly believed she'd write the story?"

Yolande gave it a few moments of thought. "No. He's determined and he's loyal, but I also think he's a moral person who just massages that morality when it comes to politics. Murder is a totally different thing."

J.J. sat thinking for a few moments. "If so, none of this makes any sense, or maybe it does and it doesn't tie into the murder." She stood, thanking Yolande for being so candid.

Yolande remained seated but looked her in the eye. "I trust you won't spread this around?"

"No, I won't," J.J. said, and meant it. "I can see myself out."

She thought about it all the way to the office. She truly believed Yolande didn't do it. But what about Fletcher? Despite Yolande's protestations, was he willing to go for the win at any cost?

CHAPTER 34

She sat at her desk typing up her notes for next Monday's meeting with the teachers association. But the question kept nagging at her. Would Fletcher kill Miranda if he truly believed she was the type of person to torch her brother's career in favor of her own? J.J. didn't have an answer for that, but what she did have was an invitation to help out tonight at the campaign office. Dawn had sent her an e-mail asking for help stuffing more envelopes. Did they ever come to the end of those mailings envelopes? she wondered.

"You're smiling. What are you reading?" asked Skye from her desk.

"I'm going to spend my evening stuffing envelopes. Can you think of anything more exciting for a single gal to be doing?"

Skye laughed. "Actually, yes. Most anything else. Is this part of the Gary Myers campaign?"

"Uh-huh. I've just received a request from Dawn, the volunteer I told you about, to help tonight. So, I'm going. It might be a good chance to get some more intel, too."

"Hmm, intel. Now you're really sounding like you're in supersleuth mode. Why don't you ask that hunky private eye to help stuff?"

"Not his thing, I'm certain."

"But he might come in handy if you encounter hostiles when doing your sleuthing."

"Hostiles? Good word, but hardly applicable. No, I'll just be trying to get a better picture of Fletcher Kane, the campaign manager. He's pretty high up on my suspect list at the moment, but I'm very sure he won't be there tonight. Pretty tame stuff, really. What are your plans?"

"Well, we, Nick and I, are going shopping at the Pottery Barn in the Town Center." Skye stood and stretched. "I'm hoping we'll leave with some homey accent pieces for the condo. He hasn't yet gotten over his man cave phase."

"Okay. At least one of us will have an exciting evening."

"How is Connor doing?"

"He's lying low these days. He's planning to go back to work next week, but I think he's in a funk. I hope working will help. I just wish I could think of something else to do for him."

"I don't think you can do that. He's going to have to come to terms with all that's happened and find his own way back. But I'm sure your support helps."

"Thanks."

Skye's phone rang and J.J. was left to ponder Connor and then her to-do list for the day. By quitting time, she had tackled most things and placed a check mark beside them. She decided to grab a quick bite at Rocco G's before heading to her evening chores.

Rocco greeted her with a smile, a hug, and an espresso before asking what else she'd like.

"Do you have any of that wonderful rolled eggplant with smoked provolone left?" She was eyeing the chalkboard behind the counter. "How do you say that in Italian?"

"*Involtini di melanzane e provola*. And I do have one left. I can warm it up just a touch to bring it back to life."

"Sounds perfect." She took her espresso and went to sit in what was becoming her favorite spot, a table for two beside the window.

"How are things, Rocco?" she asked when he brought the plate with her food over to her.

"Life, it's *è bella*. Business is good and my new chef, she has magic in her fingers. And how about you, my friend. Is all good with you?"

"Well, I'm going to spend the evening stuffing envelopes for Gary Myers's campaign. How's that for exciting?"

"That is quite the sacrifice for one so in demand," he teased.

"It is, Rocco. Life is not so bad. And it's about to get better." She took a bite and nodded her appreciation.

CHAPTER 35

J.J. was surprised to see so few people at the campaign office. She'd thought it might be an "all hands on deck" kind of night. But besides Dawn, there were only two other women, whom she hadn't met. After introductions, Dawn steered J.J. into the back room. Fletcher Kane's office was dark as they passed by, so J.J. had been right to think stuffing envelopes would not require a campaign manager's scrutiny.

"I sure hope you don't mind working in here by your-self, but there's a lot more space to spread everything out," Dawn said, switching on the light.

"No, that's fine by me."

"Great. And I do want to thank you so much for coming to help tonight. I took you at your word. We really have fallen behind, and Fletcher wants these letters out this weekend. I don't think it will take too long to finish off. Not with all of us working at it."

"I'm happy to help, and I'm glad you called on me. Now, those letters into those envelopes?" She pointed from one box to the other.

"That's right, along with a copy of that small flyer. Just call me if you need anything." Dawn left the door open, and J.J. could hear her talking to the others.

After about twenty minutes, the other two women poked their heads around the corner and wished J.J. a good night.

"You're all finished?"

"Oh yes. We've been here since four. Time to head home for dinner. Nice to meet you and thanks. If you hadn't come in, we'd still be here."

"Glad to help." J.J. wondered how many times she'd be saying that tonight.

After a few minutes, Fletcher stepped into the room. J.J. almost dropped the envelope she was stuffing. *Where did he come from?*

"Uh, it's good of you to help us out, especially since I may have been a bit curt with you last time we met." He eased the door behind him but didn't totally close it.

J.J. wondered if she should be worried. But no, Dawn was still here. She glanced out the window into the main room, just to be sure. "That's okay. You have your turf to protect. I understand."

"What do you mean by that?"

"I knew you weren't being that forthcoming, but I wasn't sure why. I talked to Yolande today." She might as well get this out in the open and over with. She had noticed that Dawn was keeping a close eye on them. She'd be safe.

"Oh?"

"I know about the affair."

Fletcher now totally shut the door. "If she was foolish enough to tell you about it, I can only hope you'll keep that knowledge to yourself. There's still the election to think about."

"I was thinking that it could be a possible motive for murder."

"What? Why? To keep Miranda from talking? She

wouldn't do anything to hurt her brother. And Yolande would never harm her."

"Is that what you truly believe?"

"Of course. What?"

J.J. just looked at him.

"Do you think I killed her in order to keep her quiet? That's crazy." He sounded as angry as he looked. J.J. wished he weren't standing between her and the door.

He took a deep breath and unclenched his fists. "I will tell you this one time and one time only. I did not kill her. I don't think we have anything more to say to each other."

He stomped out of the room, slamming the door behind him. J.J. let out the breath she'd been holding. Maybe she should have told Devine where she was going, after all. But strangely enough, she did believe Fletcher. That wasn't an act. So, where did that leave her? With a large stack of envelopes to be stuffed. She opened the door, preferring not to be shut in so totally. About half an hour later, she saw the overhead lights in the front office flick off. Only some light from what she believed to be the lamp on Dawn's desk remained on. Must be time to close up. She worked faster.

"How is it going?" Dawn asked.

J.J. looked up in surprise. She hadn't heard Dawn enter the room. "Just a few more envelopes, then I'm done. Are you finished for the evening?"

"All finished. Everyone else has left. I have just a few loose ends to deal with." Dawn smiled. She'd worn her hair pulled back in a ponytail, which made her face look gaunt, even a bit haunted.

J.J. smiled back. "Anything else I can help with?"

"Oh yes. You can." She moved a step closer "I heard you and Fletcher talking earlier. He seemed angry when he left."

"He always seems to get mad at me. I need to filter what I say to him."

"About that. I heard you tell him you knew about the affair."

J.J. looked startled. She hoped Dawn wouldn't ask her any questions about it. "I should also learn to speak more softly."

Dawn smiled again. "That really is too bad."

"What do you mean? What does it have to do with you?"

"She said the same thing to Fletcher, namely that she knew about the affair."

"Who?" J.J. was getting a bad feeling about this conversation.

"Miranda. They were arguing in his office, and I heard her say that as I walked by."

"And?"

Dawn shrugged. "And I had to deal with it. Just like now."

"What do you mean, 'deal'?"

"Well, I couldn't let Miranda go telling anyone else about me and Gary. If his wife knew, who knows what she would do?"

She said it so matter-of-factly, J.J.'s mind went blank. But only for a few seconds.

"Wait a minute. You and Gary Myers? The two of you? You're having an affair?"

Dawn smiled again. "For quite a few months now."

Is she for real? "Did you kill Miranda?"

There had been a woman in one of the blurry photos they'd rejected who looked a bit like Dawn. She should have followed up on it. She'd meant to follow up on it.

"I had to, for Gary's sake. He needs to win this election. It means a lot to him." She pulled a knife from behind her back. A big one.

Is she nuts? J.J. tried to glance around the room, looking for a weapon. Where was her smartphone? In her purse, which was on a chair in the corner with her jacket on top of it. Could she call 911 in time? Not likely. There wasn't much space between them.

"But what about Fletcher?" J.J. knew she had to keep her talking. "If he knows, why haven't you killed him, too?"

"Because he's devoted to Gary. He wouldn't do anything to hurt his chances in the election. Fletcher might not like the idea of our affair, but I know he won't say anything."

Lovely. Now what? "Fletcher knows we're here together. Don't you think he'll put two and two together? First Miranda, now me." She shivered. "And both of us talked to him about the affair. Only it's not your affair we knew about. It's Yolande's."

"What?" Dawn looked momentarily stunned. "Yolande is also having an affair?"

"That's right. And what's more, that's what both Miranda and I talked to Fletcher about. Yolande's affair. Not yours."

Dawn's grip wavered, but she regained her concentration before J.J. had a chance to make a move. "I don't get this."

"What it means is that you killed her for nothing. And if you kill me, it will be two huge mistakes on your part."

"Oh, but I have to kill you now, because you know about Miranda. So, only one mistake." She smiled.

Is this girl for real? "What do you plan to do? Several people have seen us together tonight."

"Well, we're going to leave, and I'll tell the police that we said good-bye at our cars. And I'll actually drive off, but you will be found at some point, dead in your car."

A frisson of cold slithered down J.J.'s back. She knew about good-byes in parking lots and bodies left behind. She couldn't think of a thing to do while they were inside, though, unless she could spot a weapon or at least a shield. Maybe she'd have a chance of getting away once outside. If she could distract Dawn. And then run.

"All right. Let's get it over with." J.J. tried to keep her voice calm. She didn't want Dawn to realize how she was almost paralyzed with fear.

Dawn looked surprised but gestured for J.J. to grab her jacket and purse. "You lead the way. Stop at my desk while I grab my things but don't get too close to it."

J.J. did what she was told, all the while keeping her eyes moving around the room, looking for anything that might help. Dawn reached for the front door, then once she'd opened it, ordered J.J. outside, pulling the door shut behind them both. "I'll lock up after. Now, walk normally to your car."

She was right beside J.J., knife poking in her side.

Can I trip her? No, she might slice me. I can't call out to anyone, either, not that there's anyone on the street. Why did the office have to be in a quiet section of town? No local nightlife going on. No homes with lights on front porches. She noticed there was no light shining in the parking lot, either.

J.J. stumbled over a raised joint in the sidewalk. That hadn't been on purpose. She felt the knife cut through her jacket and cried out.

"Sorry. I didn't mean to do that, but watch where you're going. And keep quiet," Dawn hissed.

J.J. nodded. It felt more like she'd been burned rather than cut. They reached her car.

"Unlock the door."

"My keys are in the front section of my purse."

"Grab them slowly, and no funny stuff."

J.J. stifled a giggle. This was beginning to sound like an old-time gangster movie. Her hand paused on her smartphone. Could she use it? Probably not. She grabbed the key fob and pointed at the door.

"Okay. Now unlock the freaking door." Dawn sounded like she was starting to stress out.

J.J. did as she was told, and when the double beeps sounded, she swung her purse around to clip Dawn on the side of the head. She felt another slice in her side but elbowed Dawn and started running back to the office and pulled open the front door. She could hear Dawn's heels clicking on the sidewalk, close behind her.

She made it through the door but had to fight to close it. Dawn had grabbed the outside handle and was pushing hard. J.J.'s side felt like she was being stabbed multiple times. She gritted her teeth but yelled out as the door crashed open, knocking her to the side, followed by Dawn rushing at her.

They both fell to the ground, Dawn on top.

J.J. closed her eyes. Her side hurt like hell. There was a searing pain at the back of her head where she'd hit the side of something hard. *Sorry, Mom* was all she could think. If these were to be her last few moments, she should do better than that.

She felt the floor beside her. Anything of use? She felt Dawn searching also. Where was the knife? Somebody grunted. Nobody spoke.

With one final burst of energy, J.J. managed to push Dawn off, and rolled to the side. Her hand hit the small iron doorstop. Dawn clamped a hand down on J.J.'s leg. J.J. grabbed the doorstop and lashed out with it, hitting Dawn. She heard a groan.

J.J. collapsed backward. She heard a scuffle; someone crying out. It could have been her own voice. She was too tired to open her eyes.

"J.J. Are you okay?" Devine's voice never sounded so sweet.

She willed her eyes open and struggled to sit up. "I guess."

Devine turned on the light switch next to the door. J.J.

followed his gaze to the floor and the small pool of blood beside her. "I guess I got stabbed."

She felt dizzy and slowly settled back onto the floor.

Devine cursed and knelt down beside her, peeling back her jacket and doing a quick check of her side.

"It doesn't look too deep. Just lay quietly. I'm calling an ambulance." He had his smartphone out and punched it three times.

She listened while he gave the necessary information.

"Where is Dawn?"

"She's not going anywhere," Devine said, taking off his jacket, balling it up and placing it under her head. "And neither are you until the paramedics arrive."

CHAPTER 36

J.J. leaned against the pillows on her hospital bed. The meds had reduced the pain in her side to a dull throb, and she was having a hard time focusing on all the talking going on around her.

Skye stood on one side of the bed, holding her left hand. Devine stood on the other side, holding her right. She felt safe.

"How did you know?" she asked once the nurse had left the room.

"Rocco told me." His grip tightened.

She tried to raise her eyebrows but it hurt to do so.

"I stopped in to buy some olive oil on the way home," Devine explained.

J.J. sighed. "I know. Dumb move on my part."

"You think?"

"I thought I'd be stuffing envelopes."

"I doubt that."

"I didn't clue in about Dawn."

"Nobody did." He shook his head. "But it doesn't

surprise me one bit that you ended up in this position. Again."

J.J. glanced toward the door as Hastings walked in. "I think that goes for a lot of us," he said with a slight grimace.

"Ah, Detective Hastings. So nice," J.J. said, feeling woozy. It was an effort to talk.

"I'm actually just passing by to ask that you come to the station as soon as you're able to make a statement. I'm not sure if that sunk in when we were talking in the ER. And to give you this." He held out a small package.

J.J. winced as she reached for it. Skye took it instead. She looked at J.J., who nodded, so she tore the wrapping off and held up a package.

"Lake Champlain Chocolates."

"My favorite," said J.J. "Thanks."

Hastings smiled. "My pleasure. They've got a dandy gift shop here. See you later."

J.J. felt Devine's grip twitch.

Skye grinned and ran a hand along J.J.'s arm. "I love those chocolates but wouldn't nearly get myself killed in order to get some. I really wish you'd just stick to event planning. I'm starting to get gray hairs already. And I'm not even your mom."

J.J. turned her head to face Skye and felt a jolt down her side. She winced. "Don't tell Mom about this. Promise."

"I won't tell her, but you will when you're all better. What about going home next weekend? It will be obvious something's wrong. And what if she comes to live here? She has to be forewarned what to expect with her daughter being so nosy and all." Skye smiled but J.J. could hear the tough note in her voice.

"She'd better be forewarned, because I don't think anyone this stubborn is going to change," Devine threw in. "I've given up."

"I know you have, and look where it got her," Skye

challenged. "If you'd keep a closer watch on her, these things wouldn't happen."

"Hold it, you two. I am in this room. And I do appreciate your concern. But I have a splitting headache. And a sore side. I'm going to be a bad host and ask you to leave."

"Amen," said the nurse just entering the room.

CHAPTER 37

"I'm just breathing a sigh of relief that we're able to actually have our monthly Culinary Capers dinner," Beth said, taking her chicken dish out of the oven.

"You and me both," J.J. agreed. She grabbed the bottle of wine but was relieved of it by Evan before she even made it to the table.

"Allow me," he said with great aplomb. "You are still in recovery mode. You're sure it's all right that you came today? We could have postponed for a week."

J.J. shook her head. "I'm all right. Really. It was just an overnight in the hospital. I've stopped hearing bells, and I see only one of you now."

Evan almost dropped the wine.

"Just kidding. You guys are making too much of this."

The doorbell rang, and J.J. exchanged glances with Beth. "Who's that?" she asked. "Did Connor change his mind?"

Beth shook her head and flung her oven mitts onto the counter. "I'll get it."

J.J. took a last look at the chicken and entered the hall just as Devine walked in the door. J.J. just stared.

"Thanks for the invitation, Beth. Here's my contribution." He passed over a covered dish.

"Thank you, Ty. You really needn't have bothered, but I'm sure we'll enjoy it. J.J., will you get a glass of wine for our guest?"

J.J. nodded, still speechless. She grabbed a glass from the counter and Evan filled it.

"Hi, Ty. Welcome to our cozy dinner party." Evan saluted him with the bottle.

"I didn't realize," J.J. said, still at a loss for words. She looked at Beth. "When did this happen?"

"Well, Connor is out for this month, so we had an extra dish needing to be made. And besides, I thought Ty deserved a thanks for saving your life and also helping with my problem."

J.J. opened her mouth to protest that he hadn't saved her life, but who knew? Dawn had been stunned by the hit on the head but not knocked unconscious. It might have ended very differently if Devine hadn't shown up at that point. She looked over at him and smiled.

She introduced him to Alison, who winked at J.J. and spent most of the evening glancing at her and grinning. J.J. tried to ignore it all. She already felt a bit awkward having Devine there.

They enjoyed appetizers and wine in the living room, talking mainly about Beth's choice of cookbook and what was happening at Cups 'n' Roses. Then they moved into the dining room for the dinner. The extra center leaf that had been added to Beth's antique oak dining room table, along with the five chairs, filled most of the floor space in the small room. J.J. and Devine ended up sitting beside each other on one side, Alison and Evan on the other, with Beth at the head of the table near the door to the kitchen.

After the open concept of J.J.'s apartment, she found it

cozy but confining being in Beth's. The building had been built in the '50s and had a major dollop of charm, along with some very small rooms with high ceilings.

"Now this," Beth said, picking up her platter and passing it to Devine, "is Sara Paretsky's recipe for Chicken Gabriella. If you've read any of her V. I. Warshawski books, about a private eye, by the way, Ty, Gabriella is her mom's name. She was an Italian immigrant living in Chicago, and her daughter, V. I., is one of my favorite female sleuths. Next to our own J.J., that is."

J.J. blushed as the others laughed. She waited until the dish had gone around, and then picked up her own. "And this is from author Cathy Pickens. It's Fried Yellow Squash." She handed it across the table to Evan. "I dared to play around a bit with the recipe and added a blend of dried herbs to the flour mixture. I was tempted to add some red pepper flakes, too, but I admit, I chickened out."

"So to speak," Beth added, with a wink.

"Yeah."

"Why fry the squash?" Alison asked.

"Well, my author writes the Southern Fried mysteries, and being set in the South, there's a lot of food talk, too. She says that next to fried okra, fried squash is pretty much a staple at any Southern meal. Her sleuth, Avery Andrews, is a small-town lawyer, also female, who has a restaurant that's a local haunt, but she also takes us to real restaurants. And those are going on my list if I ever visit down South."

J.J. dished out a spoonful as the bowl came back to her. "There aren't any recipes in her mysteries, which is sort of unusual for cozies, I think, but she makes up for it by including this one in *The Mystery Writers of America Cookbook*. Enjoy."

"My turn," Evan said. "I chose the Eggplant Caprese Salad with Basil Chiffonade and Olive Vinaigrette. It speaks for itself. I like to think of it as the big brother of a summer caprese salad."

Alison spooned some onto her plate. "It looks delicious and very Italian. So, eggplant's been added. Anything else?"

"My author, Lisa King, suggested using smoked mozzarella but I went straight to buffalo mozzarella. I've just discovered it at Baak's Cheese Shop and now I can't get enough of it."

"Oh, I love it, too," Alison agreed.

"Tell us about your author," Beth prompted as she took her own serving.

"She writes about Jean Applequist, a wine writer—my kind of writer—in San Francisco. She likes her recipes simple, something else in common with one of our members"— he winked at J.J.—"but she sure knows her wines. I read *Death in a Wine Dark Sea*, and like its title, it was kind of dark but it had a lot of twists and some lighter scenes, too. I'd read another by her."

"I'm glad we've gotten you started on a new series, Evan." Beth grinned. "And even though I told Ty he didn't have to bring anything, he insisted."

"I wanted to do Kinsey Millhone's Famous Peanut Butter and Pickle Sandwich"—he paused for effect, then grinned—"but Beth suggested a carb instead. So, here's the Simplest Ever Potato Pancakes from author Hallie Ephron." He grabbed the dish and passed it to J.J.

"You're a Sue Grafton fan?" J.J. asked. "Or do you just like peanut butter and pickles?"

"I'm a reader and have kept up with all of her alphabet. Don't look so surprised."

"Pleasantly so."

"And, I grew up eating peanut butter sandwiches, although not with pickles. Yet."

"And for our finale," Beth continued, "Alison brought the dessert, didn't you?"

"Uh-huh. I'll tempt you with the name right now but you'll have to wait and eat all your veggies first. It's author

Mary Jane Clark's Sinfully Delicious Siesta Key Lime Pie."

"Oh man, I can hardly wait," J.J. said, mouth already watering. "You're not usually a pie person, though, Alison."

"I've decided to branch out." She stuffed a forkful of chicken in her mouth.

"This chicken is so moist, Beth. And what's that flavor?" Evan asked.

"Probably the Armagnac and pinot grigio. Do I get extra points?"

"You bet."

They ate in silence and, J.J. knew from the looks on everyone's faces, in total enjoyment of the feast. She'd learned over her months with the group that this was a good thing. The chef was being honored when everyone concentrated on eating.

"Wonderful idea, Beth," J.J. acknowledged, finally breaking the silence.

"Hear! Hear!" Evan added. "To Beth."

"To us all," she countered as they toasted one another. "And to our J.J. So, who's going to fill us in on what's been going on?"

J.J. took a sip of wine. "I don't really know all the details. My guess is that Dawn, who's been a volunteer on Gary Myers's campaign for quite some time, heard Miranda arguing with the campaign manager about an affair. She assumed it was about her affair with Gary and that everyone would find out about it. So she decided to take matters into her own hands. She was at the casino night especially for that reason. I don't know how she managed to get away undetected. She must have had a lot of blood on her." She shuddered just thinking about it.

"She made a quick trip to the head to change her clothes and wash up. Then she tossed the knife and her dress overboard and neither have been found as yet," Devine said. "It was a good plan for such a flake."

"What do you mean?" J.J. asked.

"There was no affair between her and Myers. It was totally in her head."

"You know that for a fact?"

"Yes."

"But what if Myers is lying about it? He has a lot to lose, after all."

"I don't believe he is. And there's no proof. Nothing she says makes sense. Either way, the motive still stands."

"That's very sad," Beth said. "She must have really needed to be loved."

J.J. sat staring at her plate. How had she missed that?

Devine covered her hand with his. "It was so real for her and continues to be. She'll get the help she needs, though."

"I'm glad about that. But poor Miranda. It shouldn't have happened."

"Most murders shouldn't," Alison added. "But right now, we're here celebrating J.J.'s recovery and another Culinary Capers dinner. Let's party."

Devine gave J.J.'s hand a squeeze. She squeezed back. And smiled.

Hmm, maybe we'll have to give that first date a try.

RECIPES

It's been such fun having the Culinary Capers dinner club use *The Mystery Writers of America Cookbook* in *Roux the Day. And I'm particularly delighted that noted authors Sara Paretsky, Cathy Pickens, and Lisa King have given their permission to reprint their recipes. Enjoy!*

CHICKEN GABRIELLA

By Sara Paretsky

- Enough olive oil to cover the bottom of a skillet, plus 1 tablespoon
- 2 garlic cloves, finely chopped
- 1 fryer chicken, cut into pieces
- ¼ cup Armagnac
- 1 cup pinot grigio (or other dry white wine)
- 6 Calimyrna figs, cut into quarters

Coat the bottom of a skillet with olive oil and heat for about 30 seconds. Add garlic and sauté until golden brown, stirring constantly. Remove garlic and reserve.

Add the additional 1 tablespoon olive oil to the skillet. Turn heat to high, quickly add chicken, and sear each piece on both sides.

Remove the skillet from the heat. Pour the Armagnac into the skillet and flame it with a match. (Light the Armagnac the instant you put it in the pan or it will not flame.) Return the pan to the heat.

Once the Armagnac has cooked off, add the pinot grigio and simmer the chicken, covered on low heat until tender, approximately 30 to 45 minutes.

Add the figs and sautéed garlic for the last 10 minutes of cooking.

Serve with a green salad and a crisp, cold white wine.

YIELD: 4 SERVINGS

FRIED YELLOW SQUASH

By Cathy Pickens

- Oil for frying
- 1 to 2 eggs
- ½ cup milk (or buttermilk)
- 1 to 4 medium yellow squashes, sliced into rounds about ¼ inch thick
- 1 cup flour
- 1 cup cornmeal
- Salt and black pepper to taste

Heat about 2 inches of oil in a large Dutch oven or very large skillet. The oil has to be hot (350°F or 400°F) to cook the squash properly.

Layer some paper towels on a large plate and set it beside the stove.

Lightly beat the eggs in a bowl and add the milk. Soak

the squash in the milk-egg mixture for a few minutes while you prepare the flour mixture.

In a bowl or large plastic bag, mix the flour, cornmeal, salt, and pepper.

Remove some squash from the milk mixture (enough for one layer in your Dutch oven or pot) and add to the flour mixture. Dredge or gently shake to thoroughly coat.

Add the squash to the hot oil in a single layer and fry until toasty brown (about 3 minutes). The oil should sizzle when you drop in a test piece. Lift out the cooked squash and drain on the paper towels. Cook the remaining squash in batches and serve immediately, while hot.

YIELD: 2-4 SERVINGS

Eggplant Caprese Salad with Basil Chiffonade and Olive Vinaigrette

By Lisa King

- ○ 1 medium eggplant, about 1 pound
- ○ ¼ cup extra virgin olive oil, plus more for brushing the eggplant
- ○ Sea salt and freshly ground black pepper, to taste
- ○ 1 8-ounce ball smoked mozzarella
- ○ 4 Kalamata or other brine-cured black olives, pitted and chopped fine
- ○ 1 garlic clove, minced
- ○ 1 tablespoon sherry vinegar (you can substitute red wine vinegar)
- ○ 6 to 8 large basil leaves

Preheat a broiler with a rack placed about 4 inches from the heat. Line a sheet pan with foil.

Trim the eggplant and cut it crosswise into ½-inch slices. You should have 8 slices. Brush them on both sides with oil and season lightly with salt and pepper.

Put the slices in one layer on the foil-covered sheet pan and broil until browned and tender, turning once and moving slices around to ensure even cooking. (You can also grill the eggplant over medium coals.) Let cool to room temperature.

Arrange the eggplant slices on a platter. Trim the rounded ends from the smoked mozzarella ball and cut it crosswise into 8 slices. Put one on each eggplant slice.

Make the vinaigrette: Put the olives, garlic, and vinegar in a small bowl. Whisk in the olive oil and season with salt and pepper.

Make the basil chiffonade: Stack the basil leaves on a cutting board and roll up the long way. Slice the rolled-up basil into thin strips.

Scatter the basil chiffonade over the eggplant and mozzarella. Stir the vinaigrette and spoon it over the salad.

Serve at room temperature, accompanied by any remaining vinaigrette.

YIELD: 4 SERVINGS

Turn the page for a preview of
the next Dinner Club mystery

MARINATING IN MURDER

Available soon from Berkley Prime Crime

The horn of a passing car blared so loudly J.J. Tanner almost knocked herself out when her head snapped up and hit the doorframe of the SUV she was helping to pack.

"Ouch, ouch, ouch!"

"Are you okay, J.J.? It's that idiot Darrel Moses making a fool of himself each time he passes by." Alison Manovich glared at the taillights of the old, beat-up Ford pickup.

J.J. rubbed the back of her head and tried not to wince too much. "An admirer, is he?"

Alison made a face. "Just erase that thought from your head, girl. He's the last guy on earth I'd be interested in, if I were even interested in meeting someone." She leaned the folding camp chairs up against the side panel inside the back of her silver SUV. "There should be enough room for a couple of coolers in here. Surely all the food we need for the picnic will fit into two."

J.J. joined her at the back of the SUV and glanced in. "I'd say that's plenty of room. In fact, there's also lots of space for Beth, Connor, and me. And if Evan decides to drive his new sports car, he can put some food on his passenger seat, after all." She grinned. "It will serve him right. Show-off."

Alison shook her head, her blonde ponytail flipping from side to side. "Who would have thought those two would just up and buy a sports car? It's a totally new image for Evan and Michael. It must have cost a small fortune."

"Well, it's not as if they have a family to support. They both have very good jobs and a house, so they're entitled to play with a car."

Alison sighed. "You're right of course. I'm just seeing a little green, I guess."

"I can see you behind the wheel of a convertible, especially in your cop uniform. Now that would be an attention getter."

Alison's answer was drowned out by the very loud arrival of a motorcycle. Both girls stared in surprise, wondering who'd joined the party. When the Harley Davidson came to a stop just inches away from them and Connor Mac lifted off his helmet, they broke into shrieks.

"OMG, when did you get that?" Alison asked, dancing around the shiny black bike, giving it a thorough once-over.

"I picked it up this afternoon. What do you both think?"

"I love it." Alison answered first. "I'm in awe. I need a ride and soon."

Connor looked delighted. "Happy to oblige anytime."

J.J. eyed it skeptically. "I think the next time we go to a movie, I'm walking."

She smiled to keep it light. They'd gone out to one movie since the murder last fall of his on-again, off-again girlfriend. It was complicated. He was still grieving. The bike was a total surprise. Maybe it was part of the recovery process. She had to admit, it looked like it might be working.

"So, are you driving it to the picnic tomorrow?" Alison queried.

"Of course. It's going to be great weather and that's exactly what a bike is for."

"What about your food?" J.J. asked. She wasn't fond of motorcycles, feeling they were too loud and much too dangerous, but she tried not to let that show and put a damper on his obvious delight.

Connor's smile was all little-boy-begging. "I thought you might take it up for me, J.J. Maybe you could swing by on your way over here tomorrow morning?"

J.J. sighed. She was such a pushover. "All right. But I have dibs on any extra chocolate that may find its way there."

"Are we going to convoy?" Alison asked, back to packing her SUV, stuffing a large golf umbrella behind the chairs.

"I'm up for anything," Connor answered, climbing off his bike and releasing the kickstand. He looked around. "No Evan or Beth yet?"

"Well done," J.J. said, as Beth's red van pulled into the driveway, stopping a few inches from the bike. "You must have conjured her up."

Connor had thrown up his hands to warn Beth away from his bike, an exaggerated look of terror on his face.

Beth opened her driver's door and leaned out. "Oh, no. Don't tell me. Connor, you didn't go over to the dark side, did you?"

"Yup."

"Lord help us." Beth struggled out of the car and leaned against it, taking a few deep breaths and glaring at the bike.

"Are you all right, Beth?" J.J. asked. Beth looked even more tired than usual. Maybe it had been a hard day at her Cups 'n' Roses café. She hoped that's all it was. J.J. marveled at the amount of energy her older friend seemed to always have.

"A little fatigued, that's all." Beth tucked her short gray hair behind both ears and turned to the street. "Evan wanted to drive his new baby over so I expect he'll be making his big entrance any minute now."

On cue, a shiny red Miata, top down, pulled up in front of Alison's townhouse. Evan parked, blocking the driveway, and took his time getting out and sauntering over to the rest of the Culinary Capers Dinner Club.

"Do you like it?" He beamed like a proud papa. Then he noticed the Harley. "What's this? Am I to be outdone by a biker?" He added a note of scorn to his voice but smiled.

"Boys and their toys," Beth said in a loud voice, and wandered over to Alison's SUV. "Is there anything I can do to help?"

"Nope," Alison said. "I think with the chairs pushed up against one side, there'll be plenty of room for most of the food. You're riding with me tomorrow, aren't you?"

"I'd be happy to." Beth looked at Evan. "And just what are you going to be able to bring along to the picnic in that cream puff?"

"I thought I'd bring J.J."

J.J.'s mouth dropped open. "First I've heard of it but I'd be delighted. Can I drive?"

Evan sputtered. "In a word, no."

He leaned into the car, pulled out a long red scarf, and passed it to J.J. "But you can wear this. Don't you think it brings a certain *je ne sais quoi*?"

"Very continental, sir. But I seem to remember that a long scarf and a sports car can be a deadly combination." J.J. grimaced, thinking of Isadora Duncan. "And where did you get the scarf? Did it come with the car?"

"It was a gift from the salesperson I bought the car from. A woman." He grinned and wrapped it around his neck. "Now, what's the final game plan?"

"I was just saying we could meet here around ten, load up and then convoy over to North Island," Alison suggested. "It shouldn't take too much more than a half hour to reach the beach and if we get there early, we can snag a good picnic table."

J.J. shot a covert glance at Connor. North Island had

played a big part in all that had happened in the fall. He didn't let on if he was upset.

"I have a wonderful fold-up table that would be perfect," Beth offered. "It would be sort of dreamy with a flowing white lace tablecloth, which I just happen to have."

"Oh, and I could bring candles with hurricane covers," J.J. offered, getting into the spirit.

"Very glam," agreed Evan. "Flowers. I'll pick up a small floral centerpiece on my—on our way."

Alison folded her arms. "It all sounds delightful but I think I'm the hostess this month and, although I do appreciate the input, I'd really like just an old-fashioned picnic table with an oilskin cloth that I'll bring. It's what my mom always used for our family picnics."

Beth looked apologetic. "I tend to get carried away sometimes. I'm sorry, Alison. Not my month so not my place to take over. I look forward to a good old-fashioned picnic."

"We all do," J.J. added. "Your turn to host the dinner, your choice of cookbook, your choice of, well, everything. And I just wanted to thank you, Alison, for picking a cookbook this month with such wonderful photos. *Summer Days and Balmy Nights* is a real delight to thumb through."

Alison smiled. "I did it just for you, J.J. But I do hope you've actually read through it and picked a recipe from it."

J.J. made the sign of crossing her heart. "I always play by the rules, Alison. And I know that tomorrow will be most memorable."

She caught the scarf that Evan threw to her. Hmm. An omen?

J.J. shivered even though the evening was unusually warm for May.

ABOUT THE AUTHOR

Linda Wiken is the author of the national bestselling Ashton Corners Book Club Mysteries under the pseudonym Erika Chase, and is the former owner of a mystery bookstore.

The Dinner Club Mysteries

By Linda Wiken

The Culinary Capers dinner club creates delicious and inventive meals together—and solves the occasional murder along the way.

Find more books by Linda Wiken
by visiting prh.com/nextread

"Wiken serves up generous portions of suspense and food lore."—Victoria Abbott, national bestselling author of the Book Collector Mysteries

lindawiken.com
 LindaWiken.Author
🐦 LWiken